A WOMAN NAMED DALE

A WOMAN NAMED DALE

In the Shadows of Grace

An epistolary novel

by Kae R. Nelson

A WOMAN NAMED DALE

In the Shadows of Grace

An epistolary novel

By Kae R. Nelson

Author

For the letter writers and secret keepers, the ones who leave paper trails of truth.

For families learning that love is louder than fear, and grace is stronger than tradition.

For everyone still writing their way home.

God loves you, and so do I.

"And now these three remain: faith, hope and love. But the greatest of these is love."

    -   *1 Corinthians 13:13, NLT*

CONTENT NOTE

This book contains depictions and discussions of:

- Family rejection and estrangement
- Religious trauma and conversion therapy attempts
- Anti-LGBTQ+ discrimination and violence
- Sexual assault and molestation
- Physical and emotional abuse
- Suicide ideation
- Death and complicated grief
- Stalking and kidnapping

While these difficult topics are handled with care and are integral to Dale's story of healing and hope, readers should be aware of this content before proceeding.

If you or someone you know is struggling with any of these issues, please reach out for support. Resources are available through:

National Suicide Prevention Lifeline: 988

The Trevor Project: 1-866-488-7386

Trans Lifeline: 877-565-8860

PFLAG National: pflag.org

This story ultimately celebrates God's unconditional love, resilience, family healing, and the power of chosen community, but the journey includes real pain that some readers may find triggering.

Take care of yourself. You matter.

COLLECTED DOCUMENTS
COVER PAGE

From the Personal Collection of Dale Elizabeth Morrison
With the permission of the author

Additional Sources:
LGBTQ+ History Project, Atlanta, GA
Third-party requests and public records
Donated: September 2025

COLLECTION STATUS:
All documents have been obtained through Dale Morrison's personal archives, institutional donations, or formal requests to third parties. Some requests were denied due to privacy concerns, medical confidentiality, or institutional policies, so this collection is incomplete.

ARCHIVAL COMPLETENESS:
The narrative presented here spans 2018-2025, focusing on Dale's transformative journey from age 17-24. While certain materials remain unavailable, the collection provides a comprehensive view of this period.

MISSING ELEMENTS:
Some family correspondence (privacy restrictions)
Complete medical records (confidentiality)
Institutional records (access denied)
Documents destroyed during family estrangement
Deliverance documentation from Cedar Ridge Baptist Church

EDITORIAL NOTE

Where documents are missing, narrative gaps have been noted. The story that emerges is necessarily incomplete, but no less powerful for its human imperfections.
This collection represents one young woman's courage to document her truth, even when that truth was painful to live.

Greg Whittaker
LGBTQ+ History Project, Journalist
Atlanta, Georgia September 2025

Document 1: Letter to God - The Prayer

Written by Margaret Morrison

Dated: September 12, 1999

Dear God,

I'm writing this letter at 2:30 in the morning because I can't sleep· Earl is snoring beside me, and I'm trying not to wake him, but my heart is so full of hope and hurt at the same time·

We've been trying for three years now· Three years of hoping every month, of disappointment, of doctor visits and tests and treatments· Three years of watching other couples announce pregnancies while we smile and say, "how wonderful" and go home· Me in tears and him in anger·

But Lord, I know it's Your will that we be parents· I can feel it in my bones, in my heart, in the way Earl's face lights up when he sees children at church· We have so much love to give· Our home is ready· Our hearts are ready·

I pray that You bless us with a healthy child· A baby we can love and cherish all the days of our lives· I promise You we'll be good parents· We'll raise this child in Your love, in Your light, in Your truth· We'll teach them right from wrong, help them grow into the person You intend them to be·

I can picture our baby, Earl singing lullabies, all of us together as a family· I've already picked out names - if it's a girl, maybe Elizabeth, after my grandmother· If it's a boy, maybe David, after Your beloved king. Earl doesn't want a junior. He likes the name Dale.

Lord, I know You have a plan. I know You see the bigger picture when all I can see is this empty nursery and this aching heart. But I believe - I have to believe - that You're going to give us the child we're meant to have.

Help me be patient. Help me trust Your timing. Help me remember that Your love is bigger than my fear, Your plan better than my dreams.

I promise I'll love this child with everything I have. No matter what challenges come, no matter what struggles we face, I'll never stop loving them. They'll always be wanted, always be cherished, always be home.

Please, God. Please bless us with a baby.

I'm signing this letter and putting it in my Bible. Someday, when our child is old enough to understand, I'll show them this letter, so they'll know how desperately they were wanted, how fervently they were prayed for.

Our baby will know they were loved before they were even born.

With all my faith and hope,

Margaret

ARCHIVAL NOTE
Written by Gene Whittaker

This letter was found tucked inside Dale Morrison's personal Bible, along with hospital bracelets, baby photos, and a birth announcement dated November 3, 2001: "Earl and Margaret Morrison joyfully announce the arrival of their son, Dale Earl Morrison. 7 lbs., 4 oz. A perfect blessing from God."

The letter appears to have been given to Dale at some point, as evidenced by a note in her handwriting on the back:

"Mama kept her promise. She loved me before I was born."

Ms. Morrison, now a celebrated author and advocate, has graciously donated these documents from her personal collection to help other families navigate similar journeys. The documents that follow chronicle Dale's transformation from a scared teenager to a young woman who learned that sometimes the greatest gift we can give our parents is the courage to become who we truly are.

PERSONAL NOTE FROM DALE MORRISON

I'm sharing these documents because I believe stories have the power to heal. My mother prayed for a child to love and cherish all the days of her life. It just took her a while to recognize that the child was me.

If you're reading this as a parent struggling to love your LGBTQ+ child, know that love is always possible. If you're reading this as a young person who feels unloved, know that you are worthy of the love my mother prayed for.

If you are reading this and you are religious, if you believe in God's love, please know that this story is not an attack on faith. It's a story about faith finding its way to love. My mother's prayers were answered—just not in the way she expected.

Nobody is perfect. We all fall short, we all make mistakes, and no sin is excusable on our own merit. But God's grace is bigger than our failings. He is the one who opens the gates of heaven—for murderers who find redemption, for the homeless who cry out in need, for gay people seeking love, for straight people seeking forgiveness, for all of us who are broken and in need of grace.

Sometimes the greatest test of faith is learning that God's love reaches everyone—that His mercy extends to all who seek it, regardless of who they are or who they love. We don't get to decide who deserves God's grace. That's His decision, and His love is bigger than our understanding.

If you are a person of faith who struggles with LGBTQ+ identity—either your own or someone you love—please know that you are not outside of God's love.

Sometimes the answer to our prayers looks different than we expected. But love recognizes love, eventually.

Dale Morrison
Atlanta, Georgia
June 2025

Document 2: Letter to God
Written by Dale Morrison
Dated: September 3, 2018

Dear God,

I love You. I need You to know that before I write another word. Before my father's fists. Before my mother's silence. Before the world called me a mistake, You were the first voice I ever heard. I don't want to lose You. But I feel like I already have.

I don't understand why You made me this way. If I was supposed to be a boy, why does every part of me say that's a lie? If I was supposed to be a girl, why did You put me in this body? People tell me I have to choose—between You and me. But is that true? If You are the God of love, if You are the One who sees every wound and every broken piece, then why would You ask me to erase myself to prove I love You?

People at church say You don't make mistakes. My father says I am one. I don't know who to believe.

I've heard the sermons. I've read the scriptures. I know what people say. But I also know that they pick and choose their sins like fruit at a market. They tell me I am lost while they cheat on their wives. They tell me I am an abomination while they lie and steal and gossip and hurt. But I don't want to use their sins to excuse mine. I just want to know the truth.

If I become that Dale, fully and completely, will You still love me?

Please, God. I need to know.

Document 3: Diary Entry
Written by Dale Morrison
Dated: September 16, 2018

I can barely hold the pen. My hands are shaking so badly.

I don't know why I did it. I knew better. I KNEW better. But Mama had left her black heels by the door when she got home from church. Dad was already three beers deep watching the game, and I just... I wanted to know what it felt like. To be tall like that. To hear that click-click sound when I walk. To feel... I don't know. Different.

I only had them on for maybe two minutes. I was just walking back and forth in the hallway, trying to get used to the feeling, when I heard his chair creak. The game had gone to commercial. I tried to kick them off fast, but they were too small, and I tripped and fell right there in the doorway where he could see everything.

The look on his face. I'll never forget that look. Like I had just killed something precious right in front of him.

"what the hell are you doing?"

I couldn't say anything. I just lay there on the floor with Mama's heels stuck to the top of my feet like stickers.

He walked away from me. Real slow. That's when you know you're in trouble - when Dad moves slow like that. Predators stalk before they pounce. He walked to the kitchen, and I heard him open another beer. Then another. Then the whiskey bottle. Panthers 24, Falcons 31.

I stayed on the floor. I knew better than to move even the slightest.

Mama came out of the bedroom where she'd been folding laundry. She saw me on the floor, saw the shoes, saw Dad drinking harder than usual. She didn't say anything, but I saw her face just... close. Like she was putting shutters over her windows.

"Margaret," Dad said without turning around. "Take the boy to his room."

"Earl, maybe we should just-"

"I said take him to his room."

Mama slowly helped me up. Her hands were shaking too. "Come on, baby," she whispered. "Let's go pray."

But praying didn't help because an hour later Dad came into my room, and he wasn't walking slowly anymore.

"You want to know something?" he said, and I could smell the whiskey on him from across the room. "You want to know why I drink? I drink because it's the only time you don't look like some kind of... some kind of mistake."

Then he took off his belt.

I won't write about the rest. My body still hurts. I can't lie down right.

Mama brought me some ice wrapped in a dish towel and said we needed to pray for Dad's forgiveness and for God to help me resist these "temptations."

She said the Bible tells us to honor our fathers and mothers, and that means not doing things that bring shame to the family.

I don't understand. If God made me, why does who I am make Dad so angry?

I hid Mama's heels under my mattress. I don't know why. I should throw them away or, even better, give them back to her. I should forget this ever happened.

But for those two minutes, I felt... right. Maybe there was a person inside me that made sense.

Even if nobody else can see her.

Especially if nobody else can see her.

Maybe she's been here all along, just waiting for me to find her.

Document 4: Diary Entry

Written by Dale Morrison

Dated: October 22, 2018

I have a secret, and she works at the Walgreens on Fifth Street. She's maybe 25, has short blonde hair, kind eyes, and she doesn't know she's saving my life.

It started three months ago when I went in to buy deodorant, and she was working at the register. I was wearing my usual costume - baggy jeans, oversized jersey, baseball cap backwards and pulled low. The costume I wear to keep everyone happy.

"You know," she said while scanning my items, "you have really beautiful eyes. Most guys have lashes like that, and it's not fair, but your eyes are gorgeous." I didn't know what to say. Nobody had ever called any part of me beautiful before.

I started making any excuse to go back. Just little things like toothpaste, shampoo, candy bars I didn't need. Always when she was working. Always hoping she'd say something else nice.

Last week, I was buying a pack of gum, and she said, "You're here a lot. I'm Christina." She held out her hand.

"Dale," I said, shaking her soft hand.

"Dale. I like that. It's a strong name. Works for a boy or a girl, you know?"

My heart stopped. Did she know? Could she tell?

"I had a friend in college named Dalia. She went by Dale," she continued. "She was this amazing girl. People poked at her because she wanted to go by Dale, but she didn't care. Dale was confident, smart, and didn't let anyone push her around. You remind me of her somehow."

She. She said she.

I couldn't speak. I just paid for my gum and left.

But I kept thinking about what she said. How she looked at me when she said it. Like maybe she saw something I thought I was hiding.

Today I went back. I'd been practicing in the mirror for a week, trying to figure out how to ask her something without sounding crazy.

"Christina," I said when I got to the counter. "That friend of yours from college. Dale. What was she like?"

Christina smiled. "She was brave. She knew who she was even when other people tried to tell her different. She used to say that names don't have genders - people do. And people get to decide for themselves who they are."

My hands started shaking. "What if... what if someone wasn't sure? About who they were?"

"Then I'd tell them they have time to figure it out. And that whoever they are, they deserve to be happy."

I bought my gum and left, but her words keep echoing in my head.

"They deserve to be happy."

Do I deserve to be happy? Does the person inside me, the one who tried on Mama's heels, the one who feels right when people say "she," does she deserve to exist?

At home tonight, Dad was passed out in his chair by 7 PM. Mama was in the kitchen humming hymns while she cooked. I went to my room and looked at myself in the mirror.

"Dale," I whispered to my reflection. "You're a woman named Dale."

It felt like coming home.

I don't know what I'm going to do with this feeling. I can't tell Mama. She'd pray harder and make me talk to Bishop Patterson. I can't tell Dad. The belt would be the least of my worries.

But maybe... maybe I don't have to tell anyone yet. Maybe I can just be Dale in secret for a while. Maybe I can figure out what that means.

Christina gave me hope. Hope that somewhere out there, people like me get to be happy.

Hope that maybe someday, I can be one of them.

The girl in the mirror smiled back at me. For the first time in my life, I liked what I saw.

Document 5: Therapy Notes

Written by Dr. Jasmeen Greene

Dated: November 8, 2018

HEARTS AND MINDS COUNSELING CENTER

Confidential Patient Notes

Date: November 8, 2018

Therapist: Jasmine Greene, LMFT

Session Type: Family Consultation

Attendees: Earl Morrison (father), Margaret Morrison (mother)

Reason for Visit: Parents contacted the office expressing concern about their teenager's "concerning behaviors and attitude problems." Father insisted on consultation without the main person present.

Session Notes:

Mr. Morrison dominated the entire 50-minute session. Spoke continuously about patient's "rebellion against God's plan" and "unnatural tendencies." Became increasingly agitated when discussing specific incidents involving patient wearing women's clothing/shoes.

Key quotes from Mr. Morrison:

- "That boy is an abomination. The Bible is clear about this."

- "God doesn't love what he's becoming. Neither do I."

- "I've tried everything - discipline, prayer, keeping him busy with sports. Nothing works."

- "He's choosing to be this way to hurt us. To hurt me."

- "If he doesn't stop this devil's behavior, he's no son of mine."

Concerning observations:

- Mr. Morrison referred to patient exclusively as "that boy" or "him" - never by name

- Described physical punishments in detail with no apparent awareness of severity

- Showed signs of alcohol use during session (smell on breath, slight slur at 2 PM appointment)

- Made multiple references to "beating the devil out of him"

- Expressed belief that patient's identity exploration is "a choice" and "rebellion"

Mrs. Morrison's behavior:

- Remained silent for 47 of 50 minutes

- Avoided eye contact throughout session

- Visible anxiety - wringing hands, shallow breathing

- When directly asked "Margaret, what are your thoughts about Dale?" she hesitated for nearly 30 seconds and responded: "My husband is... Earl is correct. The Bible is clear. Children should obey their parents."

- When pressed further about her own feelings toward her child, she stated: "My feelings don't matter. A wife should submit to her husband's wisdom."

- Appeared to be dissociating during husband's more violent descriptions

Clinical Impressions:

- Mr. Morrison exhibits signs of alcohol abuse and potential domestic violence

- Mrs. Morrison shows classic signs of psychological abuse/learned helplessness

- Patient does not present but appears to be experiencing severe family rejection and potential physical abuse
- Religious fundamentalism being used to justify harmful treatment
- Strong concern for patient's safety and psychological well-being

Recommendations Made:
- Individual therapy for patient
- Family therapy with all members present
- Alcohol assessment for Mr. Morrison
- Support resources for Mrs. Morrison

Parents' Response: Mr. Morrison rejected all recommendations. Stated: "We don't need some liberal therapist telling us how to raise our boy. The Bible and the belt are all the therapy he needs." Mrs. Morrison nodded agreement but avoided eye contact.

Follow-up: Parents left session early when I explained mandatory reporting requirements regarding child abuse. Mr. Morrison stated they would "handle this God's way" and would not be returning.

Action Required:
- File report with Child Protective Services
- Attempt to contact patient through school counselor
- Document all interactions for potential future legal proceedings

Personal Note: In 19 years of practice, rarely encountered such concerning family dynamics. Patient is likely experiencing severe psychological trauma. Worried about escalation if patient continues to explore gender identity. Will monitor situation closely.

Next Steps: <u>Reaching out to Millbrook High School counseling office to check on student welfare.</u>

Jasmine Greene, LMFT License #: MFT-4428

Document 6: Spiritual Consultation Notes

Written by First Lady Dorothy Patterson
Dated: November 15, 2018

CEDAR RIDGE BAPTIST CHURCH
Spiritual Consultation Notes
Date: November 15, 2018

Present: Bishop Patterson, First Lady Dorothy Patterson, Earl Morrison (Deacon), Margaret Morrison

Opening Prayer led by Bishop Patterson

Brother Earl's Concerns: Brother Earl came seeking Biblical guidance regarding his son's "unnatural and sinful behavior." Reports finding the boy wearing women's clothing and shoes on multiple occasions. States he's tried correction through discipline, but the behavior persists.

"Bishop, I've done everything the Good Book tells us to do. Spare the rod, spoil the child. I haven't spared the rod. But this boy seems determined to walk in wickedness."

Brother Earl mentioned they attempted secular counseling but found it "worldly and useless." The therapist tried to fill their heads with nonsense about accepting the boy's behavior instead of correcting it.

"That woman tried to tell us we needed to support him in this sin. Can you imagine? She wanted us to encourage an abomination!"

Sister Margaret's Input: Sister Margaret remained mostly quiet during the consultation, as is proper for a godly woman. When asked directly, she confirmed her husband's account and expressed her commitment to following his spiritual leadership in the home.

- 19 -

First Lady Dorothy's Counsel: First Lady Dorothy reminded the family that children are given to parents by God to be shaped according to His will. "The devil comes to steal, kill, and destroy - and he often targets our children. This behavior is clearly demonic influence trying to corrupt this young man's soul."

She recommended increased prayer, fasting, and firm Biblical discipline. "Some children require more correction than others. The Bible is clear - foolishness is bound in the heart of a child, but the rod of correction shall drive it far from him."

Pastor's Biblical Guidance: After much prayer and consultation of Scripture, I provided the following Biblical counsel:

1. Romans 1:26-27 - God's condemnation of unnatural affections is absolute

2. 1 Corinthians 6:9-10 - Those who practice such things will not inherit the kingdom of God

3. Proverbs 22:15 - Foolishness is bound in the heart of a child; the rod of correction will drive it far from him

4. Deuteronomy 22:5 - A woman shall not wear that which pertaineth unto a man, neither shall a man put on a woman's garment: for all that do so are abomination unto the Lord thy God

The boy's behavior is clearly contrary to God's design for masculinity. Brother Earl is correct to take firm action.

Recommendations:

- Increased discipline when inappropriate behavior occurs

- Remove all temptations from the home (lock away feminine items)

- Mandatory church attendance at all services

- Extra time in men's ministry activities with strong male role models
- Consider military school if secular high school is not providing proper masculine environment
- Prayer and fasting for deliverance from this spirit of confusion

First Lady Dorothy's Additional Counsel: "Sometimes the Lord allows us to face great trials with our children to test our faithfulness. Brother Earl, your willingness to stand firm against this wickedness shows your commitment to raising this boy in the fear and admonition of the Lord. A godly wife supports her husband's spiritual leadership, especially in times of trial. Your submission to Earl's authority in this matter honors God."

Closing Observations: This family is facing a spiritual battle for their son's soul. Brother Earl's firm hand and Biblical discipline may be the only thing standing between this young man and complete moral destruction.

We must remember that secular psychology seeks to normalize what God calls sin. The Morrison family was wise to reject worldly counsel in favor of Biblical truth.

Prayer Request: Added the Morrison family to our prayer list. Specifically praying for:
- Deliverance of their son from spirits of confusion and rebellion
- Strength for Brother Earl to continue standing firm
- Grace for Sister Margaret to support her husband's leadership
- Wisdom for church leadership to guide this family through this trial

Follow-up: Scheduled monthly consultations to monitor

progress. Suggested the boy begin attending our "Men of Valor" youth group on Wednesday evenings for additional masculine influence.

Scripture for Meditation: "Train up a child in the way he should go and when he is old, he will not depart from it." - Proverbs 22:6

In His Service, Rev. William Patterson Senior
Bishop, Cedar Ridge Baptist Church

First Lady's Note: Will organize the ladies' prayer circle to intercede specifically for this family's situation. Sister Margaret needs our support during this difficult season.

Document 7: Letter to God

Written by Dale Morrison
Dated: November 17, 2018

Dear God,

I don't want to be here anymore.

I've tried to be what they wanted. I've tried to be what You wanted. But I don't know who that is anymore.

I could disappear, and it would be easier. For them. For me. I know what my father would say. He'd tell people it was for the best. That he never had a son, just a mistake, and the Lord corrected it for him. My mother... I don't know what she would say. Maybe nothing. Maybe she'd cry in a room where no one could hear, wipe her face, and go back to pretending.

I think she loves me. I think she always has. But love should make a sound, shouldn't it?

The world has already decided who I am. They have already measured my worth and found me lacking. And I am tired. So tired of holding up my hands in a fight I never wanted to be in.

But I can't leave that way.

Not because of my father. Not because of the world. But because of me. Because if I leave, I will let them win. I let them write the ending to a story they never cared about reading. I won't leave despite them or turn my life into a battle just to prove them wrong. That would still mean they control me.

I will live regardless of them. Regardless of their hate, their silence, their misinterpretations of You.

I don't know if that's faith. I don't know if that's strength. But it's all I have left.

And for now, it's enough.

Document 8: Diary Entry

Written by Dale Morrison
Dated: November 18, 2018

They think I don't know, but I heard them talking after church Sunday.

Bishop Patterson pulled Dad aside after service, and I saw them whispering with First Lady Dorothy. Mama stood there with her hands folded, nodding at everything they said. When we got home, Dad was different. Angrier. More determined.

"Boy, we're going to fix this once and for all," he said. "No more playing around. No more being soft."

He's locked everything away now. Every dress, every pair of heels, every piece of makeup in this house is in a box in their bedroom closet with a padlock on it. Even her jewelry box. He's treating me like I'm some kind of thief who can't be trusted.

But the worst part isn't the locks. It's the way Mama looks at me now. Or doesn't look at me. She used to at least try to talk to me, even if it was just Bible verses. Now she won't even make eye contact. It's like I've become something too shameful to acknowledge.

Wednesday night Dad made me go to that "Men of Valor" meeting at church. Twelve teenage boys sitting in a circle talking about being "warriors for Christ" and "biblical masculinity." Brother Johnson kept staring at me like I was a science experiment. He made us all stand up and declare that we would "reject the feminization of American culture" and "embrace our God-given role as men."

I stood there and said the words. But inside, I was screaming.

They don't understand. This isn't something I'm choosing. This isn't rebellion or the devil or whatever they want to call it. This is just... me. The person I've always been, underneath all the costumes and acting.

I've been thinking about what Christina said at Walgreens. About her friend who knew who she was even when other people tried to tell her different. I wonder if that girl ever felt like she was drowning in other people's expectations.

Last night I had a dream. I was standing in front of a mirror, but instead of my reflection, I saw her - the real Dale. She was beautiful. She was wearing a simple blue dress, and her hair was long and soft. She looked happy. At peace.

    "Don't let them kill me," she said. "Please don't let them kill me."

I woke up crying.

I'm not going to let them kill her. I don't know how, but I'm not going to let them erase the person I really am just because they can't understand her.

Dad can lock up every dress in this house. Bishop Patterson can quote Bible verses until he's blue in the face. But they can't lock up what's inside me. They can't padlock my heart.

I'm still Dale. I'm still a woman named Dale. And someday, when I'm strong enough and far enough away from here, I'm going to let her out into the world.

They think they're saving my soul. But they're the ones who are lost.

I just have to survive long enough to prove it.
The girl in my dreams is counting on me.
I won't let her down.

Document 9: Letter to God

Written by Dale Morrison
Dated: December 8, 2018

Dear God,

I tried.

I put on the jersey. I ran the laps. I took the hits and gave them back harder. My father grinned at me from the sidelines, drink in one hand, expectation in the other. I thought maybe if I did this, if I pushed hard enough, the thing inside me would die.

I even thought about finding a girlfriend. Just to prove I could. Not one I knew, of course. That would be too real. I thought about paying someone so no one would ever find out. Get in, get out, prove something to myself, to them, to You.

But nothing fits. Not the jersey. Not the girls. Not the way they talk about women like they're trophies to be won instead of people. I sit in locker rooms and feel like a fraud. I stand beside my father and feel like a disappointment.

How do they make it look so easy? How does my father wear manhood like a badge while I wear it like a mask that never quite fits?

I don't want to be like this. I don't want to be him.

But if I'm not this, then what am I?

I need an answer, God. Before my father asks me to prove myself again. Before I lose what little of me that's left.

Document 10: Letter to Mother

Written by Dale Morrison
Dated: December 12, 2018

Dear Mama,

I don't know if you'll read this. I don't know if you'll throw it away or show it to Dad or take it straight to Bishop Patterson. But I have to try and tell you the truth, even if it hurts both of us.

I'm not your son, Mama. I know that's what the birth certificate says. I know that's what everyone expects. But I'm not him. I never was. I'm your daughter. I've always been your daughter. And I've been dying inside trying to pretend to be someone I'm not.

Do you remember when I was little, maybe five or six, and I asked you why God made me wrong? You told me God doesn't make mistakes. You said God has a plan for everyone, and we have to trust His wisdom even when we don't understand it.

I've held onto those words for so long, Mama. Because if God doesn't make mistakes, then maybe He made me exactly who I'm supposed to be. Maybe the mistake isn't me being a girl. Maybe the mistake is everyone expecting me to be a boy.

I know this is hard to hear. I know it goes against everything you've been taught, everything Dad believes, everything our church preaches. But I'm begging you to look at me - really look at me - and see your child is hurting.

I've tried so hard to be what you want. I've played football even though I hate it. I've worn these clothes that feel like a costume. I've cut my hair short and tried to walk, talk, and be different.

But I can't keep doing it, Mama. It's killing me.

When you used to tuck me in at night and call me your "sweet boy," my heart broke. Not because I don't love you, but because I want so badly to be your sweet girl instead. I want to braid your hair and learn to cook your recipes and talk to you about the things mothers and daughters share. I want you to see me for who I really am. You always tell me that God loves me. But then you and Dad treat me like I'm an embarrassment when I try to be myself. If God loves me the way He made me, why can't you?

I see how other kids' mamas look at them. With pride. With joy. With love that doesn't come with conditions. I want that so bad, Mama. I want you to look at me the way Mrs. Rodriguez looks at Jenny - like I'm something wonderful instead of something that needs to be fixed.

Don't you want me to be happy? Don't you want me to be healthy? Because pretending to be someone I'm not is making me sick inside. I can't sleep. I can't eat. I spend every day wishing I could disappear because existing as a lie is too painful.

I'm not asking you to understand everything right away. I'm not asking you to go against Dad, I know how scary that would be. I'm just asking you to see me. To love me. To maybe, just maybe, consider that the child you've been praying for isn't broken - she's just different than what you expected.

You always say the Lord works in mysterious ways. Maybe this is one of those mysteries. Maybe He gave you a daughter when you were expecting a son because He knew you could love her if you tried.

I'm still the same person who helps you fold

laundry and brings you wildflowers from the backyard. I'm still the one who makes you laugh when I make my silly voices. I'm still your child, Mama. I just need you to love all of me, not just the parts that are easy.

If you can't accept me as your daughter, I understand. But please don't stop loving me completely. Please don't let Dad's anger become your anger too. I need at least one person in this family to see that I'm not an abomination or a mistake or something to be ashamed of. I'm just Dale. I've always been just Dale. And Dale is a girl who loves her mama and wants more than anything to be loved back.

Please, Mama. Please just think about it. Please just pray about it. Not for God to change me, but for God to help you see me the way He made me. I love you more than all the stars in the sky. That will never change, no matter what happens.

Your daughter,

Dale

PS - I hid this letter in your Bible, in the book of Ruth. I picked that one because Ruth said "Where you go, I will go" to someone she loved. I want you to know that no matter how far apart we grow, my love for you will always follow you. I just hope someday your love can follow me too.

Document 11: Spiritual Consultation Notes

Written by First Lady Dorothy Patterson
Dated: December 19, 2018

CEDAR RIDGE BAPTIST CHURCH
Spiritual Consultation Notes
Date: December 19, 2018

Present: Bishop Patterson, First Lady Dorothy Patterson, Earl Morrison (Deacon), Margaret Morrison

Emergency Nature of Meeting: Brother Earl contacted the church office in distress after discovering a letter written by his son to Sister Margaret. The letter contained what Brother Earl described as "pure demonic deception designed to corrupt my wife's heart."

Brother Earl's Report: "Bishop, I found this letter hidden in Margaret's Bible - IN THE HOLY SCRIPTURES! This boy is like that serpent in the Garden, whispering lies to Eve, trying to make her question God's design. But I caught it before Margaret could be fully deceived, just like Adam should have done."

Brother Earl read portions of the letter aloud. The content revealed deep spiritual deception - the boy claiming to be female, questioning God's creation, and attempting to manipulate his mother's natural maternal instincts to enable sin.

"This isn't just rebellion anymore, Bishop. This is demonic influence trying to destroy my family from the inside out."

Sister Margaret's Condition: Sister Margaret appeared deeply disturbed by the letter's contents. When asked directly, she admitted to having "confusing feelings" after reading it.

"I know Earl is right. I know the Bible is clear. But when I read those words... for a moment, I felt sorry for him. I wanted to comfort him. That's not natural, is it Bishop? A mother shouldn't feel sympathy for her child's sin."

First Lady Dorothy counseled Sister Margaret that these feelings were evidence of the enemy's attack on her discernment as a godly woman.

Spiritual Assessment: After much prayer and consideration, I believe we are dealing with a spirit of sexual perversion and gender confusion that has taken hold of this young man. The letter demonstrates several concerning spiritual markers:

1. **Blasphemous theology** - claiming God made him as a female

2. **Manipulation tactics** - using scripture to justify sin

3. **Family division** - attempting to turn mother against father's spiritual authority

4. **Persistent rebellion** - continuing in sin despite correction

This level of deception indicates demonic stronghold requiring spiritual warfare intervention.

Deliverance Ministry Recommendation: I am recommending a full deliverance session for this young man. However, I must warn the family that this is not to be undertaken lightly.

Requirements for Deliverance Session:

- Must have complete family unity in faith and purpose

- Parents must be prepared for an intense spiritual battle

- Subject must be brought willingly (by parental authority if necessary)
- Session requires overnight stay in the sanctuary for a complete spiritual breakthrough
- Minimum 12-hour fasting period beforehand to weaken demonic hold
- Prayer circle of mature believers (I recommend Brothers Johnson, Smith, Davis, Martinez, and Williams)

Warnings and Expectations: Brother Earl, Sister Margaret - deliverance ministry is intense spiritual warfare. The demons will not leave quietly. Expect:

- Violent physical reactions from the subject
- Blasphemous language and accusations
- Attempts to manipulate your emotions
- Possible temporary worsening of behaviors as spirits are challenged
- Need for physical restraint during prayer

The young man may say things designed to break your hearts and make you doubt. Remember, this is not your child speaking, but the enemy using his voice.

Biblical Precedent:

- Mark 9:14-29 - The boy with an unclean spirit required prayer and fasting
- Matthew 17:21 - "This kind goeth not out but by prayer and fasting"
- Luke 8:26-33 - The demoniac of Gadara required Jesus's direct intervention

Proposed Timeline:

- Bring subject to church after evening service
- Begin fasting and prayer circle at 9 PM
- Continue through Saturday morning until breakthrough achieved

- Parents remain present throughout to maintain spiritual authority

First Lady Dorothy's Counsel: "Sister Margaret, this will be the hardest thing you've ever done as a mother. You will hear your child's voice saying things that will make you want to give up. But remember, you're not fighting for the boy you see, you're fighting for his eternal soul."

Final Decision: Brother Earl has agreed to the deliverance session. Sister Margaret, though hesitant, has submitted to her husband's spiritual leadership in this matter.

Preparation Instructions:

- Subject should not be informed of plans until Friday evening
- Remove all food from home Thursday evening to begin family fast
- Brothers Johnson, Smith, Davis, Martinez, and Williams to be contacted for prayer support
- Church sanctuary to be prepared with necessary materials
- First aid supplies to be available given physical nature of spiritual warfare

Closing Prayer Focus: We are entering battle for this young man's soul. The enemy will not surrender easily what he believes he owns. But greater is He that is in us than he that is in the world.

Scripture for Meditation: "For we wrestle not against flesh and blood, but against principalities, against powers, against the rulers of the darkness of this world, against spiritual wickedness in high places." - Ephesians 6:12

In His Service, Rev. William Patterson Senior
Bishop, Cedar Ridge Baptist Church

Document 12: Diary Entry
Written by Dale Morrison
Dated: December 19, 2018

He found my letter.

The letter I wrote to Mama, the one I poured my whole heart into, the one where I begged her to see me as her daughter. He found it.

Dad came home tonight with this look in his eyes I've never seen before. Not just anger - something worse. Something that looked almost like excitement. Like Christmas morning, but twisted and dark.

"Margaret!" he called out the second he walked through the door. "Pack that boy some clothes. We're taking him to the church Friday night."

Mama's face went white. "Earl, can we – "

"Did you forget we figured out what's wrong with him. It's not just rebellion - there's a demon in that boy. A demon of sexual perversion that's been whispering lies in his ear and now it's trying to get to you too."

"You found my letter," I said. It wasn't a question.

Dad's face twisted with disgust. "I found the devil's words written in your handwriting, hidden in the Holy Bible like some kind of blasphemy. Trying to corrupt your mama's heart, trying to make her think God made a mistake. Bishop said 12 hours of fasting, but we'll make sure the Lord sends an angel and fast now til then."

"Earl," Mama whispered, "maybe we should just-"

"No!" Dad slammed his fist on the kitchen table so hard the saltshaker fell over. "This ends now.

This thing cannot have my son. Bishop Patterson knows how to handle this. We're gonna get that demon out of him once and for all."

I don't understand what they're planning, but the way Dad's talking about it scares me more than his belt ever did. He keeps saying things like "spiritual warfare" and "whatever it takes" and "the demon won't go quietly."

He made Mama throw away all the food in the house. Says we have to fast until Friday to "weaken the demon's hold." I'm not even allowed to drink anything but water.

"This is gonna be hard on all of us," Dad said, looking at me like I was something diseased. "But Bishop says it might get violent. Says you might say things, do things that ain't really you. Just the demon fighting back."

Violent? What are they planning to do to me?

Mama won't look at me. She's been crying on and off all evening, but when I tried to talk to her, she just shook her head and walked away.

"I can't," she whispered. "I can't listen to any more lies."

But they weren't lies, Mama. Every word in that letter was true. I am your daughter. I was just trying to help you see that.

Instead, I've made everything worse. Dad is more convinced than ever that I'm possessed. Mama thinks I'm trying to trick her into sin. And now they're planning to do something to me at the church that Dad describes as if I'm going to need medical attention afterward.

I'm scared. I'm really, really scared.

I keep thinking about what Dad said - that it

might get violent, that I might say and do things that "aren't really me." What does that mean? Are they going to hurt me until I agree to pretend to be a boy forever? Are they going to try to beat the girl out of me literally?

I feel so stupid about writing that letter. I thought maybe, just maybe, if I explained it right, Mama would understand. I thought if I reminded her that she always said God doesn't make mistakes, she might realize that meant He didn't make a mistake with me either.

Instead, Dad thinks I'm literally possessed by demons.

One day. One day until whatever they're planning.

I don't know what's going to happen to me Friday night. But I have this terrible feeling that the Dale who goes into that church isn't going to be the same Dale who comes out.

If I don't survive this - if they hurt me too badly, or if they somehow managed to break the part of me that knows who I really am - I want someone to know the truth.

My name is Dale. I'm 17 years old. I'm a girl who was born in the wrong body in the wrong family in the wrong town. I never chose to be this way, but I'm not ashamed of it either. I tried to love my parents and be what they wanted, but I can't kill the person God made me to be just to make them comfortable.

I'm not possessed. I'm not sick. I'm not broken.

I'm just Dale. And Dale is enough, even if nobody else can see it.

Please, God, if you're listening - protect the girl inside me. Don't let them kill her. She's the only real thing I have left.

Document 13: Letter to Parents

Written by Dale Morrison

Dated: December 20, 2018

Mom and Dad,

By the time you read this, I'll be gone. I can't stay here anymore. I can't let you do whatever you're planning to do to me at the church tomorrow night.

I know you think I'm possessed. I know you think there's something evil inside me that needs to be cast out. But you're wrong. There's nothing evil about me except the pain you've caused by refusing to love who I actually am.

Dad, you like to talk about sin. Let's talk about sin.

Is it a sin that I know in my heart I'm a girl? Or is it a sin that you get drunk and beat your wife and daughter? Because I've seen the bruises on Mama's arms, Dad. I've seen her flinch when you so much as sneeze in her direction because she's never sure if you're about to hit her. I've worn my own bruises from your "Biblical discipline" more times than I can count.

The Bible says "Be sober, be vigilant" but you come home drunk most nights. It says "Husbands, love your wives as Christ loved the church" but you terrorize Mama until she's afraid of her own shadow. It says "Fathers, do not exasperate your children" but you've spent my whole life trying to beat me into being someone I'm not. So, tell me, Dad - what makes my "sin" worse than yours? What makes me being true to who God made me worse than you being a drunk who hurts his family?

You always quote "spare the rod, spoil the child" but you never seem to remember "love your neighbor as yourself" or "judge not lest ye be judged." You pick and choose Bible verses like weapons to justify hurting people, but that's not what Jesus taught.

Jesus ate with tax collectors and sinners. He loved the outcasts and the different ones. If Jesus was here today, I think He'd sit with me and love me exactly as I am, not try to beat me into being someone else.

Mama, I know you're scared of Dad. I know you think if you agree with everything he says, maybe he won't hurt you as much. But your silence is killing me. Every time you tell me to "listen to your father" when he's destroying my soul, you're choosing his comfort over my life.

I wanted so badly for you to love me. Not the boy you wanted me to be, but me - Dale, your daughter who braids friendship bracelets and cries at sad movies and dreams about being pretty someday. I wanted you to see that being different doesn't make me wrong. But you can't see me because you're too busy trying to disappear yourself.

I'm not running away because I'm rebellious or because the devil is tempting me. I'm leaving because I'd rather be homeless and hungry than dead inside. I'm leaving because I refuse to let you kill the person God made me to be.

God doesn't make mistakes, Mama. Remember? If God doesn't make mistakes, then He made me exactly who I'm supposed to be - a woman named Dale who happened to be born in the wrong body. The mistake isn't how He made me. The mistake is how you've treated His creation.

I forgive you both, even though you've never asked for forgiveness. I forgive you, Dad, for the bruises and the cruel words and the nights you made me feel like I'd rather be dead than disappoint you again. I forgive you, Mama, for choosing fear over love, for letting him hurt both of us, for never once standing up and saying "enough." But forgiving you doesn't mean I have to stay here and let you destroy me.

Somewhere out there, there are people who will love me for who I am. Somewhere out there, there are families that don't use the Bible as an excuse to hurt their children. Somewhere out there, there's a place where being Dale isn't a sin that needs to be beaten out of me.

I'm going to find that place.

Don't look for me. If you really love me, let me go. Let me find people who can love all of me, not just the parts that make them comfortable.

If you ever change your mind and want to know me as your daughter instead of trying to force me to be your son, I'll find a way to let you know where I am. But until then, I have to protect myself, because you won't.

Maybe someday you'll understand that you didn't lose a son. You threw away a daughter.

I love you both, even though you can't love me back.

Your daughter,

Dale

Document 14: Spiritual Consultation Notes

Written by First Lady Dorothy Patterson
Dated: December 21, 2018

CEDAR RIDGE BAPTIST CHURCH
Spiritual Consultation Notes
Date: December 21, 2018
Time: 6:00 AM (Emergency call-in)

Present: Bishop Patterson, First Lady Dorothy Patterson, Earl Morrison (Deacon), Margaret Morrison

URGENT SITUATION: Brother Earl contacted me at 5:30 AM after discovering his son was missing and finding another letter. The timing, being just hours before our planned deliverance session confirms the demonic nature of this situation.

Brother Earl's Report: "Bishop, the demon knew. It knew we were coming for it Friday night, so it made the boy run. This letter... Bishop, this is pure Satan speaking through that child's hand."

Brother Earl read the letter aloud. The content reveals escalating demonic deception:

- Direct blasphemy claiming God made the boy as female
- Accusations against godly parental authority
- Attempts to justify sin through twisted scripture
- Manipulation tactics targeting Sister Margaret's maternal instincts
- Rebellion against Biblical family structure

Most Concerning Elements: The letter demonstrates advanced demonic strategy:

1. **False victimization** - claiming abuse when receiving Biblical correction

2. **Scripture twisting** - using God's word to justify abomination

3. **Family division** - attempting to turn wife against husband's spiritual leadership

4. **Emotional manipulation** - exploiting natural parental love to enable sin

5. **Escape timing** - demon fled before deliverance could occur

Sister Margaret's Condition - CRITICAL: Sister Margaret is in severe spiritual distress. The letter has shaken her faith in her husband's spiritual leadership.

"Bishop, what if... what if we were wrong? What if Earl, we, have been too hard? The letter talks about bruises, about me being afraid... What if the boy is just hurting and we've been making it worse?"

IMMEDIATE SPIRITUAL INTERVENTION REQUIRED Sister Margaret is experiencing dangerous doubt about Biblical family order. First Lady Dorothy provided emergency counseling:

- Reminded her that children often lie to escape discipline

- Explained that demons use partial truths to create convincing deceptions

- Counseled that a wife questioning her husband's spiritual authority opens doors for Satan

- Emphasized that the boy's "pain" is the demon being confronted by righteousness

URGENT SPIRITUAL ASSESSMENT: This escalation confirms my worst fears. We are not dealing with simple rebellion - this is high-level demonic possession. Evidence:

EMERGENCY ACTION PLAN: The demon has escalated to open warfare. We must respond immediately:

Phase 1 - Immediate (Today):

- Contact law enforcement to report runaway minor
- Alert church prayer chain for emergency intercession
- Organize search teams from Men's Ministry
- Secure Sister Margaret's spiritual stability through intensive counseling

Phase 2 - Recovery Mission:

- Canvas local areas where troubled youth congregate
- Contact other area churches about harboring runaways
- Check bus stations, shelters, known teenage gathering spots
- Use all available resources to locate subject

Phase 3 - Emergency Deliverance: When found, deliverance must occur IMMEDIATELY. The demon will not be given time to plan another escape.

- Mobile deliverance team ready for deployment
- Secure location prepared for extended spiritual warfare
- Medical support on standby given violent nature of advanced possession

- Legal consultation about parental rights in extreme cases

Biblical Precedent for Urgency:

- Mark 5:1-13 - The Gerasene demoniac required immediate intervention
- Acts 16:16-18 - Paul cast out the spirit immediately upon discernment
- Matthew 12:43-45 - Delayed action allows demons to return with greater force

First Lady Dorothy's Counsel: "Sister Margaret, this letter is exactly what Satan wants you to see. He's using your child's voice to attack your husband's godly leadership and your own faith. The bruises Dale mentions. Sometimes love looks harsh to those who don't understand discipline. The fear he claims you have? That's not fear - that's godly reverence for your husband's authority."

WARNING TO CONGREGATION: All members must be alert. This demon may attempt to corrupt other families through:

- Seeking shelter with church members
- Spreading lies about Biblical family structure
- Targeting other vulnerable youth with deceptive "acceptance"

Any member who encounters the subject must contact church leadership IMMEDIATELY. Do not attempt to counsel or help - this level of demonic influence requires Spiritual intervention.

Final Assessment: This is spiritual warfare at its most dangerous level. The enemy has taken a child of this congregation hostage and is using him to attack the very foundations of Biblical family order.

We will not rest until this young man is found and delivered from the powers of darkness that have claimed him.

Scripture for Battle: "The thief cometh not, but for to steal, and to kill, and to destroy. I am come that they might have life, and that they might have it more abundantly." - John 10:10

Prayer Focus:

- Swift location of the subject
- Protection of Brother Earl and Sister Margaret's marriage
- Binding of demonic forces preventing the boy's return
- Strength for the deliverance team when the time comes

In His Service, Rev. William Patterson Senior
Bishop, Cedar Ridge Baptist Church

CONFIDENTIAL NOTE: Have contacted Brother Martinez who has connections with local law enforcement. They will treat this as a runaway case but understand the spiritual dimensions.

Document 15: Incident Report

Written by Officer Ronald Jackson
Dated: December 21, 2018

MILLBROOK POLICE DEPARTMENT INCIDENT REPORT

REPORT NUMBER: MP-99-1208-003

DATE/TIME REPORTED: December 21, 2018 / 07:45

REPORTING OFFICER: Officer R. Jackson, Badge #T9-341

REPORT TYPE: Missing Person - Juvenile Runaway

SUBJECT INFORMATION:

NAME: Dale Morrison **DOB:** November 3, 2001

AGE: 17 **SEX:** Male **RACE:** Blk **HEIGHT:** 5'9"

WEIGHT: 165 lbs. **HAIR:** Blk, short **EYES:** Brown

LAST KNOWN LOCATION: 1247 Maple Street, Millbrook, AL

REPORTING PARTIES:

PRIMARY: Earl Thomas Morrison (Father)

DOB: 04/05/62 **ADDRESS:** 1247 Maple Street, Millbrook **PHONE:** (256) 555-0847

SECONDARY: Margaret Ann Morrison (Mother)

DOB: 06/08/81 **ADDRESS:** Same as above

PHONE: Same as above

CIRCUMSTANCES OF DISAPPEARANCE: Per Mr. Morrison, the subject was last seen at residence on evening of 12/20/2018 at approximately 22:00 hours.

The subject was discovered missing on the morning of 12/21/2018 when parents attempted to wake him for breakfast. The bedroom window was found open, screen removed. No signs of forced entry or struggle.

ITEMS MISSING:

- Subject's backpack (black JanSport)
- clothes
- Toiletries
- Birth certificate and Social Security card

FATHER'S STATEMENT: Mr. Morrison states the subject has been "acting out" recently and "getting into trouble at church." Reports subject has been "rebellious" and "influenced by bad ideas." When asked to elaborate, Mr. Morrison stated family had been receiving counseling from their Bishop regarding subject's "behavioral problems." Mr. Morrison emphasized that the subject is "confused" and may be "dangerous to himself or others" due to "spiritual influences." Requested immediate location and return of subject.

MOTHER'S STATEMENT: Mrs. Morrison appeared visibly distressed during the interview. Confirmed husband's timeline of events. When asked directly about the subject's state of mind, Mrs. Morrison stathe subject had been "troubled" and "saying strange things."

ADDITIONAL INFORMATION:

- A handwritten letter was left by subject (parents declined to provide copy, stating it contained "private family matters")

- No history of previous runaway attempts
- No known drug or alcohol use
- Subject described as "good student" but "withdrawn lately"
- Parents report no known friends subject might contact
- No access to vehicles

RISK ASSESSMENT:
Low Risk ____ Medium Risk X High Risk____

Juvenile with no street experience, limited resources, December weather conditions present exposure concerns. No indication of self-harm ideation, but parents' statements suggest ongoing family stress.

INVESTIGATIVE ACTIONS TAKEN:
- NCIC/FCIC entry completed
- Local hospitals and shelters contacted
- School resource officer at Millbrook High notified
- Area patrol units provided subject description
- Bus station and truck stops checked

OBSERVATIONS/CONCERNS: While interviewing the family, I noticed several inconsistencies:
- Parents claim subject "never had problems before" but also describe ongoing behavioral issues
- Father appeared angrier than concerned about son's welfare
- Mother seemed fearful during questioning, particularly when father spoke

- Religious overtones in father's description of situation unusual for standard runaway case
- Parents' refusal to share subject's letter limits investigation

FOLLOW-UP REQUIRED:

- Daily patrol checks of known juvenile gathering areas
- Contact with area churches and youth organizations
- School interview with subject's teachers/counselors
- Welfare check if subject located (note family dynamics for CPS review)

DISPOSITION: Case remains ACTIVE. Subject entered NCIC as endangered runaway. Parents advised to contact department immediately if subject makes contact.

SUPPLEMENTAL REPORTS:

- Interview with school counselor scheduled 12/21/2018 via emergency line.
- Canvas of local businesses ongoing
- Coordination with neighboring jurisdictions initiated

REPORTING OFFICER NOTES: Family dynamics appear strained. Father's emphasis on "spiritual" aspects of son's behavior and mother's visible anxiety suggest possible underlying issues. Recommend social services consultation if subject is

located and returned to home. Parents insist that the subject be returned immediately upon location, citing concerns about "outside influences" affecting the minor.

APPROVED BY: Sergeant J. Williams, Badge #T9-201
Date: December 21, 2018
Distribution: Detective Division, Patrol Division, CID, Juvenile Division

Document 16: Diary Entry
Written by Dale Morrison
Dated: December 21, 2018

Day 1

I'm writing this in the bathroom at McDonald's on Highway 72. My hands are shaking so bad I can barely hold the pen.

I've been walking since 3 AM when I climbed out my bedroom window. I took the back roads to take me out of town, staying away from the main streets where Dad might look for me. My feet are already blistered, and I've only got about 8 miles behind me.

The bus station was my first stop, but a ticket to anywhere costs more than the forty dollars cash I have. The lady behind the counter kept staring at me like she knew something was wrong. I got scared and left before she could ask questions.

It's cold. Colder than I thought it would be. I'm wearing three layers but the wind cuts right through everything. I found an old coat in a dumpster behind Goodwill that's too big, but it helps.

A trucker at the truck stop offered me a ride to Birmingham. He seemed nice enough, but something about the way he looked at me made my stomach turn. I said no and walked away fast.

I'm so hungry. I spent $8 on a burger and a bottled water, but I need to make my money last. I don't know how long I'll be out here.

Document 17: Diary Entry
Written by Dale Morrison
Dated: December 22, 2018

Day 2

Slept under the bridge by Miller Creek last night. I woke up covered in frost and couldn't feel my fingers. A homeless man named Charlie found me shivering and shared his blanket. He didn't ask questions, just said "rough night for sleeping outside, kid."

Charlie told me about a shelter in Huntsville, but it's thirty miles away and they ask for ID. He said they'd call my parents for sure if they knew I was a minor.

"You running from something bad at home?" he asked while we shared a can of beans he heated over a little fire.

I nodded but didn't say what.

"Sometimes home ain't safe," he said. "But the streets ain't safe either, especially for someone like you. You got a kind face. People gonna try to take advantage."

I know what he means. Three different men have approached me today. One offered me money to "come hang out." Another said he had a warm place where I could stay. I ran from both. Charlie was the third.

My money's almost gone. I bought a sandwich and a Coke and I'm down to $26.

I'm scared. I'm hungry. I'm dirty and I smell, and people look at me like I'm something disgusting. But I'm still not ready to go home. I can't face whatever they're planning to do to me at that church.

Document 18: Police Department Incident Report

Written by Officer Richard Martinez

Dated: December 23, 2018

MILLBROOK POLICE DEPARTMENT
INCIDENT REPORT

CASE NUMBER: 2018-0312-0847 **DATE:** December 23, 2018 **TIME:** 22:30 hours

LOCATION: Walmart Supercenter, 3801 Main Street, Millbrook, AL

REPORTING OFFICER: Officer Richard Martinez, Badge #247

SUPERVISOLR: Sergeant James Thompson

INCIDENT TYPE: Welfare Check / Runaway Juvenile

DISPOSITION: Turned over to parents

NARRATIVE:

At approximately 22:30 hours, I was dispatched to Walmart Supercenter on Main Street for a welfare check on a juvenile reportedly hiding in the restroom facility. Store manager Janet Cole reported that an employee had stated he could not clean the women's restroom because he observed someone go in and they have been in there for an extended period. She stated she entered the restroom and saw the juvenile in the handicap stall creating a sleeping mat. After informing the minor they could not remain in the store, Cole returned to her office and called 911. Upon arrival, I entered the restroom and found the subject, later identified as Dale Earl Morrison (DOB: 11/03/1982), sitting on the floor in a locked stall, crying. Subject appeared unharmed but emotionally distressed. I knew the subject but still requested identification. Subject initially refused to give name and was reluctant to provide identification. After questioning, subject provided a name and date of birth. I contacted parents Earl Morrison (256-555-0923) and Margaret Morrison, who arrived at the scene at 23:15 hours. Parents confirmed subject's identity and that subject was welcome to return home. Subject was released to parents' custody at 23:20 hours. Store management declined to press trespassing charges.

INJURIES: None observed
PROPERTY DAMAGE: None
WITNESSES: Janet Cole (Store Manager), Employee "Mike" (last name not provided)
FOLLOW-UP: None required **CASE STATUS:** Closed
OFFICER ON SCENE: Richard Martinez, Badge #247
DATE: December 23, 2018
SUPERVISOR ON DUTY: Sergeant James Thompson
DATE: December 23, 2018

Document 19: Diary Entry

Written by Dale Morrison

Dated: December 23, 2018

Day 3

I was trying to clean up in the bathroom at the Greyhound station when the police walked in. Two officers, and one of them looked familiar. Officer Martinez, I think. He goes to Cedar Ridge Baptist Church.

They found me.

"Dale Morrison?" he said, even though he already knew it was me.

I thought about running but there was nowhere to go. I was trapped in a bathroom with two grown men blocking the door.

"Your parents are worried sick about you, son," Officer Martinez said. "They've been looking everywhere."

"I can't go home," I said. "Please. You don't understand what they're going to do to me."

"What do you mean? Are you in some kind of trouble?" His partner asked.

I wanted to tell her everything. About the planned exorcism, about Dad's drinking and hitting, about how they think I'm possessed just because I know I'm a girl. But how do you explain that to police officers, one who goes to church with your parents?

"They think I'm... they think there's something wrong with me," I said.

"Well, we'll get you some help," the officer said. "But first you need to go home. Your parents love you."

Love. They keep using that word, but I don't think it means what they think it means.

They didn't handcuff me and let me have my notebook while they drove. I wanted to explain that I am not a criminal, but I guess technically I am - a runaway, a disappointment, a demon-possessed child who needs to be delivered back to her captors.

In the police car, Officer Martinez kept talking about how my parents were "good people" and how the church was "praying for me." He said Bishop Patterson had personally called to check on the search efforts.

Of course he did.

"You know your dad's a deacon at Cedar Ridge," Officer Martinez said. "He's a pillar of the community. You're lucky to have parents who care so much."

A pillar of the community that did things in the dark that would blot out the sun if they were ever brought to light.

We just turned into my neighborhood. I can see the familiar streets getting closer. In a few minutes I'll be back in that house, and they'll drag me to that church.

I tried. I really tried to save myself.

I'm not strong enough to survive on my own.

Maybe I'm not strong enough to survive what's coming either.

But I guess I'm about to find out.

The girl in the mirror is going to have to fight for her life now. I just hope she's stronger than I am.

Document 20: Police Department Witness Statement

Written by Janet Cole

Dated: December 31, 2018

MILLBROOK POLICE DEPARTMENT
WITNESS STATEMENT

CASE NUMBER: 2018-0312-0847 **DATE:** December 31, 2018 **TIME:** 10:45pm

LOCATION: Walmart Supercenter, 3801 Main Street, Millbrook, AL

WITNESS INFORMATION Janet Cole, Store Manager

PHONE: (334) 555-0892

STATEMENT:

At around 10:00pm on December 31, 2018, my maintenance employee Mike Thompson came to my office saying he could not clean the women's restroom because he saw someone go in and they had been in there for an extended period. He guessed about 45 minutes. I immediately went to the women's restroom to check on the situation. I saw a young person in the handicap stall, and it looked like they were trying to create a sleeping mat using their clothes. I couldn't see everything because the door was closed. The person was sitting on this makeshift bedding. I knocked on the stall door and identified myself as the store manager. I told the person that they could not remain in the store overnight and that I would need them to leave the premises. The individual responded that they had "nowhere to go" and asked if they could "just stay until morning." I explained that the store policy did not allow overnight stays and that I was concerned about their safety and wellbeing. The individual became distressed and refused to leave the stall. I left the restroom, told Mike to close it off, and returned to my office and called 911 for assistance. I was concerned about their safety and emotional state. I remained in the store until Officer Martinez arrived. The individual did not damage any store property and was cooperative with the officer. No merchandise was stolen or damaged during the incident. //End of Statement ///------------------- _JC_

I certify that the above statement is true and accurate to the best of my knowledge.

SIGNATURE: _Janet Cole_

DATE: December 31, 2018

Witnessed by: Officer Maria Martinez, Badge #247

Document 21: Diary Entry

Written by Dale Morrison

Dated: December 31, 2018

I don't know how to write about what happened tonight. There are rope burns on my wrists, and my throat is raw from screaming.

Dad, Bishop Patterson, Brother Johnson, Brother Smith, Brother Davis, and Brother Morck. Six grown men to handle one seventeen-year-old girl, though they don't know that, after everything that happened, that's what I still am.

It all started with Officer Martinez ringing the doorbell.

I dropped my bag on the porch when Dad answered the door. Mom was sitting ramrod straight in the same chair she always sat, looking at the dead tv screen. As I stepped through the threshold, I noticed Bishop Patterson standing in the space between Mama and me. Dad grabbed my shoulder with pressure no one could see, but I could feel it. He didn't' even let me sit down.

The cops drove away, and Dad gripped my shoulder tighter.

    "Let's go, Margaret." There were no hugs for my return. There was no worry in their eyes. "Time to go, boy," Dad said. His voice was different - harder than usual, like he was preparing for war.

Mama unfolded herself from the couch, wringing her hands. She looked like she wanted to say something, but Bishop Patterson put his hand on her shoulder.

    "Sister Margaret, this is men's work," he said. "You pray for us from here."

They loaded me into Brother Johnson's van. Nobody talked during the drive to the church, but I could feel their eyes on me. Like they were studying an enemy.

The sanctuary was different at night. Darker. Scarier. They had moved all the pews and made a circle of chairs in the center. There were ropes, bottles of oil, and a wooden cross that looked heavy enough to use as a weapon.

But then Bishop Patterson surprised everyone.

"Brothers, I've been praying about this," he announced. "The Lord has shown me that this level of deliverance requires a more... personal approach. I have enough Holy Ghost fire in me to handle this demon alone. Sometimes too many voices can confuse spiritual warfare."

Dad looked uncertain. "Bishop, are you sure? This boy has been—"

"Brother Earl, do you trust my spiritual authority?" Bishop Patterson's voice carried that tone that ended all arguments in our church.

"Of course, Bishop."

"Then trust me now. I'll call you when it's finished. This may take all night."

The other men filed out, looking back at me with a mixture of concern and relief. Dad was the last to leave.

"You do whatever Bishop Patterson tells you, demon," he said. "I want my son back."

Then I was alone with Bishop Patterson in that dark sanctuary.

"Sit down, son," he said, pointing to a chair in the middle of the circle.

when I hesitated, he grabbed my arms and forced me into the chair. Then he tied my wrists to the armrests.

"This is for your own protection," he explained. "When the demons fight back, you might try to hurt yourself."

He started reading from the Bible about casting out unclean spirits, but something was different. His hands weren't just on my head for prayer. They wandered. Touched places that made my skin crawl.

"DEMON OF SEXUAL PERVERSION," he shouted, but his own hands were doing things that felt like perversion. "I COMMAND YOU COME OUT OF THIS BOY!"

I tried to pull away, tried to tell him to stop, but my voice didn't work. He just prayed louder.

"The demon is making you feel shame about godly touch," he said, his voice still taking on that preacher cadence even as his hands violated me. "This is how we drive out the spirit of confusion about your gender, son. Through prayer and proper masculine guidance."

His prayers never stopped. Even when he was doing things that no man should ever do to a minor or someone who isn't willing. Even as I cried and begged him to stop, he continued. The Bible verses kept flowing from his mouth like they made his actions holy.

"Oh Lord, cast out this demon of femininity," he prayed while assaulting me. "Show this boy what it means to submit to masculine authority. Let him understand his proper role."

Hours passed.

I struggled against the ropes, screamed until my

ears hurt, and cried for someone to come save me.

"IT'S FIGHTING HARD," he announced to the empty sanctuary. "THIS IS A STRONG DEMON. BUT THE POWER OF GOD IS STRONGER."
I stopped fighting because fighting only made him pray harder, touch more. I learned that if I stayed very still and very quiet, he would focus more on his prayers and less on the other things.

I don't want to write about everything that happened. I can't. Some things are too dark to put into words.

What I will write is this: I didn't break. Through all of it - the violation disguised as prayer, the abuse hidden behind spiritual authority, the hours of being told that what he was doing to me was God's will - I held onto the truth inside me.

What he did to me wasn't deliverance. It was evil wearing a collar and carrying a Bible.

Around 4 AM, I had retreated so far inside myself that I stopped responding to anything. Not because any "demon" had left, but because I had found a place in my mind where his voice and his hands couldn't reach me.

He thought he had won. He thought my silence meant success.

"The demon has been cast out," he announced, exhausted and sweating as he untied my wrists and zipped his pants. "The boy is free. The spirit of sexual confusion has been driven out through proper masculine authority."

He called Dad to come pick me up. When Dad arrived, Bishop Patterson was back to his normal spiritual demeanor, as if nothing had happened.

"How do you feel, son?" Dad asked. For the first time in months, his voice was gentle.

I looked at him. At the man who had handed me over to a predator wearing holy robes.

"Empty," I said. Which was true, but not in the way they thought.

Dad drove me home as the sun was coming up. Mama was waiting in the kitchen with breakfast. She looked over my wrists, looked at Dad, and back at me. She said nothing. Just grab bandages and ointment.

"The Lord has delivered you," she whispered, dabbing medicine on my rope burns. "Bishop Patterson says you're healed now. You can be our good boy again."

I'm not their good boy. I never was. And one night of religious abuse disguised as spiritual warfare didn't change that.

I'm still Dale, and now I know that some of the people who claim to speak for God are the very ones He would be most ashamed of.

What Bishop Patterson did to me was evil. What he called deliverance was assault. What he called God's will was his own sick desires hidden behind prayer.

The girl inside me survived. Violated, traumatized, but alive.

And someday, somehow, I'm going to make sure the world knows what really happens in some of those churches when they claim to be casting out demons.

They have no idea how strong she really is. Or how angry.

DOCUMENT REQUEST
CEDAR RIDGE BAPTIST CHURCH
Requested by

Contact Attempted: Pastor William "Willie" Patterson

Church: Cedar Ridge Baptist Church

Address: 892 Old Montgomery Road, Millbrook, AL 36054

Request Date: April 22, 2025

Follow-up Attempts: April 29, May 5, May 12, 2025

Documentation Sought: Process and procedures or institutional records pertaining to the December 30, 2018 "deliverance ceremony" involving Dale Earl Morrison (later Dale Elizabeth Morrison) and family intervention proceedings.

Response: Pastor Patterson declined to provide any documentation related to the requested incident. When contacted by phone on May 5, 2025, Pastor Patterson stated that "church disciplinary matters are confidential" and that the church would not be participating in this archival project.

Additional Contact: Mrs. Dorothy Patterson (Pastor's wife) was approached during a September 12, 2024 phone call. Mrs. Patterson refused to answer questions regarding the incident and referred all inquiries back to her husband. She terminated the call when the nature of the research was explained.

Outcome: No documentation obtained from Cedar Ridge Baptist Church. The church's institutional records regarding this incident remain inaccessible for research purposes.

Document 22: Spiritual Consultation Notes

Written by First Lady Dorothy Patterson

Dated: December January 4, 2019

CEDAR RIDGE BAPTIST CHURCH
Post-Deliverance Counseling Session
Date: January 4, 2019

Present: Bishop Patterson, Earl Morrison (Deacon), Margaret Morrison

Session Opening: Opened with prayer of thanksgiving for God's victory over demonic forces. Brother Earl and Sister Margaret appeared relieved but exhausted from the spiritual battle their family had endured.

Deliverance Results: I am pleased to report complete success in casting out the demon of sexual perversion and gender confusion that had taken hold of the Morrison boy. After an intensive night of spiritual warfare, the unclean spirit was fully expelled.

Brother Earl's Response: "Bishop, I can't thank you enough! When I saw that boy this morning, I could tell immediately that something had changed. He was quiet, respectful - not that defiant look in his eyes anymore."

Brother Earl became emotional, shouting "HALLELUJAH!" and praising God for the deliverance. His faith throughout this trial has been exemplary.

"Bishop, you saved my boy's soul. You saved my family. I don't know how to repay you."

Bishop Response: I explained to Brother Earl that no repayment was necessary - this is simply the work of the Lord. "Give it to God, Brother Earl. All glory belongs to Him."

Sister Margaret's Demeanor: Sister Margaret remained quiet throughout the session. When asked directly about her observations of her son's condition, she simply nodded and said, "He seems... different."

I sensed some concern in her spirit and reminded her that deliverance can be emotionally difficult for family members to witness, even secondhand.

Details of Spiritual Warfare Session: I shared with the parents that this was one of the most challenging deliverances I have performed in twenty years of ministry. The demon was far stronger than initially assessed and required... non-traditional spiritual warfare techniques.

"Brother Earl, Sister Margaret, I want you to understand that what I had to do last night went beyond typical prayer and laying on of hands. Some demons require more intensive spiritual intervention. The enemy fought hard for this boy's soul."

Brother Earl's Concern: Brother Earl immediately expressed concern for my well-being: "Bishop, are you alright? Did the demon try to hurt you? Do you need anything? Medical attention? Rest?"

His concern was touching. I assured him that while the spiritual battle was intense and I had to employ methods that were both physically and emotionally demanding, the Lord sustained me throughout.

"I won't lie to you, Brother Earl - there were moments when I wondered if my spiritual armor was strong enough. But God gave me the strength to do what was necessary."

Ongoing Care Instructions: Provided the following guidance for maintaining the boy's spiritual freedom:

1. **Vigilant Monitoring:** Watch for any signs of the demon attempting to return

2. **Increased Biblical Study:** Boy should spend extra time with masculine Biblical role models

3. **No Isolation:** Boy should not be left alone for extended periods during vulnerable recovery phase

4. **Physical Activity:** Continue masculine activities like sports to reinforce proper gender roles

5. **Regular Check-ins:** Monthly Spiritual consultations to ensure spiritual stability

Brother Earl's Gratitude: "Bishop, I owe you everything. That boy is my son again because of what you did. If you ever need anything - anything at all - you just say the word."

I reminded Brother Earl that his faithfulness as a deacon and his willingness to trust spiritual authority in difficult circumstances was payment enough.

Sister Margaret's Questions: When pressed for her thoughts, Sister Margaret asked quietly: "Bishop, when you say non-traditional methods... what exactly...?"

I explained that some spiritual warfare techniques are not appropriate to discuss in detail, as they can be misunderstood by those not called to deliverance ministry. "Sister Margaret, sometimes God calls his servants to make sacrifices in the battle for souls. Trust that everything I did was guided by the Holy Spirit."

Final Assessment: The Morrison family should experience no further issues with their son's gender confusion or rebellious behavior. The demon has been fully cast out, though vigilance must be maintained to prevent re-infestation.

Brother Earl's Closing Statement: "Bishop, you went above and beyond the call of duty. You put yourself at risk for our family. I'll never forget what you've done for us."

Closing: Reminded the family that this victory belongs to God alone. "I was simply His vessel. Give all glory to the Almighty."

Follow-up Scheduled: Monthly check-ins with the boy to monitor spiritual condition. Parents instructed to contact me immediately if any concerning behaviors return.

Prayer Focus:

- Continued freedom for the Morrison boy
- Healing any trauma the family experienced during this spiritual battle
- Strength for Spiritual ministry in difficult cases
- Protection against any retaliatory attacks from defeated demonic forces

---

In His Service, Rev. William Patterson Senior
Bishop, Cedar Ridge Baptist Church

Document 23: Diary Entry

Written by Dale Morrison

Dated: March 3, 2019

I'm writing this from my hospital bed. My left hand is in a cast, my ribs are taped up, and I can barely see out of my right eye. But I'm alive.

It started last Friday night. I couldn't take another evening of sitting in that house, pretending to be their good little boy while Dad drank himself into his usual stupor. I waited until they were asleep, then snuck out through my bedroom window.

I'd been planning this for months. I bought the fake ID from a kid at school for fifty dollars - it said I was 21 and my name was Dana Morrison. Close enough to Dale that I'd remember to answer to it, but feminine enough that it felt like stepping into my real skin.

The club was in Huntsville, far enough from home that I wouldn't run into anyone I knew. I'd been saving up for months to buy the dress - a simple black one that made me feel beautiful for the first time in my life. I borrowed some makeup from Walgreens when no one was looking and did my best to learn how to use it from YouTube videos at the library.

When I walked into that club, I felt like I was home. The music was loud, the lights were dim, and nobody looked at me like I was an abomination. For three hours, I was just another girl dancing, laughing, being alive.

"Can we buy you a drink, beautiful?"

That's when I met Marcus and his friend Tyler. They were cute, maybe in their early twenties, and they bought me drinks and told me I was pretty. We danced together, and for the first time in my life, I felt what it was like to be seen as a woman.

Marcus asked if I wanted to go outside for some air. I should have said no. I should have stayed in the safety of the club. But I was seventeen and stupid and drunk on the feeling of being desired for who I really was.

"You two have been nothing but gentlemen. Thank you for showing me a good time." I declined the invite and left the club smiling as I walked. I heard footsteps and turned to see they were walking out also.

"Just wanted to make sure you stayed safe out here," Tyler said, making his way behind me.

"You're too pretty to be walking in the dark alone," Marcus cooed, standing in front of me. Tyler made a joke about taking me home. Marcus laughed and put his hand on my waist, and I felt like I was in a fairy tale.

Then his hand moved lower, rounding my butt. His fingertips found the hem of the dress. He smiled at me as he changed directions and slid his hand up. He stopped immediately.

The look on his face changed so fast it was like watching someone flip a switch. Confusion. Disgust. Rage.

"What the hell?" he said, jerking his hand away. "You're a dude?"

"I'm not—" I started to say, but Tyler was already grabbing my arm.

"You sick freak," he snarled. "You were trying to trick us."

I tried to explain, tried to tell them I was just being

myself, but they weren't listening. Marcus hit me first - a punch to the stomach that doubled me over. Then Tyler kicked me in the ribs, and I went down hard on the asphalt.

"Fucking tranny," Marcus said, and then they were both on me, spitting, hitting and kicking, calling me names I won't repeat.

I remember thinking, "This is how I die. Beaten to death behind a club, wearing a black dress, finally being myself."

But I didn't die. Someone heard the noise and called the police. The paramedics said I was lucky - broken ribs, broken hand, concussion, but nothing that wouldn't heal.

The hospital called my parents. I was seventeen, so they had to.

Mama came alone.

"Where's Dad?" I asked when she walked into my room, her face white as a sheet.

"He's... he's at home," she said, not meeting my eyes.

"Why didn't he come?"

Mama was quiet for a long time. Finally, she said, "He said this wouldn't have happened if the deliverance worked. If you were really back."

Even drugged up on painkillers, that hit harder than any punch Marcus had thrown.

"Mama," I said as she sat down in the chair beside my bed, her hands folded in her lap like she was praying.

"I'm not your son," I said. "I never was. I'm your daughter. I've always been your daughter. And last night was the first time in my life I got to be myself, even for a few hours."

She didn't say anything. Just sat there, staring at her hands.

"Those men beat me, but I'm not ashamed of who I am, Mama. I'm ashamed of who I've been pretending to be."

Mama finally looked at me. Really looked at me. And for the first time, I saw her seeing me - not the boy she wanted me to be, but who I was.

"You were wearing a dress," she said quietly.

"Yes."

"And makeup."

"Yes."

"And you looked..." She struggled for words. "You looked like a girl."

"Because I am a girl, Mama. I've been trying to tell you that for years."

She was crying now, but quietly, the way she always cried when she didn't want Dad to hear.

"What am I supposed to do with that?" she whispered.

"Love me," I said. "Just love me for who I am instead of who you want me to be."

We sat in silence for a long time. The machines beeping, the nurses talking in the hallway, the sound of her crying softly in the chair beside my bed.

Finally, she said, "I don't know how."

"Then learn," I said. "Please, Mama. Just try to learn."

She stayed with me for two more hours. She helped me drink water when my hands were shaking too much to hold the cup. She adjusted my pillows when

I couldn't get comfortable. She even brushed my hair back from my forehead the way she used to when I was little and sick.

Just before she left, she leaned down and kissed my forehead.

"My child," she whispered. Not "my son" or "my boy." Just "my child."

It wasn't everything I needed to hear. But it was a start.

Dad still hasn't come to see me. He sent words through Mama that he's "disappointed in my choices" and that I "brought this on myself by living a lie."

But I wasn't living a lie that night. For the first time in my life, I was living my truth.

And even though it nearly killed me, I'm not sorry.

I'm done apologizing for existing.

The girl in the mirror finally got to come out and dance.

Now she's ready to fight for her right to stay out.

Document 24: Poem

Written by Dale Morrison

Dated: March 11, 2019

I said yes to the drink.

I fluttered my eyelashes and smiled as I sipped. Feeling bits of romance and possibility slide down my throat as I looked into eyes that promised white picket fences and suburban life.

I smiled as stories of how I'd been the subject of attention danced around me; tickling my cheeks. I smiled the whole night. Smiled so much it hurt not to. The gentle caresses were promises of happiness. Sweet nothings licked my ears, the only thing sweeter than the drink. It felt good to be wanted.

I scribbled my number on a napkin. It was romantic in the movies. My flirtatious smile wobbled as faces stretched and dimmed in my blurry mind. I told myself to quit while I was still cute. I slid from the bar while the napkin was folded by manicured hands and slid into a pocket. The memory of my sudden confidence turned my cheeks red. They burned so good.

It's hard to walk silently on gravel, so when I heard the footsteps I turned to see the person. All smile and charm was the face, but the words were not.

The warmth moved from my cheeks to cover my body; from excitement to warning. Each goosebump an indication to run. Well dressed and respected, each blur did what the next did, and I was surrounded by rage hidden by smiling masks. The masks got closer, and the smiles distorted.

One mask told me I was too pretty to be alone on a night like this. Another said I didn't pay for the drink. They asked me why I looked so scared and the last told me this would be fun.

I fought and I scratched, I screamed, and I cried. I put keys in between my knuckles. But no whistle blowing would have made this stop. It's supposed to be safe in the brightness. A kick forced me to give the drink back and it burned, all sweetness gone.

I woke up on the gravel. The air still. I was alone. I shoved my dress back over my hips and picked up my blue heels. Scared. Confused. Lost.

Document 25: Diary Entry

Written by Dale Morrison

Dated: March 15, 2019

I graduate in 12 weeks.

12 weeks until I can leave this house, this town, this life that was never mine to begin with. I've been counting down the days since that night at the church over a year ago. 546 days of pretending Bishop Patterson "fixed" me. 546 days of being the quiet, obedient son they think they created.

They have no idea who I really am now.

I've gotten good at being invisible. I do my chores, I go to school, I sit in church every Sunday and Wednesday and listen to Bishop Patterson preach about God's love while he watches me from the pulpit with those eyes that remember what he did to me. I even shake his hand after service and say "Good sermon, Bishop" because that's what good boys do.

But inside, I'm planning.

I've been working at the grocery store after school, telling Dad the money is for college. He's so proud that his "delivered" son is responsible. What he doesn't know is that I've been saving every penny. $2,847 so far. Enough to get me far away from here.

I've been researching cities with good support systems for people like me. Places where being different isn't a sin that needs to be beaten out of you. San Francisco. Portland. Atlanta. Cities with real communities, real people who understand that God makes all kinds of folks.

Christina from Walgreens graduated from nursing school and moved to Birmingham last year. Before she left, she slipped me a piece of paper with her address. "If you ever need somewhere safe to land," she said. I think she knew. I think she always knew.

I've been writing letters to myself - practicing what I'll say when I finally get to live as Dale, the real Dale. Not the broken boy they think they created, but the woman who survived everything they did to her.

The hardest part is Mama. She's gotten quieter since that night at the church, if that's even possible. Sometimes I catch her looking at me with this expression I can't read. Like she's seeing something she doesn't want to understand.

Last week, she was folding laundry, and she held up one of my t-shirts. Just held it there, staring at it.

"You're so thin," she said quietly. "You used to be such a sturdy little boy."

"I'm fine, Mama."

"Are you?" She looked at me directly for the first time in a while. "Are you really fine?"

For a second, I thought about telling her everything. About the girl inside me who never died despite everything they did to kill her. About Bishop Patterson and what really happened that night. About how I lay awake planning my escape from the life they forced me into.

Instead, I said, "I'm exactly what you and Dad wanted me to be."

She didn't say anything after that. Just folded the shirt and put it away.

Dad's been drinking more lately. Not just at night - sometimes I smell it on him when he comes home for lunch. He's louder when he drinks now, more emotional. Last Sunday after church, he cornered Bishop Patterson and started thanking him again for "saving my boy."

"That deliverance changed everything," Dad said, his voice too loud for the church lobby. "My son is a man now. A real man."

Bishop Patterson just smiled and patted Dad's shoulder. "God's grace is sufficient, Brother Earl."

But I saw the way he looked at me over Dad's head. Like he was remembering. Like he was wondering if I remembered too.

I remember everything.

The truth is, I'm not the person any of them think I am. I'm not the demon-possessed boy they "delivered." I'm not the grateful son who learned his place. I'm not even the victim they think they broke.

I'm Dale. I've always been Dale. And in 12 weeks, I'm going to finally start living like it.

I've been practicing walking in heels in my bedroom when they're not home. I found some at Goodwill that almost fit. I've been letting my hair grow out just a little - not enough that anyone notices, but enough that I can see the person I'm going to become.

I've been reading books about people like me. Stories of other girls who were born looking like boys, who had to fight for the right to exist as themselves. I'm not alone. I never was alone.

That's what they could never understand - you can't cast out someone's soul. You can't beat the truth out of someone's heart. You can't pray away who God made them to be.

They thought they won that night at the church.

They thought they destroyed the woman inside me.

They have no idea how wrong they are.

In 12 weeks, I'm going to disappear from their lives forever. And somewhere else, in a place where people don't use the Bible as a weapon, Dale is going to finally come alive.

The girl in the mirror has been waiting patiently for 18 years.

She's not waiting much longer.

Document 26: Diary Entry

Written by Dale Morrison

Dated: April 17, 2019

I've been home from the hospital for two weeks now. The physical wounds are healing, but everything else feels more broken than before.

Dad still hasn't spoken directly to me since the attack. When he needs to communicate something, he tells Mama, and she tells me. Like I'm dead to him but he hasn't figured out how to bury me yet.

"Tell him he needs to keep his bedroom door open when he's in there," Dad said yesterday while I was sitting right at the kitchen table.

"Earl," Mama said quietly, "Dale is sitting right here."

"Tell him," Dad repeated, then walked out of the room.

The open-door rule is new. So is Dad removing the lock from my bedroom.

But the strangest thing is how he looks at me now. Not with the usual anger or disappointment. With fear. Like I'm something dangerous that might contaminate the house if he's not careful.

Mama is different too, but in ways I can't quite figure out.

She brings me my meals without being asked. She changes the bandages on my hand herself instead of making me do it. When I have nightmares about the attack - which happens most nights - she sits on the edge of my bed until I fall back asleep.

But she won't talk about what I told her at the hospital. Every time I try to bring it up, she gets this look on her face like she's trying to solve a puzzle that doesn't have all its pieces.

"Mama, can we talk about—"

"Your ribs feeling better today?" she'll interrupt. Or "Did you take your pain medicine?" Or "What do you want for lunch?"

It's like she heard me that day in the hospital, but she doesn't know what to do with what she heard.

Yesterday I caught her staring at me while I was reading on the couch. Just staring, like she was trying to see something she'd missed before.

"What is it, Mama?"

She blinked, startled. "Nothing, baby. Just... nothing."

But it wasn't nothing. I could see her mind working, processing, trying to reconcile the son she thought she knew with the daughter she's starting to see.

The worst part is church. We still have to go every Sunday and Wednesday, and Bishop Patterson still shakes my hand and asks how I'm "recovering from my ordeal."

"The Lord protected you from worse harm," he said last Sunday, his hand lingering on mine just a little too long. "He has plans for you yet, young man."

Something has changed in how other people at church look at me. Word got around about why I was in the hospital - not the whole truth, but enough. People whisper when I walk by. I hear fragments: "dressed like a girl," "asking for trouble," "what kind of parents..."

Mrs. Henderson cornered Mama after service last week.

"Margaret, honey, you know I don't like to gossip, but people are talking about your boy. They're saying he was... well, you know. At some kind of club. Dressed inappropriately."

I watched Mama's face from across the fellowship hall. For a second, I thought she might defend me. Might tell Mrs. Henderson to mind her own business. Might stand up for her child the way mothers are supposed to do.

Instead, she just nodded and said, "We're handling it."

Handling it. Like I'm a problem that needs to be managed instead of a person who was nearly killed for being herself.

The police caught Marcus and Tyler. They're being charged with assault, but their lawyer is already talking about how I "deceived" them, how I "provoked" the attack by "presenting falsely." Even the justice system wants to make this my fault somehow.

At night, when the house is quiet and my ribs ache and I can't sleep, I think about that moment in the club when I felt beautiful. When I felt whole. When I looked in the bathroom mirror and saw Dale - the real Dale - looking back at me.

It lasted maybe three hours. Three hours of being myself, and it nearly cost me my life.

But I'd do it again. Even knowing how it ends, even knowing the price, I'd do it again.

Because for those three hours, I wasn't pretending. I wasn't performing. I wasn't apologizing for existing.

I was just Dale.

The girl in the mirror has scars now. Physical ones on my face and ribs, emotional ones that go deeper. But she's still here. Still fighting. Still refusing to disappear just because other people can't handle her existence.

Dad thinks he can make me go back to being his son by taking away locks and hiding makeup and pretending I never told the truth about who I am.

He's wrong.

You can't put a person back in a closet once they've tasted freedom. You can't make someone forget who they really are just because it makes you uncomfortable.

I'm Dale. I'm a woman. I'm a survivor.

And I'm done hiding.

The question now is: what am I going to do about it?

Graduation is still two months away. Two more months of living in this house, pretending to be someone I'm not, letting Dad ignore me and Mama struggle with a truth she doesn't know how to handle. Two more months of Bishop Patterson's knowing looks and the church's whispers and my own reflection looking back at me like a stranger.

Two. More. Months.

And then? Then I'm going to find out what it means to live as myself every day, not just for three stolen hours in a club.

The girl in the mirror is counting down the days.

So am I.

Document 27: Diary Entry
Written by Dale Morrison
Dated: May 8, 2019

Dad's been coughing for weeks now. A deep, rattling cough that echoes through the house at night and makes Mama flinch every time she hears it. He keeps saying it's just allergies, just the changing weather, just getting older.

But this morning he coughed up blood.

I was eating breakfast when I heard him in the bathroom, that same terrible cough followed by a sound I'd never heard before - like choking mixed with panic. Then Mama screamed.

"Earl! Earl, there's blood!"

I ran to the bathroom doorway and saw him standing over the sink, bright red streaks across the white porcelain. His face was pale, but his jaw was set in that stubborn way that meant he was going to pretend nothing was wrong.

"It's nothing," he said, splashing water to wash away the evidence. "Just coughed too hard."

But Mama was crying now, that quiet, scared crying she does when she's trying not to make Dad angry.

"Earl, that's not normal. That's not nothing. We need to call Dr. Roberts. We need to—"

"I said it's nothing!" Dad's voice ricochetted through the small bathroom, but there was something different about it. Something that sounded almost like fear.

He looked at himself in the mirror, and for a second, I saw him really look. Saw him notice how thin his face had gotten, how gray his skin looked, how his shirt hung loose on his shoulders.

"Maybe... maybe I should get it checked out," he said quietly. "Just to shut you up about it."

Mama was already reaching for the phone.

An hour later, they were getting ready to leave for the hospital. Dad was moving slower than usual, and I could hear that wheeze in his breathing even when he wasn't coughing.

"I can drive," Mama offered, reaching for the car keys.

"The hell you can," Dad said, snatching them away from her. "I've been driving for thirty years. I don't need my wife to chauffeur me around like I'm some kind of invalid."

"But Earl, you're not feeling well—"

"I'm fine." He was already walking toward the garage, that stubborn set to his shoulders that meant the conversation was over. "And I'll be damned if I'm going to let some woman drive me to the hospital like I can't take care of myself."

Even sick, scared, and coughing up blood, he couldn't let go of control. Couldn't let Mama do something as simple as drive him to get help.

I watched from my bedroom window as they backed out of the driveway. Dad behind the wheel, gripping it tight with both hands. Mama in the passenger seat, twisted around to look at him with that worried expression she wore whenever he was drinking too much or angry about something.

But this was different. This wasn't anger or alcohol. This was something Dad couldn't yell at or ignore or beat into submission.

I'm alone in the house now, and it's so quiet without

Dad's coughing echoing through the halls. Part of me hopes it's nothing serious. Maybe a cold that got out of hand. Just something minor that antibiotics can fix.

But another part of me, the part that's watched him terrorize this family for seventeen years, wonders what would happen if it's not nothing.

What would happen to Mama if she didn't have to walk on eggshells anymore? What would happen to me if I didn't have to pretend to be his son anymore?

What would happen to this house if the person who filled it with anger and fear and the smell of whiskey wasn't here anymore?

I feel guilty for even thinking about it. He's my father, even if he can't see me as his daughter. Even if he's spent my whole life trying to beat me into being someone I'm not. Even if he refused to come see me in the hospital when I almost died.

But I can't help wondering: what would freedom look like?

For me. For Mama. For both of us.

The phone hasn't rung yet. They've been gone three hours now. That seems like a long time for "just allergies."

I keep looking out the window, waiting for the car to pull back into the driveway. Waiting to see if Dad walks back into this house the same man who left it, or if everything is about to change.

The girl in the mirror looks different today. Not hopeful, exactly. But not hopeless either.

Like maybe, just maybe, the future might hold something other than hiding and pretending and apologizing for existing.

Maybe that makes me a terrible person. Daughters aren't supposed to wonder what life would be like without their fathers. But then again, maybe fathers aren't supposed to make their daughters feel like they'd be better off dead.

The phone is ringing now. Mama's calling from the hospital.

I guess I'm about to find out what the rest of my life looks like.

Time to answer the phone.

Mama's voice was so small I could barely hear her over the hospital noise in the background.

"Dale? Baby, can you hear me?"

"I'm here, Mama. What did the doctor say?"

There was a long pause. I could hear her breathing, that shaky way she breathes when she's trying not to cry in public.

"It's... it's not good, baby. It's not allergies."

My stomach dropped. "What is it?"

"Lung cancer." The words came out in a rush, like she had to say them fast or she wouldn't be able to say them at all. "Advanced lung cancer. The doctor says it's... it's bad."

I sat down hard on the kitchen chair. Cancer. The word hit me like a physical blow.

"How long?" I asked, though I wasn't sure I wanted to know.

"Six months. Maybe less." Mama was crying now, not trying to hide it anymore. "Dale, what am I going to do? What are we going to do?"

I should have said something comforting. Something about fighting it or hope or about miracles. But all I could think about was Dad coughing up blood this morning and still refusing to let Mama drive. Still needing to be in control even when his own body was betraying him.

"Where is he now?"

"They're running more tests. He's... he's angry, Dale. So angry. He keeps saying the doctors don't know what they're talking about, that he's going to get a second opinion, that this is all wrong."

Of course he was angry. Dad's solution to everything was anger. Couldn't yell cancer away, though.

"Is he in pain?"

"He won't admit it if he is. You know your father. He just keeps saying he's fine, that he doesn't need anybody feeling sorry for him."

I could picture it perfectly. Dad in a hospital bed, probably trying to intimidate the nurses, demanding to speak to whoever was in charge, and blaming everyone but himself for years of cigarettes and whiskey.

"Mama, are you okay?"

Another long pause. "I don't know how to do this, Dale. I don't know how to... how to watch him die. I don't know how to be alone."

The words came out before I could stop them: "You're not alone. You have me."

"I know, baby. I know. But your father... he's been my whole life for so long. I don't know who I am without him."

That broke my heart more than the cancer diagnosis. Mama had made herself so small, so invisible, that she couldn't even imagine existing without the man who spent decades making her afraid of her own shadow.

"When are you coming home?"

"They want to keep him overnight for more tests. I'm going to stay here with him. There's leftover casserole in the fridge for your dinner."

"Mama, you don't have to worry about me. Just take care of yourself, okay?"

"I will, baby. I love you."

"I love you too, Mama."

After I hung up, I sat in that quiet kitchen for a long time, trying to figure out what I was feeling.

Sad? Yes, because cancer is a terrible way to die, and because Mama was scared and alone at the hospital.

Guilty? Definitely, because part of me wondered if this might finally give me and Mama a chance to have a real relationship without Dad's anger poisoning everything.

Angry? God yes, because even dying, Dad was still making everything about his need to control, his refusal to show weakness, his inability to let anyone help him.

But mostly, I felt something I didn't expect, grief. Not for the father who was dying, but for the father I never had. The one who might have loved his daughter instead of trying to beat her into being his son. I imagine he would have protected me instead of handing me over to a predator in Bishop's clothing. He would have rushed to the hospital when I was attacked instead of staying home because he was ashamed of who I am.

I was grieving for a relationship that never existed, and now, would never exist.

Document 28: Medical Record

Written by James Crawford, MD

Dated: May 8, 2019

MILLBROOK MEDICAL CENTER PATIENT MEDICAL RECORD

Patient: Morrison, Earl Thomas **DOB:** 10/12/1982 **Age:** 38 **MRN:** 4472891

Date of Service: 05/08/2019 **Attending Physician:** James Crawford, MD - Pulmonology

CHIEF COMPLAINT: Patient presents with persistent cough x 6 wks, progressively worsening. Reports hemoptysis beginning this morning. Accompanied by a wife who reports pt loss, fatigue, and night sweats.

HISTORY OF PRESENT ILLNESS: 38-year-old male construction worker with chronic cough that has significantly worsened over past 6 weeks. Patient initially attributed symptoms to "allergies" and "getting older." Wife reports patient has lost approximately 15-20 pounds over the past 3 months, though patient denies intentional weight loss. Patient admits to increased shortness of breath with minimal exertion. Denies chest pain. This morning experienced the first episode of hemoptysis, which prompted today's visit.

PAST MEDICAL HISTORY:
- No significant past medical history
- No previous hospitalizations
- Patient reports occasional alcohol use (wife indicates outside of the room that there is heavy daily consumption)

SOCIAL HISTORY:

- Married, one child
- Works in construction and Deacon at his church
- Heavy drinker per wife's report (patient minimizes)
- Lives in Millbrook, AL

PHYSICAL EXAMINATION:

Vital Signs: BP 145/92, HR 98, RR 22, Temp 99.1°F, O2 Sat 89% on room air **General:** Thin, pale male appearing older than stated age, in mild respiratory distress **HEENT:** Pale conjunctiva, no lymphadenopathy **Chest:** Decreased breath sounds right lower lobe, dullness to percussion, coarse rales bilaterally **Cardiovascular:** Regular rate and rhythm, no murmurs **Abdomen:** Soft, non-tender, no masses **Extremities:** No clubbing, mild peripheral edema

DIAGNOSTIC STUDIES:

Chest X-Ray: Large right lower lobe mass approximately 6cm with pleural effusion. Multiple bilateral pulmonary nodules consistent with metastatic disease.

CT Chest with Contrast:

- Primary mass, lower right lobe 6.2 x 5.8 cm
- Multiple bilateral pulmonary nodules
- Mediastinal lymphadenopathy
- Moderate right pleural effusion
- Possible liver lesions requiring further evaluation

Laboratory Results:

- WBC: 12,500 (elevated)
- Hemoglobin: 9.2 (low)

- LDH: 485 (elevated)
- CEA: 28.5 (significantly elevated)

CLINICAL IMPRESSION: Primary lung carcinoma with metastatic disease. Given imaging findings and tumor markers, appear to be advanced non-small cell lung carcinoma (Stage IV).

HOSPITAL COURSE: Patient underwent bronchoscopy with biopsy. Pathology confirmed adenocarcinoma of the lung. Oncology consultation obtained. Patient and family informed of diagnosis and prognosis.

ONCOLOGY CONSULTATION:

Dr. Maria Santos, MD: Reviewed imaging and pathology with patient and spouse. Discussed poor prognosis given advanced stage at presentation. Patient became agitated during discussion, demanding "second opinion" and stating doctors "don't know what they're talking about." Wife appeared to understand severity better than patient.

PROGNOSIS: Terminal. Given extent of metastatic disease, prognosis is measured in months. Median survival for Stage IV adenocarcinoma ranges from 4-8 months without treatment, potentially 8-14 months with palliative chemotherapy, though patient's overall condition and comorbidities may limit treatment options.

DISCHARGE PLANNING:

- Referred to oncology for treatment planning discussion
- Palliative care consultation recommended
- Home health services arranged
- Family education regarding disease progression and end-of-life planning

MEDICATIONS ON DISCHARGE:
- Morphine sulfate 15mg q12h PRN pain
- Lorazepam 0.5mg BID PRN anxiety
- Prednisone 20mg daily x 5 days for inflammation
- Proton pump inhibitor for stomach protection

FOLLOW-UP:
- Oncology appointment scheduled within 1 week
- Return to ED if increased respiratory distress, severe pain, or other concerning symptoms occur
- Primary care follow-up in 2 weeks

DISCHARGE CONDITION: Stable but guarded. Patient remains in denial regarding diagnosis and prognosis. Wife demonstrates better understanding of situation and appears to be primary caregiver.

PHYSICIAN NOTES: Patient exhibited significant denial and anger upon receiving diagnosis. Refused to discuss end-of-life planning, insisting he would "beat this thing." Wife appears overwhelmed but more realistic about prognosis. Social work consultation may be beneficial for family support. Patient's alcohol use history concerning given need for pain management.

PROGNOSIS UPDATE: Given rapid progression of symptoms and extensive metastatic disease at presentation, survival may be on the shorter end of predicted range. Patient's overall health status and apparent alcohol dependency may further compromise response to treatment.

Attending Physician: Dr. James Crawford, MD **Date:** 05/08/2019 **Dictated:** 05/08/2019 23:45 **Transcribed:** 05/09/2019 08:30

Document 29: Diary Entry

Written by Dale Morrison

Dated: May 12, 2019

I went to see him today. After everything - after he refused to visit me in the hospital when I was beaten nearly to death, after months of pretending I don't exist, after a lifetime of trying to beat the woman out of me - I went to see my dying father.

I don't know why. Maybe because I'm a better person than he ever taught me to be. Maybe because I wanted to give him one last chance to see his daughter instead of the disappointment he created in his mind. Maybe because I knew if I didn't go, I'd spend the rest of my life wondering "what if."

The nurse smiled when she saw me in the hallway. "Are you here for Mr. Morrison in room 314?"

"I'm his... I'm Dale. His child."

"Oh wonderful! He could use some company. Let me tell him you're here."

She knocked gently and poked her head into his room. "Mr. Morrison? You have someone here to see you."

I walked in before he could refuse. Before he could tell her to send me away.

He looked so small in that hospital bed. The cancer had eaten away at him until he was just skin and bones and anger. But his eyes... his eyes still held all that familiar rage when he saw me.

"What the hell are you doing here?" His voice was weak, but the venom was as strong as ever.

"I came to see you, Dad. I heard you were sick."

"Don't call me that." He tried to sit up straighter, but the effort made him cough. "You lost the right to call me that a long time ago."

I stood at the foot of his bed, my hands clasped in front of me. I'd practiced what I wanted to say, but looking at him now - dying and still so full of hate - all my words seemed meaningless.

"You know this is all your fault," he said, gesturing weakly at the machines around him. "All of it."

"Dad, you have cancer. That's not—"

"I drank because of you!" His voice cracked with the effort of yelling. "You think I wanted to spend my life drunk? You think I enjoyed it? I drank because it was the only time I could look at you and see my son straight. When everything else in the world was wobbly and crooked, at least then you looked like what you were supposed to be."

The words hit me like physical blows, but I didn't move. I'd heard variations of this my whole life. It was always my fault. His drinking, his anger, his inability to love the child he had instead of the one he wanted.

"I'm sorry you felt that way," I said quietly. "But I'm not sorry for being who I am."

"Who you are?" He laughed, a bitter sound that turned into another coughing fit. "You're nobody. You're nothing. You're a mistake I can't fix no matter how hard I try."

Tears were running down my face now, but I stood my ground. "I'm your daughter, Dad. I always have been. I always will be."

"SHUT UP!" He slammed his hand against the bed rail, making the IV tubes shake. "Don't you dare say that in here! Don't you dare!"

"It's the truth."

"The truth?" His eyes were wild now, desperate. "You want to know the truth? Bishop Patterson told me to call him if that demon ever came back. Said there were more... options. More permanent solutions. Maybe I should have taken him up on that years ago."

The blood drained from my face. More options. More permanent solutions. I thought about that night at the church, about Bishop Patterson's hands, about the hours of torture disguised as prayer. And I realized there were worse things they could have done to me. Things they might still do if they got the chance.

"You're sick," I whispered. "You're really sick, and I don't just mean the cancer."

"GET OUT!" He was screaming now, thrashing in the bed despite the machines. "GET OUT OF HERE! I don't want to see you! I don't want to know you! I wish you'd never been born!"

Nurses were rushing into the room. Someone was saying something about sedation, about calming him down. But all I could hear was his voice screaming that he wished I'd never been born.

I ran. Just turned around and ran out of that room, down the hospital corridor, past the elevators, down the stairs, out into the parking lot where I finally stopped and fell to my knees on the cold asphalt.

I cried for the father I never had. I cried for the little girl who spent years thinking if she just tried harder, maybe Daddy would love her. I cried for all the times I wasted hoping he would change, hoping he would see me, hoping he would choose love over hate.

But mostly, I cried with relief. Because I finally understood something I'd been fighting my whole life: his rejection of me was never about who I was. It was about who he was. His hatred, his fear, his inability to love - that was all his. I didn't cause it, I couldn't fix it, and I didn't have to carry it anymore.

I'm done. I'm done trying to earn love from someone who doesn't know how to give it. I'm done apologizing for existing. I'm done making myself smaller so he can feel bigger.

He's dying, and he's going to die angry and alone and full of regret. Not because of me, but because of the choices he made every single day of my life.

I'm not going back to that hospital room. I'm not going to his funeral. I'm not going to pretend to grieve for a man who told me he wished I'd never been born.

I have a life to live. A real life, as the woman I was always meant to be. And I'm not going to waste another second of it trying to make peace with someone who chose war every time.

The girl in the mirror doesn't need his approval anymore.

She never did.

Goodbye, Dad. I hope you find whatever peace you can in the time you have left.

But I'm done trying to give you mine.

Document 30: Diary Entry
Written by Dale Morrison
Dated: May 12, 2019 - Later

Something strange happened after I left Dad's room. Something I can't quite explain, but I need to write it down before I forget the details.

I was rushing toward the elevator, tears streaming down my face, just wanting to get out of that hospital as fast as possible. I wasn't watching where I was going, and I crashed right into this elderly woman coming out of the gift shop.

"Oh, my goodness, I'm so sorry!" I said, helping her steady the small paper bag she was carrying.

She was probably in her seventies, with silver hair pulled back in a neat bun and the kindest eyes I'd ever seen. She was wearing a simple blue dress and a cream-colored sweater, and she smelled like lavender and something else I couldn't identify - something warm and comforting, like cinnamon or vanilla.

"No harm done, dear," she said, her voice soft but clear. "Are you alright? You look upset."

I tried to wipe my face with my sleeve. "I'm fine. Just... family stuff."

She studied my face for a moment, then reached into her paper bag and pulled out a small, wrapped piece of candy. It looked handmade, the wrapper a soft yellow paper tied with a thin ribbon.

"Here," she said, pressing it into my palm. "This always helps when the world feels too heavy."

I stared at the candy, confused. "I can't take your—"

"Nonsense. I have plenty." She smiled, and when

she did, I swear the harsh hospital fluorescent lights seemed warmer somehow. "I'm Evelyn, by the way."

"Dale."

"Dale. That's a strong name. Good for carrying important things."

Before I could ask what she meant by that, she was gathering up several shopping bags at her feet.

"I don't suppose you could help an old woman get these to her car?" Evelyn asked. "My arthritis is acting up today, and these bags feel heavier than they should."

I couldn't say no to those kind eyes, even though all I wanted was to go home and hide under my blankets. "Of course."

We walked slowly through the hospital corridors, her bags in my hands. They weren't heavy at all - mostly felt like they were full of fabric or something soft. But I didn't mention it.

"So," Evelyn said as we made our way to the parking garage, "family stuff can be the hardest stuff. Want to tell me about it?"

I don't know why I opened up to a complete stranger. Maybe it was her voice, so gentle and non-judgmental. Maybe it was the way she walked beside me without rushing, like she had nowhere else in the world she needed to be. It could have been that I desperately needed someone to hear me.

"I went to see my father," I said. "He's dying. Cancer."

"I'm sorry to hear that. That must be very difficult."

"It should be. But..." I stopped walking, the

words catching in my throat. "He told me he wished I'd never been born. He said I was a mistake he could never fix."

Evelyn stopped too, turning to face me with those impossibly kind eyes.

"And why would a father say such a thing to his child?"

The whole story came pouring out. Not everything - I couldn't tell her about Bishop Patterson or the deliverance or the attack at the club. But I told her about being different, about never being the son my father wanted, about years of trying to earn love that would never come.

"I'm not who he wanted me to be," I finished. "I'm not who anyone wants me to be."

Evelyn was quiet for a long moment, just looking at me with an expression I couldn't read.

"Dale," she said finally, "do you know what I see when I look at you?"

I shook my head.

"I see someone brave. Someone who kept being herself even when the world told her not to. Someone went to see her dying father even after he refused to see her in the hospital. Someone with a heart big enough to help a stranger carry her bags when her own heart is breaking."

My breath caught. "Her?"

Evelyn smiled that warm smile again. "Did I say something wrong?"

"No, I... most people don't..." I couldn't finish the sentence.

"Most people don't see what's really there," Evelyn said gently. "They see what they expect to see, what they want to see, what they're afraid to see. But some of us look a little deeper."

We'd reached her car, an older model sedan that somehow looked brand new despite its age. I set her bags in the back seat, and when I turned around, she was holding another piece of candy - this one wrapped in pale blue paper.

"For the road," she said. "And Dale? Your father's words about you? They're not true. They never were true. You're not a mistake - you're exactly who you were meant to be. The people who can't see that? That's their limitation, not yours."

She got in her car and rolled down the window. That's when I saw it - a worn leather Bible sitting on her dashboard. My whole body tensed up, and I took an instinctive step backward. There's no hate like church love.

Evelyn must have seen the change in my face because her expression softened even more.

"I sin plenty, sugar," she said gently. "That's why I don't have time to grade anybody else's paper."

"What do you mean?" I asked, still keeping my distance from the car.

"You ain't God's mistake. You just ain't your daddy's idea of easy. We all have our crosses to bear. They just look a little different."

I walked closer to the car, not believing my ears. A Christian woman with a Bible on her dashboard was telling me I wasn't a mistake?

"Do you... do you believe in God?" I asked.

"With everything I have," Evelyn replied without hesitation.

My voice came out as barely a whisper. "Do you think I'll go to hell for being like this?"

Evelyn looked at me for a long moment, her eyes full of something that looked like love.

"That's not up to me, sugar. All I can say is this: in everything you do, do it with God in mind, and you can't go wrong."

I didn't know what to do with that. A lifetime of being told I was an abomination, that God couldn't love me, that I was destined for hell - and here was this woman with her Bible and her gentle voice telling me something completely different.

"Thank you," I said, because I didn't know what else to say.

She started to roll up her window, then stopped.

"Dale?"

"Yes ma'am?"

"You're not unholy for being complicated. Remember that. For all have sinned and come short of the glory of God."

"Will I see you again?" I asked, surprising myself with the question.

"Oh, I think our paths will cross again," Evelyn said. "They have a way of doing that when they're supposed to."

She drove away, and I stood there in the parking garage holding two pieces of homemade candy, feeling something I hadn't felt in a very long time: hope.

I unwrapped the first piece when I got to my car. It tasted like honey and sunshine and something indescribable - like the feeling of being understood. And for the first time in hours, I stopped crying.

I don't know who Evelyn is or why she was at the

hospital today. I don't know how she knew to call me "her" or why her candy tasted like comfort itself. I don't know how she could have a Bible on her dashboard and still see me as worthy of love.

But I know this: sometimes angels come disguised as elderly women with shopping bags and homemade candy. Sometimes exactly the right person appears exactly when you need them most. Sometimes God's love looks different than what they taught you in church.

I'm keeping the second piece of candy for when I need to remember that someone in this world sees me for who I really am. Someone who believes in God with everything she has and still thinks I'm not a mistake.

And for the first time since I walked into that hospital room, I think maybe that's enough.

Maybe I'm enough.

The girl in the mirror is smiling again.

Maybe Evelyn had something to do with that too.

Document 31: Diary Entry

Written by Dale Morrison

Dated: May 27, 2019

It's been two weeks since I met Evelyn, and I can't stop thinking about what she said. I keep her second piece of candy in my wallet, wrapped in that soft blue paper. Sometimes I take it out just to look at it, to remember that conversation in the hospital parking garage.

"You're not unholy for being complicated."

I've never heard anyone say anything like that before. Especially not someone with a Bible on their dashboard.

I went to the library yesterday and did something I've never done before - I looked up verses about love instead of condemnation. For seventeen years, all I heard were the verses Dad and Bishop Patterson used like weapons. But there are other verses. Verses about God loving all his children. Verses about not judging. Verses about kindness and compassion.

I found one that made me cry right there in the library: "For I am fearfully and wonderfully made." Psalm 139:14.

Fearfully and wonderfully made. Not "mistakenly made" or "sinfully made." Wonderfully.

What if Evelyn is right? What if I really am exactly who I was meant to be?

I've been thinking about that a lot lately, especially as Dad gets sicker. Mama calls me with updates from the hospital - he's getting weaker, more confused, asking for pain medication more often. She always ends these calls the same way: "He keeps asking when you're coming to visit."

But I can't go back there. Not after what he said to me. Not after he told me he wished I'd never been born, that Bishop Patterson had "more options" for dealing with me. I won't put myself through that again, and I won't pretend to be the grieving son he wants me to be.

Mama doesn't understand. "He's your father," she said last week. "Whatever happened between you two, he's still your father."

But being someone's father means more than just biology. It means love, protection, acceptance. Dad was never those things to me.

I'm done playing roles that don't fit.

Something else happened this week that I can't stop thinking about. I was at the grocery store, in the cereal aisle, when I heard a little voice say, "Mama, why does that lady look sad?"

I turned around and saw a little girl, maybe five years old, pointing at me. Her mother looked mortified.

"Hush, baby. That's not... that's a..." The mother looked confused, studying my face, my clothes, trying to figure out what box to put me in.

But the little girl wasn't confused at all. "Are you okay, lady?" she asked me directly.

Lady. A five-year-old child looked at me and saw a lady.

"I'm okay, sweetheart," I said, kneeling to her level. "Thank you for asking."

"Good," she said, then skipped away with her embarrassed mother.

Children see truth differently than adults do. They

haven't learned to look for what they expect to see instead of what's actually there.

That little girl reminded me of something Evelyn said: "Some of us look a little deeper."

I've been looking deeper too. At myself, at my life, at what I want my future to look like.

I graduated. I have enough money saved to get out of this town and start over somewhere else. Somewhere I can be Dale - the real Dale - without an apology.

I've been researching cities with good support systems for people like me. I found out there are other women like me, living openly, working, loving, being themselves without shame. There are doctors who can help. There are communities that understand.

For the first time in my life, I can imagine a future where I'm not hiding.

I keep thinking about what Evelyn said about doing everything with God in mind. What if living as my authentic self - as the woman I really am - is exactly what God wants me to do? What if all this time, the sin wasn't being who I am, but pretending to be someone I'm not?

What if the real blasphemy was letting other people's fear keep me from being the person God created me to be?

I don't have all the answers yet. I'm still scared. I still have nightmares about that night at the church, about Marcus and Tyler behind the club, about Dad's voice screaming that he wished I'd never been born.

But I also have Evelyn's voice in my head, reminding me that I'm not unholy for being complicated. I have the memory of that little girl calling me "lady" like it was the most natural thing in the world. I have the taste of honey and sunshine, and hope wrapped in blue paper.

I have the verses I found at the library, the ones that talk about being fearfully and wonderfully made.

Maybe that's enough to build a new life on.

Two more months, and then I'm leaving this town forever. I'm going to find a place where Dale doesn't have to apologize for existing. Where she can work and live and maybe even love without hiding.

Where she can go to a church - if she wants to - and hear about God's love instead of God's condemnation.

Where she can be fearfully and wonderfully made, just like the psalm says.

The girl in the mirror looks different now. Still scared, still healing, but not ashamed anymore.

Evelyn would be proud.

I think God might be too.

At least, I'm finally ready to find out.

Document 32: Therapy Notes

Written by Linda Chen, MSW, LCSW

Dated: June 6, 2019

MILLBROOK MEDICAL CENTER SOCIAL WORK CONSULTATION NOTES

Date: June 6, 2019 **Time:** 2:00 PM **Social Worker:** Natalie Newtoln, MSW, LCSW

End-of-Life Care Nurse: Dannielle Ward, RN, BSN **Attendees:** Earl Morrison (patient), Margaret Morrison (spouse) **Location:** Conference Room B, Oncology Wing

PURPOSE: Treatment planning and discharge options consultation

OPENING: Meeting convened to discuss treatment options and end-of-life care planning with Mr. Morrison and his wife. Mr. Morrison appeared agitated from the start, stating he "didn't need to be here" and that "doctors are making this bigger than it is."

TREATMENT OPTIONS DISCUSSION:

Ms. Newton: "Mr. Morrison, we want to make sure you understand all your options moving forward."

Mr. Morrison: "My option is to go home and get better. That's it."

Nurse Ward: "I understand that's what you want, but let's talk about what that might look like. Your cancer is advanced, and without treatment—"

Mr. Morrison: "Advanced according to who? You people see cancer and think death. I've been through worse."

- 113 -

CHEMOTHERAPY DISCUSSION:

Ms. Newton: "The oncologist mentioned palliative chemotherapy. Can you tell us why you've decided against it?"

Mr. Morrison: "Because it's poison. You want me to pump poison into my body so I can be sick for the rest of my life? No thank you."

Nurse Ward: "The goal wouldn't be to cure the cancer at this stage, but to slow its progression and help with symptoms—"

Mr. Morrison: "Help with symptoms? The only symptom I got is the doctor telling me I'm dying. Fix that and I'll be fine."

Mrs. Morrison: (quietly) "Earl, maybe we should listen to what they're saying..."

Mr. Morrison: "Margaret, whose side are you on?"

HOSPICE CARE DISCUSSION:

Ms. Newton: "What about hospice care? It's not about giving up—it's about making sure you're comfortable and have support."

Mr. Morrison: "Hospice is where you go to die. I'm not dying, so I don't need hospice."

Nurse Ward: "Hospice can be provided in your home. It's about pain management, emotional support for you and your wife—"

Mr. Morrison: "I don't need strangers in my house telling me how to live. I've been taking care of myself for years. I can handle whatever this is."

Ms. Newton: "Mr. Morrison, what are you most afraid of about accepting help?"

Mr. Morrison: (long pause, then anger) "I'm not afraid of anything. I just don't need help I don't need."

HOME CARE DISCUSSION:

Nurse Ward: "If you're determined to go home, we can set up home health services. Nurses who can help with medications, oxygen therapy—"

Mr. Morrison: "I said no strangers in my house."

Mrs. Morrison: "Earl, I don't know how to... I mean, what if you need help and I can't..."

Mr. Morrison: "You've been taking care of me for 20 years, Margaret. You'll figure it out."

FAMILY SUPPORT DISCUSSION:

Ms. Newton: "What about your son? Would he be able to help with care?"

Mr. Morrison: (immediately hostile) "I don't have a son. Next question."

Mrs. Morrison: (tearful) "Earl, Dale might want to—"

Mr. Morrison: "I said I don't have a son. That... person... is not welcome in my house. Ever."

Nurse Ward: "Mr. Morrison, this is a difficult time for families. Sometimes people say things they don't mean—"

Mr. Morrison: "I meant every word. Don't bring it up again."

REALITY ORIENTATION ATTEMPT:

Ms. Newton: "Mr. Morrison, I need to be direct with you. The doctors are telling us you have a few months to live. How do you want to spend that time?"

Mr. Morrison: "The doctors are wrong. I'm going home, I'm going to rest, and I'm going to get better. That's how I'm going to spend my time."

Nurse Ward: "But what if you don't get better? What if you get worse at home and your wife can't manage?"

Mr. Morrison: "Then I'll deal with it then. But I'm not planning for failure."

WIFE'S CONCERNS:

Mrs. Morrison: *"What if... what if something happens at night? What if he can't breathe? What if—"*

Mr. Morrison: "Margaret, stop. You're borrowing trouble. Nothing's going to happen that we can't handle."

Ms. Newton: "Mrs. Morrison, what support do you need?"

Mrs. Morrison: (looking at husband) "I... I just want to do what's right. What Earl wants."

FINAL ATTEMPTS:

Nurse Ward: "Mr. Morrison, accepting help isn't giving up. It's being smart about your resources."

Mr. Morrison: "My resources are my wife and my house and my own two hands. That's all I've ever needed."

Ms. Newton: "What if we started small? Just a home health aide once a week?"

Mr. Morrison: "No."

Nurse Ward: "Pain medication management?"

Mr. Morrison: "I can handle pain."

Ms. Newton: "Counseling for you and your wife?"

Mr. Morrison: "We don't need counseling. We need to go home."

MEETING CONCLUSION:

Mr. Morrison: "Are we done here? I'm going home tomorrow whether you people like it or not. I'll be fine because I've always been fine. Margaret will be fine because she's got me. End of discussion."

ASSESSMENT: Patient demonstrates significant denial and control issues preventing acceptance of appropriate end-of-life care. Spouse appears willing to consider options but defers completely to patient's wishes. Patient's refusal of all support services creates high-risk discharge situation.

RECOMMENDATIONS REFUSED:

- Palliative chemotherapy
- Hospice care (home or facility)
- Home health services
- Pain management consultation
- Family counseling
- Nutritional support
- Oxygen therapy
- Emergency planning

PLAN: Patient will be discharged home against medical advice with minimal support systems. Wife provided with emergency contact information and hospice referral for future consideration.

FOLLOW-UP: Oncology appointment scheduled (patient "might attend"). Social work services declined. End-of-life care planning is incomplete due to patient refusal.

CONCERNS:

- Patient's complete denial of prognosis
- Isolation from potential family support (adult child)
- Wife's lack of preparation for caregiving demands
- No safety net for medical emergencies
- Patient is likely continued alcohol use complicating care

Linda Newton, MSW, LCSW Danniella Ward, RN, BSN Date: June 8, 2019

Document 33: Discharge Summary

Written by James Crawford, MD

Dated: June 15, 2019

MILLBROOK GENERAL HOSPITAL DISCHARGE SUMMARY

Patient: Morrison, Earl Thomas **DOB:** 10/12/1982 **Age:** 38 **MRN:** 4472891

Admission Date: 05/08/2019 **Discharge Date:** 06/15/2019 **Length of Stay:** 38 days **Attending Physician:** Dr. James Crawford, MD - Pulmonology

Consulting Physician: Dr. Maria Santos, MD - Oncology

FINAL DIAGNOSIS:

- Primary: Stage IV Adenocarcinoma of the lung with metastatic disease
- Secondary: Chronic obstructive pulmonary disease (COPD)
- Alcohol use disorder (patient denies, family confirms)
- Depression (untreated, patient refuses psychiatric consultation)

HOSPITAL COURSE: Patient admitted with hemoptysis and progressive dyspnea. Imaging revealed extensive metastatic lung cancer. Despite multiple family conferences and consultations, patient has consistently refused all recommended treatment options.

TREATMENT REFUSALS: Patient has signed AMA (Against Medical Advice) forms refusing:

1. **Palliative chemotherapy** - Patient stated "I'm not going to poison myself for a few extra months"
2. **Hospice care referral** - Patient became agitated, stating "I'm not dying in some place with strangers"
3. **Home health services** - Patient refused, claiming "I can take care of myself"
4. **Pain management consultation** - Patient suspicious of "drug doctors," prefers alcohol for pain relief
5. **Psychiatric consultation** - Patient stated "Nothing wrong with my head that fixing my lungs won't cure"
6. **Social work services** - Patient refused family support services

FAMILY MEETINGS: Multiple conferences held with wife (Margaret Morrison). Wife appears overwhelmed but defers to patient's wishes regarding all treatment decisions. Patient becomes hostile when family members attempt to discuss realistic prognosis or end-of-life planning. Notably, patient has refused to allow his adult child to visit, despite wife's requests. States child is "not welcome" and becomes agitated when the topic is raised.

DISCHARGE CONDITION: Patient being discharged home against medical advice in poor condition. Significant weight loss (18 lbs. during admission), increasing oxygen requirements, and progressive weakness. Patient ambulating with assistance but insists on independent living.

MEDICATIONS ON DISCHARGE:

- Morphine sulfate 30mg PO q12h PRN pain (patient accepted only after told it was "for breathing")
- Prednisone 20mg daily x 7 days
- Proton pump inhibitor 40mg daily
- Albuterol inhaler q4h PRN dyspnea

HOME INSTRUCTIONS:

1. Return to ED immediately for increased respiratory distress, fever, or uncontrolled pain

2. Follow-up with oncology in 1 week (appointment scheduled, patient states he "might go")

3. Oxygen therapy recommended (patient refused home oxygen)

4. No driving (patient disagrees with restriction)

5. No alcohol consumption (patient made no commitment to compliance)

PROGNOSIS: Given extent of disease and patient's refusal of all treatment, prognosis remains grave. Without intervention, survival is estimated at 2-8 months. Patient informed but states "doctors don't know everything."

FAMILY EDUCATION: Wife provided with hospice contact information for future consideration. Educated on signs of respiratory distress and when to seek emergency care. Wife appears to understand gravity of situation better than patient.

SOCIAL CONCERNS:

- Patient's isolation of family members concerning
- Alcohol is likely to continue and complicate pain management

- Wife may need additional support resources as caregiver
- Patient's refusal of help may endanger both patient and spouse

DISCHARGE PLANNING CHALLENGES: Patient's refusal of all support services creates significant safety concerns. Wife appears physically frail and emotionally overwhelmed but committed to caring for patient at home per his wishes.

FOLLOW-UP APPOINTMENTS:
- Oncology: 06/19/2019 at 2:00 PM (patient states "we'll see")
- Primary care: 06/26/2019 at 10:00 AM
- Emergency contact: Return to ED for any concerning symptoms

PHYSICIAN NOTES: This discharge is occurring against strong medical recommendation. Patient demonstrates significant denial regarding his prognosis and has refused all interventions that could improve quality of life in his remaining time. Patient's control issues and anger appear to be preventing him from accepting help, even from family members. Wife seems aware of poor prognosis but unable to influence patient's decisions. Concerned about patient's ability to manage at home and wife's ability to provide adequate care without support systems. Patient's refusal to reconcile with adult child particularly concerning given limited time remaining.

FINAL RECOMMENDATION: Strongly recommend reconsideration of hospice services and family reconciliation. Patient's current plan is not sustainable and may result in emergency readmission under more difficult circumstances.

Attending Physician: Dr. James Crawford, MD **Date:** 06/12/219 **Dictated:** 06/12/2019 16:30

DISCHARGE STATUS: Against Medical Advice - High Risk

Document 34: Spiritual Consultation Notes

Written by First Lady Dorothy Patterson

Dated: June 17, 2019

CEDAR RIDGE BAPTIST CHURCH
Spiritual Consultation Notes

Date: June 17, 2019

Location: Morrison residence, 1247 Maple Street

Present: Earl Morrison (parishioner), Margaret Morrison (parishioner) **Purpose:** Spiritual counsel and prayer during health crisis

Began with prayer for healing and God's guidance during this difficult season for the Morrison family.

Brother Earl's Condition: Found Brother Earl in good spirits despite his recent hospital stay. He appears thinner than before but maintains his strong faith and determination. Brother Earl expressed frustration with the hospital staff's "negative attitude" and their insistence on discussing "worst-case scenarios."

"Bishop, these doctors act like they're God," Brother Earl said. "They want me to give up before I even start fighting."

Spiritual Counsel: I reminded Brother Earl and Sister Margaret that while we thank God for doctors and their knowledge, they do not have the final say in our lives.

"The doctors have done their job," I told them. "They've given you information. But God is the author and finisher of our faith, and He is the author and finisher of our lives. We will lean on Him."

Scriptural Guidance: Shared several key verses with the family:

Proverbs 3:5-6: "Trust in the Lord with all your heart and lean not on your own understanding. In all your ways acknowledge Him, and He will make your paths straight."

Jeremiah 30:17: "But I will restore you to health and heal your wounds, declares the Lord."

James 5:15: "And the prayer offered in faith will make the sick person well; the Lord will raise them up."

Brother Earl's Testimony: Brother Earl shared his conviction that God is not finished with him yet. "Bishop, I've got work to do. I've got a wife to take care of. The Lord knows that."

His faith during this trial is truly inspiring. He refuses to accept the doctors' timeline, trusting instead in God's perfect timing.

Sister Margaret's Concerns: Sister Margaret appeared somewhat anxious, asking questions about "what if" scenarios. I counseled her that worry is not from God, and that she must trust in her husband's spiritual leadership during this time.

"Margaret, your job is to stand beside your husband in faith, not to question God's plan with doubt," I advised.

Discussion Of Treatment Options: Brother Earl explained that the hospital wanted him to undergo "poison treatments" (chemotherapy) and to "give up and go die somewhere else" (hospice).

I affirmed his decision to reject treatments that would compromise his quality of life. "Earl, God gave you wisdom and discernment. If these treatments feel wrong to you, trust that instinct."

Prayer For Healing: Conducted intensive prayer session for complete healing. Laid hands on Brother Earl and prayed specifically:

- For total restoration of his health
- For wisdom to discern God's will over man's counsel
- For strength for Sister Margaret to support her husband's faith journey
- For protection from doubt and fear
- For a testimony of God's healing power to emerge from this trial

Faith Declaration: Brother Earl made a powerful declaration: "Bishop, I'm going to beat this thing through prayer and faith. When I walk back into that doctor's office healthy, they're going to know it was God who did it."

Church Support: Assured the family that our entire church family is praying for them. The prayer chain has been activated, and we will continue to storm heaven on their behalf.

COMMUNION SERVICE: Served communion in their home, emphasizing Christ's broken body and shed blood for our healing. Both Brother Earl and Sister Margaret partook with strong faith.

Biblical Promises Claimed:

- Isaiah 53:5 - "By His wounds we are healed"
- Psalm 103:3 - "Who forgives all your sins and heals all your diseases"
- Matthew 19:26 - "With God all things are possible"
- Mark 11:24 - "Whatever you ask for in prayer, believe that you have received it, and it will be yours"

Spiritual Observations: Brother Earl's faith remains unshakeable. He understands that accepting the doctors' prognosis would be agreeing with the enemy rather than standing on God's promises. His determination to trust God completely is a testimony to our congregation.

Sister Margaret needs continued prayer for strength and faith. She appears to be struggling with doubt, which is natural but must be overcome through prayer and submission to her husband's spiritual leadership.

Final Encouragement: Reminded the family that God's ways are higher than our ways, and His thoughts higher than our thoughts. What looks impossible to doctors is routine for the Creator of the universe.

"Earl, you keep standing on God's promises. Don't let anyone - doctor, family member, or well-meaning friend - talk you out of believing for your miracle."

Closing Prayer: Prayed for miraculous healing, for peace that passes understanding, and for a testimony that will bring glory to God's name.

Scripture For Meditation: "He sent his word and healed them; he rescued them from the grave." - Psalm 107:20

Personal Reflection: This family's faith trial reminds us that God's power is not limited by medical diagnosis. Brother Earl's refusal to accept defeat is a powerful example of standing on God's promises rather than leaning on human understanding.

In His Service, Rev. William Patterson Senior
Bishop, Cedar Ridge Baptist Church

Document 35: Letter to Christina

Written by Dale Morrison

Dated: September 30, 2019

Dear Christina,

I don't know if you remember me - I'm the kid who used to come into Walgreens all the time when you worked there. You were always kind to me, and you once told me about your friend from college named Dale who was brave and confident. You said names don't have genders, people do.

I hope it's okay that I'm writing to you at your nursing job in Birmingham. I got your address from your mom when I told her I was your friend from high school (which isn't exactly true, but isn't exactly false either).

I graduated. Millbrook High School, Class of 2019. I should feel proud, but mostly I just feel ready to leave.

I'm writing because I need someone to know my story, and you're the only person who ever saw me - really saw me - for who I am. Even when I couldn't see it myself. You were right about your friend Dale. She was brave. And I'm finally ready to be brave too.

I'm leaving Millbrook soon. I have $3,200 saved up, a bus ticket to Atlanta, and the address of a support group I found online for people like me. People like us, I guess.

My father is dying. Lung cancer. The doctors gave him a few months, but he's refusing all treatment and insisting God is going to heal him. Our Bishop is encouraging this delusion, telling him that accepting medical help shows a lack of faith.

I went to see him once at the hospital. He told me he wished I'd never been born and that there were "more permanent solutions" for dealing with me. Even dying, he can't love the child he actually has.

But something wonderful happened that day too. I met a woman named Evelyn who had a Bible on her dashboard and still called me "her." She told me I wasn't unholy for being complicated, that I wasn't God's mistake, just not my daddy's idea of easy.

For the first time in my life, I met a Christian who acted like Christ actually would.

My mother doesn't know I'm leaving. She's too busy taking care of a man who's dying angry and alone, still refusing help, still controlling everything he can control. I wrote her a letter explaining where I'm going and why, but I'll mail it after I'm gone so she can't try to stop me.

Christina, I want you to know that what you said to me three years ago saved my life. When you told me about your friend Dale, you planted a seed that grew into hope. When you said people get to decide for themselves who they are, you gave me permission to be myself.

I'm scared about what comes next. I'm scared about living in a big city, about finding work, about the people who might hurt me for being who I am. But I'm more scared of staying here and dying a little more every day, pretending to be someone I'm not.

I want to go to college someday. I want to study social work, maybe become a counselor for kids like me who don't fit the boxes their families built for them. I want to help other people find their way to Atlanta or Portland or San Francisco - places where being different isn't a sin that needs to be beaten out of you.

I want to find a church where they talk about God's love instead of God's wrath. Where they welcome the outcasts instead of trying to fix them. I want to fall in love someday with someone who sees Dale - the real Dale - and thinks she's beautiful exactly as she is. I want to live, Christina. Really live. Not just survive.

The girl you saw in me all those years ago is finally ready to come out into the world. She's scared, but she's not ashamed anymore.

I kept your friend's name. I hope that's okay. Dale suits me, don't you think?

If you're ever in Atlanta and you see a young woman who looks a little familiar, stop and say hello. It might be me, finally living as myself.

Thank you for seeing me before I could see myself. Thank you for being kind to a confused kid who just needed someone to treat her like a human being. Thank you for showing me that some people look a little deeper.

I'll try to write and let you know how I'm doing. But if you never hear from me again, please know that you made a difference. You helped save a life.

The girl in the mirror is smiling these days. She's excited about what comes next.

Dale would be proud.

I'm finally proud too.

With love and gratitude,

Dale Morrison (The real one this time)

PS - I still have that piece of candy from Evelyn wrapped in blue paper. I'm saving it for when I get to Atlanta and find a place that feels like home. I figure that moment deserves something that tastes like hope.

Document 36: TransAtlanta Support Group Flyer

TRANSATLANTA SUPPORT GROUP

A Safe Space for Transgender Individuals and Their Families

WELCOME

Are you questioning your gender identity? Are you transgender and looking for community? Are you a family member seeking to understand and support your loved one?

You are not alone.

TransAtlanta is a peer-led support group serving the metro Atlanta area. We provide a safe, confidential space where transgender individuals and their allies can share experiences, find resources, and build community.

WHAT WE OFFER:

PEER SUPPORT GROUPS

- Weekly meetings every Thursday, 7:00-9:00 PM
- Monthly family/partners support group (2nd Saturday)
- All meetings held at Rainbow Community Center, 1247 Peachtree St NE

RESOURCE REFERRALS

- Transgender-friendly healthcare providers
- Mental health professionals experienced with gender issues
- Legal assistance for name/document changes
- Employment resources and discrimination support

EDUCATIONAL WORKSHOPS
- "Transition 101" - Monthly overview session
- Hormone therapy information sessions
- Legal rights and advocacy training
- Workplace transition guidance

SOCIAL ACTIVITIES
- Monthly potluck dinners
- Holiday celebrations
- Community service projects
- Annual Pride participation

FREQUENTLY ASKED QUESTIONS

Q: Is this group confidential? A: Yes. What is shared in group stays in group. However, please keep in mind we are mandated reporters. We use first names only and respect everyone's privacy.

Q: Do I have to be "out" to attend? A: No. We welcome people at any stage of their journey, including those who are questioning or just beginning to explore their identity.

Q: What if I'm not sure if I'm transgender? A: Our questioning support group is designed exactly for people like you. There's no pressure to label yourself or make any decisions.

Q: Are family members welcome? A: Yes! We have a monthly support group specifically for families, partners, and friends of transgender individuals.

Q: Is there a cost? A: As one of the first nonprofits of its kind, there is no fee for the services, though donations are gratefully accepted.

COMMUNITY RESOURCES

HEALTHCARE:

- Feminist Women's Health Center - sliding scale hormones
- Dr. Amy Nyguen, MD - gender therapy letters
- Planned Parenthood Southeast - LGBT-friendly services

LEGAL:

- Lambda Legal - LGBTQ+ legal advocacy
- Georgia Equality - state-level advocacy
- Legal Aid Society - low-cost legal services

EMPLOYMENT:

- Out & Equal - workplace equality resources
- HRC Corporate Equality Index - trans-friendly employers
- Georgia Department of Labor - discrimination complaints

HOUSING:

- LGBT-friendly apartment listings available at meetings
- Emergency housing assistance program
- Roommate matching services

SAFETY GUIDELINES

Your safety is our priority. We recommend:

- Using a P.O. Box for mail if you're not out at home
- Bringing a trusted friend to your first meeting
- Parking in well-lit areas

- Trusting your instincts about personal safety

CRISIS RESOURCES:

- National Suicide Prevention Lifeline: 1-800-273-8255
- Georgia Crisis & Access Line: 1-800-715-4225
- LGBT National Hotline: 1-888-843-4564

MEETING SCHEDULE

WEEKLY MEETINGS - THURSDAYS 7:00-9:00 PM

- 1st Thursday: Trans Women's Support Group
- 2nd Thursday: Trans Men's Support Group
- 3rd Thursday: Questioning/Exploring Support Group
- 4th Thursday: All-Community Social Meeting

MONTHLY MEETINGS - SATURDAYS 2:00-4:00 PM

- 2nd Saturday: Family & Partners Support Group
- 4th Saturday: Transition Workshop Series

SPECIAL EVENTS:

- New Member Orientation: 1st Saturday, 1:00 PM
- Monthly Potluck: 3rd Saturday, 6:00 PM
- Community Service: Various dates

CONTACT INFORMATION

Rainbow Community Center 1247 Peachtree Street NE Atlanta, GA 30309

TransAtlanta Hotline: (404) 873-2253 *Confidential voicemail checked daily*

Email: info@transatlanta.org **Website:** www.transatlanta.org

Mailing Address: TransAtlanta Support Group P.O. Box 12047 Atlanta, GA 30355

A MESSAGE FROM OUR COMMUNITY

"When I first came to TransAtlanta, I was scared and alone. I didn't know if I'd ever find people who understood what I was going through. Three years later, I have a chosen family, a support network, and the confidence to live authentically. This group saved my life." - Sarah M.

"As a parent, I was confused and frightened when my child came out as transgender. The family support group helped me understand that love means accepting your child for who they are, not who you expected them to be." - Patricia K.

"TransAtlanta isn't just a support group - it's a community. We celebrate each other's victories, support each other through challenges, and remind each other that we're not alone in this journey." - Michael T.

ABOUT TRANSATLANTA

Founded in 1998, TransAtlanta is one of the Southeast's oldest continuously operating transgender support organizations. We are a volunteer-run, community-based organization committed to providing education, advocacy, and support for transgender individuals and their families.

We believe that every person deserves to live authentically and without fear. Our mission is to create a world where transgender people are accepted, respected, and able to thrive.

You belong here. You are welcome here. You are valued here.

This brochure was printed in October 11, 2019. Information subject to change. Please call for current meeting times and locations.

TransAtlanta Support Group - Creating Community, Building Hope

Document 37: Letter to Mother

Written by Dale Morrison

Dated: October 12, 2019

Dear Mama,

I am writing because speaking never worked. Words feel bigger than my mouth, heavier than my body, like I have to swallow them before they can reach the air. But letters don't get swallowed. Letters sit still. Letters are seen.

I learned young that children should be seen and not heard, but I figured out that writing is a way to be both. If I put my words on paper, they exist, even if nobody reads them.

So, I write.

I write when my chest is too tight to breathe. I write when I want to cry but don't, because boys don't cry. I write when Daddy's voice shakes the walls, when your silence fills the spaces in between. I write when you tell me to listen to him because the Bible says so. I don't know if God listens when I write. Maybe He reads letters. Maybe He sees.

Do you think He does?

Love,

Dale

Document 38: Bank Statement

Written by First National Bank of Millbrook

Dated: September 15 – October 15, 2019

FIRST NATIONAL BANK OF MILLBROOK
CHECKING ACCOUNT STATEMENT

ACCOUNT HOLDER: Dale Morrison

ACCOUNT NUMBER: --4729

STATEMENT PERIOD: September 15, 2019 - October 15, 2019

ACCOUNT SUMMARY Beginning Balance (09/15/2019): $3,047.83 Total Deposits: $5,153.00 Total Withdrawals: $0.00 Service Charges: $0.00 Ending Balance (10/15/2019): $8,200.83

TRANSACTION HISTORY

DATE | DESCRIPTION | WITHDRAWALS | DEPOSITS | BALANCE

09/15/2019 | Beginning Balance | | | $3,047.83 05/18/2019 | Payroll Deposit - Morrison Grocery | | $153.00 | $3,200.83 10/11/2019 | Money Order Deposit | | $5,000.00 | $8,200.83

DEPOSIT DETAILS

Date: October 11, 2019 **Type:** Money Order **Amount:** $5,000.00 **Money Order #:** 4472891-MM **Deposited by:** Dale Morrison

Deposit Slip Note: "Please be careful. Love Mom"

ACCOUNT NOTICES

- No service charges this period
- Account in good standing
- Next statement date: November 15, 2019

CUSTOMER SERVICE For questions about your account, please call: (256) 555-BANK (2265)

Hours: Monday-Friday 9:00 AM - 5:00 PM Saturday 9:00 AM - 12:00 PM

FIRST NATIONAL BANK OF MILLBROOK
Member FDIC Your Community Bank Since 1952

Important Account Information:

- Minimum balance to avoid fees: $100.00
- Current balance exceeds minimum requirements
- ATM card expires: 12/2028
- Direct deposit available - ask about our services

Online Banking: Available 24/7 at www.fnbmillbrook.com **ATM Locations:** Downtown Branch, Walmart, Murphy's Gas Station

---

Please review this statement carefully and report any discrepancies within 30 days.

Statement Date: October 15, 2019 **Printed:** October 16, 2019 08:30 AM

Document 39: Diary Entry
Written by Dale Morrison
Dated: October 24, 2019

I went to check my account balance this morning before buying my bus ticket, and I couldn't believe what I saw. $8,200. I stared at that number for a full minute before I noticed the deposit slip note.

"Please be careful. Love Mom"

Five thousand dollars. With a note that said she loves me.

I sat in my car in the bank parking lot and cried for twenty minutes.

I don't know how she got that kind of money without Dad knowing. Maybe she's been hiding cash from the grocery budget for months. Maybe she took it from their savings account while he was too sick to notice. Maybe she borrowed it from someone. However she got it, I know it represents a huge sacrifice for her.

And I hate that I'm not more grateful.

Don't get me wrong - I am grateful. Eight thousand dollars means I can find a decent apartment in Atlanta instead of sleeping in shelters. It means I can take my time finding a job instead of having to take the first thing that comes along. It means I can afford the hormones and therapy and all the things I'll need to finally become myself.

But what I really wanted wasn't money.

What I wanted was for her to say, "Dale, don't go. Stay here and let me protect you for once. Let me stand up to your father and tell him that you're my child and I love you exactly as you are. Let me go to church and tell Bishop Patterson that what he did to you was wrong. Let me be your mother instead of just his wife."

The money feels like... like she's paying me to disappear. Like she's saying, "I can't choose you over him, but here's enough cash to make sure you can survive without me."

I know that's not fair. I know she's doing the only thing she knows how to do. She's been so beaten down, so trained to be invisible, that standing up to Dad would probably kill her. Literally. I've seen what he does when she shows even the smallest bit of independence.

But it still hurts.

I keep thinking about that conversation we had in the hospital after I was attacked. For just a moment, I thought maybe she was finally seeing me. Really seeing me. When she called me "my child" instead of "my son," I thought something had changed.

Maybe something did change. Maybe that's why she sent the money. Maybe this is her way of saying she sees me and she loves me, even if she can't say it out loud.

I just wish love didn't have to be so quiet in our family. I wish it didn't have to be hidden in money order deposits and whispered notes. I wish it could be loud and proud and fierce, the way mothers are supposed to love their children.

I wish she could have looked Dad in the eye and said, "That's my daughter you're talking about, and I won't let you hurt her anymore."

But she can't. She's spent thirty years learning to disappear, learning to make herself small enough that his anger might pass over her. I can't expect her to suddenly become someone she's never been allowed to be.

The money is her way of saying she loves me. It's the only way she knows how.

I called her this afternoon from a payphone downtown. She answered on the first ring, like she'd been waiting by the phone.

"Mama, I got your deposit."

Silence. Then, so quiet I could barely hear her: "Did you?"

"Thank you. I don't know how you—"

"Don't ask me how. Just... just promise me you'll be safe."

"I promise, Mama."

"And Dale?" She'd never called me that before. My name - my real name - in her voice. "Promise me you'll write. Not here, but... find a way to let me know you're okay."

"I will."

"I love you." She said it fast, like she was afraid someone might hear. "I've always loved you. I just... I didn't know how to show it right."

"I know, Mama. I love you too."

She hung up without saying goodbye, but I heard her crying before the line went dead.

I'm leaving tomorrow. The 6:47 AM Greyhound to Atlanta. I have a suitcase full of clothes that finally fit who I am, a wallet full of money that represents my mother's love, and a piece of blue-wrapped candy from a woman who told me I wasn't unholy for being complicated.

I'm scared. I'm excited. I'm heartbroken. I'm

hopeful.

I'm finally going to find out what it means to live as myself.

But I'm going to miss my mama. Even if she couldn't be the mother I needed her to be, she was the only mother I had. And in her own quiet, broken way, she loved me enough to let me go.

Maybe that's its own kind of bravery.

The girl in the mirror looks ready for whatever comes next. But she's crying a little too, because leaving home - even a home that never felt like home - is still leaving everything you've ever known.

Tomorrow I start over. Tonight, I'm going to let myself grieve for the family I never had and be grateful for the love I did receive, even when it came wrapped in silence and sealed with money orders.

Five thousand dollars and four words: "Please be careful. Love Mom."

It's not everything I wanted.

But maybe it's enough to build a new life on.

Maybe it's enough to forgive her for all the times she chose his peace over my protection.

Maybe love doesn't always look the way we want it to. Sometimes it looks like letting go.

I understand now, Mama. You love me the only way you know how.

It's okay. I'm going to be okay.

I'm going to make you proud.

Document 40: Diary Entry

Written by Dale Morrison
Dated: October 27, 2019

Dad was waiting for me in the living room when I came downstairs with my suitcase this morning. He looked terrible - skinnier than ever, that gray color sick people get - but his eyes were still full of that familiar rage.

"Where the hell do you think you're going?" he demanded.

"Atlanta," I said, trying to keep my voice steady. "I got a job there." (A lie, but easier than explaining.)

"Like hell you do. You're eighteen years old. You don't know anything about the world."

"I know enough to know I can't stay here."

He struggled to stand up from his chair, coughing. "You can't just leave. You've got responsibilities. Your mother needs help taking care of me."

"Then maybe you should have thought about that before you told me you wished I'd never been born."

His face went dark. "You're still my son. You live under my roof, you follow my rules."

"I'm not your son, Dad. I never was. And this stopped being my roof the day you decided Bishop Patterson's opinion mattered more than your own child's safety."

He started toward me, but the coughing fit hit him hard. When he finally caught his breath, there was blood on his hand.

"You're killing me," he wheezed. "You know that?

All this stress, all this... this nonsense. You're killing your own father."

"No, Dad. The drinking is killing you. Your anger is killing you. I'm just finally choosing to live."

I picked up my suitcase and headed for the door. Behind me, I heard him yelling, "Don't you walk away from me! If you leave, don't you ever come back! You hear me? Don't you ever come back!"

I turned around one last time. "Goodbye, Dad. I hope you find some peace before the end."

He was still shouting when I closed the door behind me.

Mama was in the kitchen, pretending she hadn't heard any of it. Somehow, she was able to get out of the back door. She met me at the end of the driveway with watery eyes. She pressed a brown paper bag into my hands - sandwiches for the bus ride - and kissed my forehead.

"Take care of yourself," she whispered.

"I will, Mama."

I walked to the bus station carrying everything I owned in one suitcase and a paper bag. Behind me, I could still hear Dad's voice echoing in my head: "Don't you ever come back!"

Don't worry, Dad. I won't.

I'm going somewhere I can finally be myself.

The girl in the mirror is free.

Document 41: Apartment Listing and Selection
Written by Dale Morrison
Dated: November 1, 2019

ATLANTA APARTMENT GUIDE
November 2019 - Budget Rentals

EASTSIDE EFFICIENCY APARTMENTS
555 Ponce de Leon Avenue
- Studio/1 Bath • $285/month • No deposit with good credit
  - Utilities included • Furnished
  - Bus line access
  - Call 404-555-0234

GRANT PARK SINGLES
1247 Memorial Drive
- 1BR/1BA • $325/month • $200 deposit
- Water/sewer included • Laundry on-site
- Near MARTA station
- 24-hour security
- Call 404-555-0891

HIGHLAND MANOR APTS
890 North Highland Ave
- 1BR/1BA • $375/month • $300 deposit
- Heat included
- Pool • Parking • Virginia-Highland area
- 404-555-0445

DOWNTOWN STUDIOS

234 Peachtree Street

- Efficiency • $295/month • $150 deposit
- All utilities included
- Furnished option available
- 24-hour security
- 404-555-0667

CANDLER PARK BUDGET RENTALS

1156 DeKalb Avenue

- 1BR/1BA • $350/month • $250 deposit
- Stove/refrigerator included • Hardwood floors • Pet-friendly
- 404-555-0523

KIRKWOOD APARTMENTS

1834 Hosea Williams Drive

- 1BR/1BA • $275/month • $200 deposit
- Water included • On-site laundry
- Bus route access
- 404-555-0789

Called Eastside Efficiency - available immediately Peachtree location - close to everything $295 is exactly what I can afford. Utilities included and furnished = good Going to see it tomorrow.

Document 42: Diary Entry

Written by Dale Morrison

Dated: November 1, 2019

I went to my first TransAtlanta meeting tonight. I've been in the city for three weeks now, and I've been carrying that brochure around like a talisman, reading it over and over but too scared to actually go.

But tonight, sitting in my tiny studio apartment eating ramen noodles for the fourth night in a row, I realized I was lonelier than I'd ever been. Even lonelier than I was back home, because at least there I had the hope of someday leaving. Here, I am where I wanted to be, but I'm still just... alone.

So I put on my best dress - the blue one I bought at Goodwill before I left Millbrook - and took the MARTA train to the Rainbow Community Center on Peachtree Street.

I sat in the parking lot for twenty minutes, watching people go in and out of the building. Some looked like me - nervous, unsure, glancing around to make sure no one was watching. Others walked with confidence, like they'd been coming here for years. A few I couldn't tell if they were trans or not, which somehow made me feel hopeful.

When I finally worked up the courage to go inside, a woman with kind eyes and graying hair welcomed me at the door.

"First time?" she asked, and when I nodded, she smiled. "I'm Janet. I run the Thursday night group. You're safe here, honey. What name would you like us to use?"

"Dale," I said, and she wrote it on a little name

tag without asking for my "real" name or looking confused about whether Dale was a boy's name or a girl's name.

"Beautiful name," she said. "Dale, welcome home."

Home. She called it home.

The meeting was in a circle of folding chairs in a room with rainbow flags and motivational posters. There were maybe fifteen people there - some who looked like me, some who looked like they'd been living as themselves for years, some who were somewhere in between.

Janet started the meeting by asking everyone to introduce themselves with their name and pronouns. When it got to me, I said, "I'm Dale, she/her," and nobody questioned it. Nobody looked confused or skeptical. They just nodded and smiled and the next person went.

It was the first time in my life I'd said my pronouns out loud in front of other people. The first time I'd claimed "she/her" as mine. It felt like... like breathing after holding your breath for eighteen years.

A woman named Carmen shared about starting hormones last month. She talked about the changes she was noticing, the way her skin was getting softer, how emotional she'd been feeling. She cried when she talked about how her sister had started calling her by her chosen name.

A man named David talked about his top surgery consultation. He'd been binding his chest since he was fifteen, he said, and now at twenty-three he was finally going to have the surgery he'd dreamed about. Everyone clapped when he showed us the photo of the surgeon's results.

A woman named Lisa shared about losing her job

when she transitioned but finding a new one at a company that had nondiscrimination policies. She said it was scary but worth it to finally live authentically.

When it came time for me to share, I didn't know what to say. I'd never told my story to anyone before. Not the whole story.

"I'm new to Atlanta," I started. "I grew up in a small town where being different was... dangerous. My family couldn't accept who I am. My church tried to... to pray it out of me. I've been hiding for so long, I almost forgot who I was hiding."

My voice broke, and Janet passed me a box of tissues.

"But I'm here now," I continued. "I'm scared and I don't know what I'm doing, but I'm here. I'm Dale. I'm a woman. And for the first time in my life, I'm in a room full of people who understand what that means."

Everyone clapped. Not the polite, obligatory clapping you get at church, but real applause. Like they were proud of me just for showing up.

After the meeting, several people came up to me. Carmen gave me her phone number and said to call if I needed anything. David recommended a therapist who specializes in gender issues. Lisa told me about job opportunities and said her company was hiring.

But it was what Janet said that made me cry again.

"Dale, I want you to know something. You are exactly who you're supposed to be. Everything you've been through - all the pain, all the hiding, all the fear - it brought you here. To us. To yourself. You survived it all, and now you get to live."

I rode the MARTA train home in a daze. The city lights looked different through the windows. Brighter. More welcoming. Like Atlanta was finally ready to be my home.

I'm still scared. I still have nightmares about Dad and Bishop Patterson. I still catch myself looking over my shoulder, expecting someone to tell me I don't belong.

But tonight, for two hours, I sat in a room full of people who saw me - really saw me - and didn't try to change me or fix me or pray me into being someone else.

Tonight, I was just Dale. And Dale was enough.

I'm going back next week. And the week after that. And the week after that.

I'm going to learn how to be myself. I'm going to learn how to live, not just survive.

I'm going to learn what it means to be home.

The girl in the mirror is smiling tonight. She's still scared, but she's not alone anymore.

She has a community now. She has a name tag that says "Dale, she/her." She has people who understand.

She has a future.

Janet was right. I am exactly who I'm supposed to be.

And for the first time in my life, that feels like enough.

More than enough.

It feels like everything.

Written by Multiple Individuals

Dated: November 3, 2019

FACEBOOK POSTS - PRAYER REQUESTS FOR EARL MORRISON

Margaret Morrison

Posted 2 hours ago

🙏 URGENT PRAYER REQUEST 🙏

My husband Earl Morrison is fighting a hard battle right now. The doctors have said some discouraging things, but we serve a God who is bigger than any medical report!

Please pray for complete healing for Earl. He is such a strong man of God and faithful deacon at Cedar Ridge Baptist Church. Pray that the Lord will touch his body and restore his health.

Also pray for wisdom for me as I care for him. I could use some meals if anyone is able to help.

Thank you all. God is still on the throne!

#PrayForEarl #GodIsHealer #MillbrookStrong

43 reactions 🖤 🖤 🙏 *27 comments 12 shares*

Cedar Ridge Baptist Church

Posted 4 hours ago

▪️ PRAYER ALERT ▪️

Church family, our beloved Deacon Earl Morrison is in need of our prayers. Earl has been diagnosed with cancer and is trusting God for his healing.

Earl has served faithfully in our church for over 20 years. He's been a pillar of strength and spiritual leadership in our community. Now it's time for us to lift him up!

CALLING ALL PRAYER WARRIORS! Please storm the throne of grace for our brother Earl. Let's believe God for a miracle!

"The prayer of a righteous person is powerful and effective." - James 5:16

Wednesday night we will have a special prayer service for Earl at 7 PM. All are welcome.

#PrayForEarlMorrison   #FaithOverFear #MiracleNeeded

127 reactions *89 comments 45 shares*

Bishop William Patterson

Posted 6 hours ago

Saints, I'm asking for your fervent prayers for one of our faithful deacons, Earl Morrison. Earl is facing a health challenge that the enemy is trying to use to discourage him and his family.

But we know that our God is a healing God! We know that nothing is impossible with Him!

I've been praying with Earl and Sister Margaret, and I can tell you that Earl's faith is unshakeable. He refuses to accept the doctor's negative report and is standing on God's promises for healing.

Let's join our faith with his! Let's pray for:

- Complete healing and restoration
- Strength for Margaret as she cares for him
- Wisdom for the medical team
- Peace that passes understanding
- A testimony of God's power

Please share this post so more people can pray! The

more people pray, the more power we have against the enemy!

"By His stripes we are HEALED!" - Isaiah 53:5

#HealingPrayers   #DeaconEarl   #GodStillHeals #PrayerWarriors

201 reactions 🙏 💜 💪 *156 comments 78 shares*

Millbrook Community Prayer Chain

Posted 8 hours ago

🔔 URGENT PRAYER REQUEST 🔔

PLEASE SHARE!!

Earl Morrison needs our prayers RIGHT NOW! He's been diagnosed with cancer and his family is asking for prayer warriors to intercede.

Earl is a good man, a faithful husband, and dedicated church member. He doesn't deserve this trial but God can use it for His glory!

If you're reading this, please stop and pray for Earl RIGHT NOW. Don't scroll past. PRAY!

Dear Jesus, we lift up Earl Morrison to you. Touch his body with your healing power. We reject this diagnosis in Jesus' name and claim complete healing for Earl. Strengthen Margaret during this time. Let your peace rule in their hearts. In Jesus' mighty name, AMEN!

Comment AMEN if you prayed! Let's flood this with prayers!

#PrayForEarl   #CancelCancer   #Jesus #HealingPrayer #MillbrookPrays

89 reactions 🙏 💜 *134 comments 67 shares*

Dorothy Patterson (First Lady)

Posted 10 hours ago

My heart is heavy tonight as I ask for prayers for a dear family in our church.

Deacon Earl Morrison has received a difficult medical diagnosis, but we are not giving up hope! Earl and Margaret Morrison have been faithful servants in our church for decades. Earl has been such a blessing to our Bishop and to our congregation.

Ladies, Sister Margaret especially needs our prayers and practical support right now. If you can provide meals, cleaning help, or just a listening ear, please reach out to her.

Sometimes God allows us to walk through valleys so that we can experience His miraculous power. I believe God is going to get glory out of this situation!

Praying for: 🙏 Complete healing for Earl 🙏 Strength and peace for Margaret 🙏 A mighty testimony of God's power 🙏 Protection from fear and discouragement

"He heals the brokenhearted and binds up their wounds." - Psalm 147:3

Much love, First Lady Dorothy

#ChurchFamily　　　　　#PrayForThesMorrisons #GodIsAbleHealer

76 reactions 🙏 💜 💜 *45 comments 23 shares*

COMMENTS SECTION

Linda Johnson: Praying right now! Earl is such a good man. God can heal him! 🙏

Robert Davis: Standing in agreement for Earl's healing! Nothing is too hard for God!

Susan Miller: Adding Earl to our church prayer list. Believing God for a miracle!

Michael Williams: Earl helped me so much when I

was going through my divorce. Time to pray for him! God's got this! 💪

Katherine Smith: Cooked a casserole for Margaret. Will drop it by tomorrow. Praying for strength for both of them.

Karen Anderson: Has anyone reached out to their son? Families need to stick together during times like this.

Margaret Morrison: Thank you all for your prayers. Earl is staying strong in his faith. Please keep praying!

Sierra Thompson: Claiming Jeremiah 30:17 over Earl - "I will restore you to health and heal your wounds, declares the Lord!"

Mark Stevens: Posted on our church page too. Getting more prayer warriors involved!

Beverly Adams: Earl is a fighter! Praying for supernatural healing! God is not done with him yet! 🙏 ♥

Document 44: Diary Entry
Written by Dale Morrison
Dated: November 6, 2019

I made the mistake of looking at Facebook today.

I don't know why I did it. Maybe because I've been in Atlanta for over a month now and I was feeling homesick. Maybe because I wanted to see if anyone back home was talking about me, wondering where I went. Maybe because I'm a glutton for punishment.

I found Mama's Facebook page first. Her profile picture is still that old photo of her and Dad from their anniversary five years ago. She looks so young and hopeful in that picture. Before the sickness, before I left, before everything fell apart.

Then I saw the post. "URGENT PRAYER REQUEST" in all caps. My heart stopped when I read it.

Dad is getting worse. The cancer is spreading. The church is rallying around him, calling for prayer warriors and miracle healing. Bishop Patterson is organizing special services. The whole community is coming together to support "Earl and Margaret Morrison" in their time of need.

Earl and Margaret Morrison. Like they're the only two people in the family.

I kept scrolling, reading post after post about what a "faithful servant" Dad is, what a "pillar of the community," what a "devoted husband and father." Father. They called him a devoted father.

Not one person - not one - mentioned that he has a child who isn't there. Not one person asked where I am or why I'm not helping take care of him. It's like

I never existed.

Even in the comments, where people are sharing memories of Dad helping them or supporting them through hard times, nobody says "Where's his son?" or "Shouldn't his boy be there?" It's like the entire town has collectively decided to pretend I was never born.

Which, I guess, is what Dad always wanted anyway.

But what hurts the most is seeing how easily they all accepted my erasure. How quickly 18 years of my existence was wiped clean from their narrative. How comfortable they all are with the story of Earl Morrison, faithful deacon, devoted husband, period. End of story.

There's no awkward gap where a child should be. No one asking uncomfortable questions about family dynamics. No one wondering why a dying man's only child isn't by his side.

I tried to imagine what they'd say if someone did ask. "Oh, Earl's son? He ran off to the big city. Got himself into some trouble. You know how kids are these days. Earl and Margaret are better off without all that drama."

That's probably how they'll explain it. Make it sound like I'm the problem, like I'm some selfish kid who abandoned his sick father instead of the daughter who fled religious abuse and a lifetime of rejection.

I saw Mrs. Henderson's comment about providing meals for Mama. Mrs. Johnson is offering to help with housework. The whole church is organizing to support them through this crisis.

Where was all this support when I was being tortured in their sanctuary? Where were all these caring Christians when their Bishop was abusing a child under the guise of deliverance? Where were these prayer warriors when I was in the hospital, beaten nearly to death for being who I am?

They can rally around a dying man who spent his life spreading hate, but they couldn't protect a child who just wanted to be loved.

I started to write a comment on Mama's post. Started to type, "I'm praying for you both too." But I stopped.

What would happen if I identified myself? Would they delete my comment? Would they block me? Would Bishop Patterson call it "demonic interference" in Earl's healing? Would Dad get angry enough to have another attack?

Or worse - would they just ignore it completely? Would my attempt to reach out be met with the same silence that's erased me from their story?

I closed Facebook without commenting. But I couldn't stop thinking about it.

I am praying for them. Not because Dad deserves it, but because Mama does. Because even though she couldn't protect me, she loved me the only way she knew how. Because she's alone now, taking care of a dying man who's probably still angry at the world, still controlling everything he can control.

I'm praying that Dad finds some peace before he dies. Not for his sake, but so Mama doesn't have to carry the weight of his bitterness after he's gone.

I'm praying that when this is all over, maybe Mama and I can find a way back to each other. Maybe without Dad's anger filling up all the space in the house, there might be room for love to grow.

But I'm not praying for a miracle healing. I'm not claiming Bible verses or rebuking cancer in Jesus' name. I'm just praying for mercy. For all of us.

The girl in the mirror looks sad tonight. Not because her father is dying - we all knew that was coming. But because even in dying, he managed to erase her from the story one more time.

Even from 300 miles away, he's still making her disappear.

But I won't disappear. I'm Dale Morrison, daughter of Earl and Margaret Morrison, whether they claim me or not. I'm part of this story, even if they've written me out of it.

Someday, when Dad is gone and the prayer warriors have moved on to the next crisis, maybe Mama will remember that she has a daughter who loves her.

Maybe that will be enough.

Maybe it will have to be.

I'm turning off Facebook for a while. I need to focus on building my new life, not mourning the old one.

The girl in the mirror is stronger than she was a month ago. She has friends now, a support group, a future.

She doesn't need their prayer chains or their false narrative.

She has her own truth.

And her own prayers.

Document 45: Facebook Posts

Written by Multiple Individuals
Dated: December 13, 2019

Dale Morrison

Posted 3 hours ago

I've been sitting here for an hour trying to figure out how to write this post. I've started and deleted it probably ten times, but I think it's time I shared what's really been going on in my life.

Three months ago, I left my hometown of Millbrook, Alabama, and moved to Atlanta. I left everything I'd ever known - my family, my church, my community - because I finally realized that sometimes you have to save yourself when no one else will.

I know a lot of you have been seeing posts about my father's illness and asking for prayers for him. I want you to know that I'm praying for him too, and for my mother who's caring for him. But I also need to tell you why I'm not there with them.

For my entire life, I've been trying to be someone I'm not. I've been trying to fit into a box that was never made for me, trying to be the person everyone expected me to be instead of the person God actually created me to be. And it was killing me. Literally.

I am a transgender woman. That's not something I chose, it's not something I can pray away, and it's not something I'm ashamed of anymore. God doesn't make mistakes, and He didn't make a mistake when He made me. I believe with everything in me that He created me exactly as I am for a reason, even if that reason isn't clear to me yet.

My family couldn't accept this truth about me. My

church tried to "pray the demon out of me" through methods that I can only describe as abuse. I was attacked and hospitalized for being who I am. And through it all, I kept trying to be the son and the church member they wanted instead of the daughter and the person of faith that I actually am.

But God kept calling me to be authentic. To stop hiding. To stop apologizing for how He made me.

So I came to Atlanta with $3,200, a suitcase full of clothes that finally felt like me, and more fear than I've ever experienced in my life. But also, more hope.

These past three months have been the hardest and the most beautiful of my life. I've found a community of people who see me for who I really am and love me anyway. I've found a therapist who doesn't try to change me but helps me understand myself. I've found a church where they talk about God's love being bigger than our fear, where being different isn't seen as being wrong.

I've found myself. The real me. Dale. She's been hiding inside for 18 years, afraid to come out because she thought no one would love her. But she's here now, and she's not going anywhere.

I'm not going to lie to you - it's been scary. There are days when I'm so lonely I cry myself to sleep. There are nights when I'm so afraid I can barely breathe. Starting over is terrifying when you're doing it completely alone.

But I'm not alone. God is with me. He's been with me through every hard day, every small victory, every moment of fear and every moment of joy. He's shown me that His love doesn't come with conditions, that His plan for my life is bigger than other people's expectations, and that being authentic isn't rebellion - it's worship.

I'm sharing this because I need your prayers. Not prayers to change me or fix me or make me go back to pretending to be someone I'm not. I need prayers for:

🙏 Strength to keep building this new life 🙏 Healing from the trauma of rejection and abuse 🙏 Wisdom as I navigate this journey 🙏 Safety in a world that's not always kind to people like me 🙏 Peace for my family back home, especially my mother 🙏 God's guidance as I figure out what He's calling me to do with this life

I also need prayers for my parents. My father is dying, and despite everything that's happening between us, I still love him. I pray that he finds peace before he passes. I pray that my mother finds strength to carry on. And I pray that someday, somehow, there might be room for reconciliation and healing.

If you're someone who can't accept who I am, I understand. I'm not asking you to understand - I'm just asking you not to judge. I spent 18 years judging myself harshly enough for all of us.

If you're someone who's struggling with your own identity, who feels like they don't fit the box everyone else wants to put them in, I want you to know you are not alone. You are not a mistake. You are fearfully and wonderfully made, exactly as you are. There is a place for you in this world, and there are people who will love you for who you really are, not who they want you to be.

God's love is bigger than our categories. His grace is wider than our understanding. His plan is more beautiful than our fears.

I'm Dale Morrison. I'm a transgender woman. I'm a person of faith. I'm someone's daughter, even if they can't see me right now. I'm a survivor. I'm a work in progress. I'm exactly who I'm supposed to be.

And I'm asking for your prayers as I continue becoming her.

Thank you for reading this. Thank you for your love, if you can give it. Thank you for your prayers, if you're willing to offer them.

God bless you all.

With love and hope, Dale 💜

P.S. - If anyone knows of job opportunities in Atlanta for someone with a high school diploma and a strong work ethic, please message me. I'm still figuring out the practical parts of this new life! ☺

#TransAndFaith   #AuthenticLife
#GodDoesntMakeMistakes   #AtlantaLife
#PrayersNeeded #LoveWins #BeingReal

287 reactions 💜 😢 🙏 🤗

156 comments

89 shares

COMMENTS ON DALE'S POST

Carmen Rodriguez (TransAtlanta Support Group) *2 hours ago* Dale, I am so proud of you for sharing your truth! It takes incredible courage to be this vulnerable publicly. You are such an inspiration to everyone in our group. Your authenticity is beautiful. Praying for you, sister! 💜 *47 likes*

Janet Miller (Support Group Leader) *2 hours ago* This is what bravery looks like, everyone. Dale, you are a light in this world. Thank you for trusting us with your story. Our community is blessed to have you. Sending love and prayers! 🙏 💜 *52 likes*

Robert Davis (Cedar Ridge Baptist Church Member) *2 hours ago* This is disgusting and ungodly.

Earl Morrison is a good man dying of cancer and his so-called "son" is on here making it all about himself and his perverted lifestyle. Have some respect for your father. You need Jesus, not surgery. *12 likes 73 angry reactions*

Lisa Poltowski (Atlanta Friend) *2 hours ago* Dale, you are so brave! I've been following your journey and I'm amazed by your strength. You're right - God doesn't make mistakes. You are exactly who you're supposed to be. If you need anything at all, please reach out. We're here for you! 💪 💜 *38 likes*

Hariette Johnson (Millbrook Neighbor) *2 hours ago* I remember you as a sweet little child always helping your mama in the garden. I don't understand all of this, but I can see that you're hurting and trying to find your way. I pray for you and your family. May God give you all peace. *89 likes*

Michael Williams (Former Classmate) *2 hours ago* Dude, what the hell? Your dad is DYING, and you're worried about playing dress-up? This is sick. You were always weird in school, but this is next level. Get help. *8 likes 156 angry reactions*

Dr. Constance Reynolds (Therapist) *2 hours ago* Dale, thank you for sharing your story with such honesty and grace. Your journey takes tremendous courage, and your faith is inspiring. You are making a difference in the world just by being authentically yourself. Many people will be helped by your words. 🙏 *67 likes*

Susan Miller (Church Member) *2 hours ago* I will pray for you, but I have to say this breaks my heart. Your parents raised you in the church and this is how you repay them? While your father is fighting for his life? Please come home and make things right with your family before it's too late. *23 likes*

David Thompson (TransAtlanta Member) *1 hour ago* Brother, you just changed my life. I've been struggling with coming out to my family and your post gave me the courage I needed. Thank you for being so real. The trans community is lucky to have you. 🖤 *71 likes*

Christina Rodriguez (Former Walgreens Employee) *1 hour ago* DALE! I remember you! I used to work at Walgreens, and you would come in sometimes. I always knew you were special. I'm so proud of you for finding yourself and living your truth. Your courage is incredible. Dale was always a beautiful name for a beautiful person. 🖤 *134 likes*

Margaret Morrison (Dale's Mother) *1 hour ago* I love you. I'm sorry I didn't know how to show it better. I'm praying for you every day. Please be safe. *312 likes 89 heart reactions*

Beverly Adams (Church Member) *1 hour ago* Margaret Morrison, you need to delete that comment right now. This child is in rebellion against God and you're encouraging sin. Earl doesn't need this stress while he's fighting cancer. Sometimes love means saying no to evil. *3 likes 245 angry reactions*

Bishop James Wilson (Progressive Church) *1 hour ago* Dale, I don't know you personally, but I want you to know that you are loved and valued exactly as you are. God's love is not conditional on other people's understanding. You are fearfully and wonderfully made. If you ever need a spiritual home in Atlanta, our doors are open. Blessings to you, sister. *198 likes*

Karen Anderson (Family Friend) *1 hour ago* I've known your family for 20 years and this is heartbreaking. Your father is such a good man, and your mother is suffering. How can you be so selfish? Come home and take care of your family instead of parading around in women's clothes. This is not what God wants. *7 likes 98 angry reactions*

Evelyn Porter (Mysterious Commenter) *1 hour ago* Sugar, I'm so proud of you for finding your voice. You're not unholy for being complicated - you're holy for being honest. Keep shining your light. The world needs more people like you. Sending you love and the sweetest prayers. 🐝 💜 *267 likes*

Marcus Webb (Threatening Comment - Later Deleted) *1 hour ago* I know where you live now. Atlanta isn't that big. You can't hide forever, you sick freak. *[Comment removed by Facebook for violating community standards]*

Linda Thompson (Supportive Stranger) *1 hour ago* I don't know you, but your post showed up in my feed and I had to comment. I'm a mother of three and if one of my children wrote something this brave and beautiful, I would be so proud. You are incredible. Your parents are missing out on an amazing daughter. *156 likes*

First Lady Dorothy Patterson *1 hour ago* This is heartbreaking. I'm praying for your soul and for your poor parents who are suffering because of your choices. Please come home and let Bishop Patterson help you. It's not too late to repent and be delivered from this deception. *12 likes 187 angry reactions*

Alex Kim (New Friend) *45 minutes ago* Dale, we just met at the coffee shop last week, but I had to comment. You are one of the most genuine people I've ever met. Your faith is inspiring, and your courage is amazing. Thank you for being you. Atlanta is lucky to have you! ● ♥ *43 likes*

Jennifer Hebert (Supportive Stranger) *45 minutes ago* I'm not religious, but I believe in love and authenticity. You are brave and beautiful, and the world is better because you're in it. Sending you strength and support from a complete stranger who believes in you! 🙏 ♥ *78 likes*

Earl Morrison (Dale's Father) *30 minutes ago* I don't have a son. *2 likes 456 angry reactions*

Dale Morrison (Replying to her father) *25 minutes ago* You're right, Dad. You don't have a son. You have a daughter who loves you and hopes you find peace. I'm praying for you. ♥ *1,247 likes 345 heart reactions*

Response Summary: *2,847 reactions 523 comments 234 shares Post has been shared to 47 different groups Trending in Atlanta LGBTQ+ community Reported 23 times (no violations found) Generated 3 news article mentions Sparked 12 copycat coming-out posts*

Document 46: Dairy Entry
Written by Dale Morrison
Dated: December 16, 2019

Janet called me this morning after my Facebook post
went viral. She asked if I could come in for an
emergency meeting with the leadership team of
TransAtlanta. I was scared - worried that maybe
I'd done something wrong, that my public coming out
had somehow reflected badly on the group.

I was wrong. So completely wrong.

I walked into the Rainbow Community Center to find
not just Janet, but Carmen, David, Lisa, and about
eight other members I'd gotten to know over the
past month. They all broke into applause when I
walked in.

"Dale," Janet said, her eyes full of tears, "do you
have any idea what you did yesterday?"

I shook my head, still confused.

"You gave hope to thousands of people," Carmen
said. "Your post has been shared over 200 times.
I've gotten messages from trans people all over the
South saying they saw your story and it gave them
courage."

David pulled out his phone and showed me
screenshot after screenshot. "Look at this - a trans
man in Mississippi said your post convinced him to
finally come out to his parents. A trans woman in
Tennessee said seeing your faith helped her realize
she could be trans and Christian. A mom in Florida
said reading your story helped her understand her
transgender daughter."

I sat down hard in one of the folding chairs. "I

just... I needed to tell my truth. I saw all those posts about my father, and I felt so erased, so invisible. I had to speak up."

"And you did it with such grace," Lisa said. "Even when you were talking about the abuse you suffered, even when your father commented that horrible thing, you responded with love. You showed the world what it means to be transgender and Christian."

Janet sat down beside me. "Dale, we need to talk about safety though. Your post got a lot of attention - good and bad. We need to make sure you're protected."

She was right. Along with all the supportive messages, there were some scary ones. Threats from people back home. Comments about finding me in Atlanta. Marcus Webb's deleted post had made my blood run cold.

"We've dealt with this before when members go public," Carmen explained. "Here's what we're going to do."

They had it all planned out. Alex, who worked in tech, was going to help me adjust my privacy settings and set up a P.O. box for any mail. Lisa's company had security contacts who could do a safety assessment of my apartment. David knew a lawyer who specialized in LGBTQ+ issues and restraining orders.

"We take care of our own," Janet said simply. "Always."

But it wasn't just about safety. They wanted to talk about the opportunity my post had created.

"Dale, people are listening to you now," said Marcus, a trans man who'd been transitioning for five years. "You have a platform. What do you want to do with it?"

I'd never thought about having a platform. I'd just wanted to exist, to be myself, to find some peace. But looking around at that circle of faces - people who'd become my chosen family in just a few weeks - I realized I did want to do something with this attention.

"I want other kids to know they're not alone," I said. "I want them to know that being trans doesn't mean you can't have faith. I want families to understand that love is more important than fear."

"We can help you with that," Janet said. "We've been wanting to start an outreach program for transgender youth, especially in rural areas. Would you be interested in helping us develop it?"

My heart started racing. "You mean like, actually helping other kids like me?"

"Exactly like that. Speaking at schools, writing resources for families, maybe even training counselors and clergy who want to be more supportive."

I thought about the letter I'd written to Christina before I left Millbrook, about wanting to study social work and help other kids who didn't fit the boxes their families built for them. This was that dream, being handed to me sooner than I'd ever imagined.

"Yes," I said without hesitation. "Yes, I want to help."

The meeting went on for two more hours. They talked about media training (apparently three news outlets had reached out about interviewing me). They discussed connecting me with other faith-affirming organizations. They gave me contact information for a trans-friendly doctor who could help me start hormone therapy when I was ready.

But what meant the most was when Janet

said, "Dale, what you did yesterday wasn't just brave. It was prophetic. You spoke truth in a way that changed people's hearts. You're going to help save lives."

As I was getting ready to leave, Carmen pulled me aside.

"I need to tell you something," she said. "When I first came to this group three years ago, I was suicidal. I didn't think I could be trans and still believe in God. I didn't think there was a place in the world for someone like me."

She paused, her eyes getting watery.

"Reading your post yesterday, seeing you claim your faith and your identity with such confidence... it healed something in me that I didn't even know was still broken. If you can do it, if you can be out and proud and Christian and transgender all at the same time, then maybe there's more hope for all of us than I thought."

I hugged her tight, both of us crying a little.

Walking home on the MARTA train, I kept thinking about what Janet had said. Prophetic. I'd never thought of myself as prophetic. I'd always felt more like a survivor, someone just trying to get by.

But maybe that's what prophecy looks like sometimes. Maybe it's not about predicting the future - maybe it's about speaking truth so clearly that it changes the present. Maybe it's about being so authentically yourself that other people remember they can be authentic too.

I'm still scared. The threats are real, the hatred is real, the danger is real. But so is the love. So is the community. So is the possibility that my pain might help someone else find their way to healing.

Tomorrow I'm going to call the reporter from the Atlanta Journal-Constitution who wants to interview me. I'm going to tell my story again, louder this time, to even more people.

Because Carmen is right - if I can be out and proud and Christian and transgender all at the same time, then maybe there's more hope for all of us than we thought.

The girl in the mirror isn't just surviving anymore. She's thriving. She's helping other people thrive too.

She's finally living the life she was meant to live.

And she's just getting started.

Document 47: Atlanta Journal Interview Transcript

Written by Michael Callaghan

Dated: December 21, 2019

ATLANTA JOURNAL-CONSTITUTION INTERVIEW TRANSCRIPT - DRAFT NOTES

Date: December 21, 2019, **Reporter:** Michael Callaghan, Staff Writer **Subject:** Dale Morrison, Transgender Rights Advocate **Location:** Java Jive Coffee Shop, Virginia-Highland

---

[OFF THE RECORD - Pre-Interview]

Callaghan: Dale, thank you for agreeing to meet with me. Before we start officially, I want to make sure you're completely comfortable with this process. This is your first major interview, right?

Morrison: Yes, and I'm honestly terrified. [laughs nervously] I never expected my Facebook post to get so much attention.

Callaghan: That's completely understandable. Look, I want you to know that we can stop at any time if you need a break. If there's any question that makes you uncomfortable, just say so. This is your story to tell, at your pace. And if you want to go off the record for any part, just let me know, okay?

Morrison: Thank you. That helps a lot.

Callaghan: I also want you to know that I've done my research. I've read about transgender issues, I've spoken with advocates, and I understand this isn't just a curiosity piece. Your story matters, and I want to tell it respectfully.

Morrison: I appreciate that more than you know.

Most of the media coverage I've seen about people like me has been... not great.

Callaghan: Well, we're going to change that today. Ready to go on the record?

Morrison: As ready as I'll ever be.

[ON THE RECORD - Official Interview]

Callaghan: Dale Morrison, you've become an unlikely voice for transgender rights after a Facebook post about your journey went viral this week. Tell me what prompted you to share such a personal story so publicly.

Morrison: I saw all these posts asking for prayers for my father - he's battling cancer back home in Alabama. Everyone was rallying around "Earl and Margaret Morrison" and their struggle. But I realized I'd been completely erased from that narrative. It was like I never existed, like I was never part of that family. I needed to claim my own story, to say "I exist, I matter, and my journey matters too."

Callaghan: Your father is dying, and you're estranged from your family. That must be incredibly painful.

Morrison: It is. The hardest part is that I still love him. I love both my parents. But they couldn't love the real me. My father spent my whole life trying to beat me into being the son he wanted instead of accepting the daughter he had. When I finally left home, he told me never to come back.

Callaghan: You mentioned in your post that your church attempted some kind of intervention. Can you tell me about that?

Morrison: [long pause] It's hard to talk about. They called it deliverance, but it was abuse. They believed I was possessed by demons and that they could pray it out of me. It involved... physical elements... that I'm not ready to discuss publicly yet. But I will say this: what happened to me in the name of God was the opposite of everything Jesus taught about love and acceptance.

Callaghan: That sounds traumatic. How did you find the strength to leave?

Morrison: I almost didn't. I was seventeen, had no money, nowhere to go. But I met someone - an elderly woman named Evelyn - who told me I wasn't "unholy for being complicated." She had a Bible on her dashboard and still saw me as worthy of love. She showed me that faith and acceptance could coexist.

Callaghan: Let's talk about your name. Dale can be used for any gender. Was that intentional?

Morrison: [smiles] Actually, that's one of my favorite parts of my story. I didn't choose the name Dale - my parents did. They named me Dale Morrison eighteen years ago, never knowing they were giving their daughter the perfect name. Dale has always been who I am. I just finally learned to live as her.

Callaghan: That's beautiful. So you didn't have to change your name to match your identity.

Morrison: Exactly. When people ask why I kept a "boy's name," I tell them it was never a boy's name. It was always Dale's name. And Dale was always a girl, even when everyone else saw something different.

Callaghan: You've faced some backlash since your post went viral. Are you concerned about your safety?

Morrison: Of course I'm concerned. Some of the messages I've received have been frightening. But I have an amazing support system here in Atlanta through TransAtlanta and the Rainbow Community Center. They've helped me take precautions while still allowing me to live openly.

Callaghan: What do you want people to understand about transgender individuals, particularly those from religious backgrounds?

Morrison: That we're not broken. We're not sick. We're not possessed by demons. We're people created by God, trying to live authentically. Many of us have deep faith - being transgender doesn't make you less spiritual, it just makes your spiritual journey different.

Callaghan: Your mother commented on your Facebook post, expressing her love. How did that feel?

Morrison: [tears up] It meant everything. My mother has been trapped in a situation where she had to choose between her husband's approval and her child's well-being. For her to publicly say she loves me, even just those simple words, took incredible courage. I hope someday we can rebuild our relationship.

Callaghan: What advice would you give to other transgender young people, especially those in rural or religious communities?

Morrison: You are not alone. You are not a mistake. You are exactly who God made you to be. It might feel impossible now, but there are places where you can be yourself safely. There are people who will love you for who you are, not who they want you to be. Hold on, find your community, and never stop believing that you deserve love and acceptance.

Callaghan: What's next for you?

Morrison: I'm working with TransAtlanta to

develop an outreach program for transgender youth, especially in rural areas. I want to create resources for families who are struggling to understand their transgender children. I want to train religious leaders who want to be more affirming. I want to make sure no other kid has to go through what I went through.

Callaghan: Any final thoughts?

Morrison: Just this: love is stronger than fear. Truth is more powerful than hatred. And sometimes the most prophetic thing you can do is simply exist as your authentic self. I'm Dale Morrison. I'm a transgender woman of faith. I'm someone's daughter, even if they can't see me right now. And I'm not going anywhere.

[OFF THE RECORD - Post-Interview]

Callaghan: Dale, that was incredible. How are you feeling?

Morrison: Better than I expected. Thank you for making this feel safe.

Callaghan: The part about your name really struck me. I'd never thought about it that way - that your parents actually gave you the perfect name without knowing it.

Morrison: It's like even when they were trying to fit me into their expectations, God was working through them to give me exactly what I needed. Dale works for who I was then and who I am now.

Callaghan: This piece is going to help a lot of people. You should be proud.

Morrison: I hope so. That's all I want - for my pain to have purpose, for my story to help someone else find their way home to themselves.

Callaghan: When can we do a follow-up? I'd love to check in with you in six months, see how the advocacy work is going.

Morrison: I'd like that. Thank you, Michael. For everything.

[Reporter's Notes:] Subject is remarkably composed for someone who's been through such trauma. Her combination of vulnerability and strength will resonate with readers. The religious angle adds important nuance to the transgender rights conversation. Story has potential for significant impact.

Planned publication: Sunday, December 29, 2019 - Front page, Living section **Photo shoot scheduled:** December 26, 2019 **Follow-up planned:** March 2020

Document 48: News Article
Written by Michael Callaghan
Dated: December 29, 2019

THE ATLANTA JOURNAL-CONSTITUTION SUNDAY, December 29, 2019 - LIVING SECTION

Finding Faith and Self: A Young Woman's Journey from Rural Alabama to Atlanta

Local transgender advocate Dale Morrison speaks about growing up in religious community that couldn't accept her identity.

By Michael Callaghan, Staff Writer

ATLANTA - In a small coffee shop in Virginia-Highland, 18-year-old Dale Morrison sits across from me, her hands wrapped around a steaming mug, speaking with a wisdom that seems far beyond her years. Just days ago, she was a quiet newcomer to Atlanta, trying to build a life away from the small Alabama town where she grew up. Today, she's become an unlikely voice for transgender rights after a Facebook post about her journey went viral.

"I never expected to become an advocate," Morrison says, her voice soft but steady. "I just needed to tell my truth."

Morrison's truth is complex and painful. Born in Millbrook, Alabama, she spent 18 years trying to be the son her parents wanted while knowing in her heart she was their daughter. Her journey from a conservative religious community that saw her identity as demonic to a thriving advocate in Atlanta illustrates both the challenges facing transgender youth and the power of authentic living.

"My parents named me Dale, never knowing they were giving their daughter the perfect name," she explains with a gentle smile. "Dale has always been who I am. I just finally learned to live as her."

Morrison's story gained national attention when her Facebook post about leaving home and finding community in Atlanta was shared hundreds of times. But it was her response to her dying father's comment - "I don't have a son" - that truly captured hearts. Morrison replied simply: "You're right, Dad. You don't have a son. You have a daughter who loves you and hopes you find peace."

"That response showed more grace than most people could muster," says Janet Miller, director of TransAtlanta, a local support group where Morrison found community. "Dale has this incredible ability to respond to hatred with love, to turn pain into purpose."

Morrison's path to self-acceptance was neither quick nor easy. She describes years of trying to conform to others' expectations, culminating in what she calls "religious abuse" designed to change her identity. She was eventually attacked and hospitalized for living authentically, leading to her decision to leave Alabama with $3,200 and a determination to build a new life.

"I realized I could either die slowly pretending to be someone I wasn't, or I could risk everything to become who I really am," she says. "The choice was actually easy."

In Atlanta, Morrison has found not just acceptance but purpose. She's working with TransAtlanta to develop outreach programs for transgender youth, particularly those in rural religious communities. Her combination of personal experience and unwavering faith makes her uniquely positioned to bridge divides between LGBTQ+ advocates and religious communities.

"Being transgender doesn't make you less spiritual," Morrison explains. "It just makes your spiritual journey different. I believe God created me exactly as I am for a reason, even if that reason isn't always clear."

Dr. Constance Reynolds, a therapist specializing in LGBTQ+ issues, says Morrison's story represents a growing trend of young transgender individuals refusing to hide their identities. "Dale's courage in living authentically, especially coming from a religious background, gives hope to countless others facing similar struggles."

Morrison's Facebook post has now been shared over 500 times and has generated responses from across the country. Parents of transgender children have reached out for advice. Young people questioning their gender identity have found courage in her words. Even some religious leaders have contacted her, seeking to understand how to better support LGBTQ+ members of their communities.

"I get messages from kids who say they're not suicidal anymore because they read my story," Morrison says, her eyes filling with tears. "If my pain can prevent someone else's, then everything I've been through was worth it."

The response hasn't been entirely positive. Morrison has received threats and harassment, particularly from her hometown community. But she remains undeterred, supported by her chosen family in Atlanta and guided by her faith.

"Love is stronger than fear," she says. "Truth is more powerful than hatred. And sometimes the most prophetic thing you can do is simply exist as your authentic self."

Morrison's mother, Margaret, commented on the viral Facebook post with a simple message: "I love you." It was the first public acknowledgment from her family, and Morrison treasures it.

"My mother has been trapped between her husband's expectations and her love for me," Morrison explains. "For her to say she loves me publicly took incredible courage. I hope someday we can rebuild our relationship."

As our conversation winds down, Morrison talks about her plans for the future. She wants to study social work, to create resources for families struggling to understand their transgender children, and to ensure no other young person has to choose between their identity and their family's love.

"I'm Dale Morrison," she says as we prepare to leave. "I'm a transgender woman of faith. I'm someone's daughter, even if they can't see me right now. And I'm not going anywhere."

In a world that often forces people to choose between their authentic selves and their communities, Morrison's story offers a different path - one where faith and identity can coexist, where love can overcome fear, and where a young woman's courage to be herself can light the way for others.

Morrison will be speaking at the Rainbow Community Center's monthly forum on December

25, 2019. For more information about TransAtlanta support services, visit

Document 49: News Article Impact Metrics

Dated: December 29, 2019

IMPACT METRICS - ONE WEEK AFTER PUBLICATION:

Media Coverage:
- Picked up by Associated Press
- Reprinted in 47 newspapers nationally
- Featured on CNN Headline News
- Discussed on NPR's "All Things Considered"
- Interviewed by local Atlanta TV stations

Social Media Response:
- Article shared 15,000+ times on Facebook
- #DaleMorrison trending on Twitter
- 500+ supportive emails to AJC
- TransAtlanta website traffic increased 800%

Community Impact:
- 23 new members joined TransAtlanta support groups
- 12 religious organizations reached out for LGBTQ+ training
- 6 schools requested anti-bullying presentations
- 3 scholarship funds established for LGBTQ+ youth
-

Personal Impact on Dale:

- Received 2,000+ messages of support
- Offered 3 speaking engagements at universities
- Contacted by book publishers about writing memoir
- Received hate mail requiring security consultation

Document 50: Notes to the Editor

Written by Michael Callaghan
Dated: December 30, 2019

NOTES TO THE EDITOR – PUBLISHED

"Inspired by Courage" *Dale Morrison's story moved me to tears. As a mother of a transgender son, I wish I had been as brave as she is. Her grace in the face of rejection shows what real Christianity looks like. - Quinn K., Decatur*

"Dangerous Propaganda" *This newspaper should be ashamed for promoting mental illness and sin. Dale Morrison needs psychiatric help, not media attention. - Robert D., Marietta*

"A Mother's Love" *I am a parent who lost my daughter when she came out as transgender. Reading Dale's story made me realize I didn't lose a daughter - I threw one away. I'm trying to rebuild that relationship now. – Anonymous*

"Medical Perspective" *As a physician, I appreciate how Dale Morrison discusses transgender identity as a medical reality, not a choice or delusion. Her story will help other families understand that being transgender is not something to be ashamed of. - Dr. James Wilson, Emory University*

FOLLOW-UP ARTICLES GENERATED:
- **Millbrook Gazette:** "Local Family Responds to National Attention"

- **Christianity Today:** "Faith and Gender: A Growing Conversation"
- **Southern Voice:** "Rural Transgender Youth: Breaking the Silence"
- **Alabama Baptist:** "Ministering to Families in Crisis"

Document 51: Diary Entry
Written by Dale Morrison
Dated: January 19, 2020

I can't believe how far this story has traveled. Janet showed me all the newspapers that picked it up, all the emails that came in. Someone in Oregon said they started a support group for transgender teens because of my article. A pastor in Texas said he's changing how his church talks about LGBTQ+ issues.

But the best part was a letter from a 16-year-old in Mississippi who said she's going to come out to her parents next week because my story gave her hope. She signed it "Another Dale - we're everywhere!"

The girl in the mirror looks different now. She looks like someone who matters, someone whose story can change the world. She looks like someone who's finally home.

I think Evelyn would be proud.

Document 52: Facebook Post
Written by Multiple Individuals
Dated: February 9, 2020

FACEBOOK POSTS - EARL MORRISON'S DECLINING HEALTH

Margaret Morrison

Posted 4 hours ago

😨 URGENT PRAYER REQUEST 😨

Friends, I need your prayers more than ever. Earl took a turn for the worse yesterday. He's back in the hospital and the doctors are saying things that I don't want to hear.

He's having trouble breathing and they've put him on oxygen full time now. He's so weak he can barely sit up in bed. But he's still fighting. He's still believing God for his healing.

Please pray for:

- His breathing to improve
- The pain to lessen
- Peace for both of us
- A miracle healing

I know some of you have seen all the news about our family situation. Please don't let that distract from praying for Earl right now. He needs our prayers, not our judgment.

Thank you all. I don't know how to do this alone.

#PrayForEarl #NeedPrayers #Scared

156 reactions 😢 💜 🙏 *87 comments 34 shares*

Cedar Ridge Baptist Church

Posted 6 hours ago

CHURCH FAMILY - CRITICAL PRAYER NEEDED 🔔

Our dear Deacon Earl Morrison has been admitted to the hospital with complications from his illness. His condition has worsened significantly, and doctors are preparing the family for difficult decisions.

BUT GOD IS STILL GOD!

We are calling for EMERGENCY PRAYER AND FASTING for our brother Earl. We will not give up on God's healing power. We will not accept the enemy's report.

SPECIAL PRAYER VIGIL - Tonight at 7 PM in the sanctuary. Come join us as we storm heaven for Earl's healing!

"The effectual fervent prayer of a righteous man availeth much." - James 5:16

Let's show the enemy what happens when God's people unite in prayer!

#EarlMorrisonPrayerVigil   #ChurchFamily #FaithOverFear #GodStillHeals

234 reactions 🙏 👍 ♥ 145 comments 67 shares

Bishop William Patterson

Posted 8 hours ago

Saints, I just left the hospital where I spent two hours praying with our brother Earl Morrison and Sister Margaret.

Earl's body is weak, but his spirit is STRONG. Even in his pain, he's praising God and declaring his faith in divine healing. What a testimony of trust in the Lord!

The enemy is attacking this family on multiple fronts - illness, family division, public scrutiny. But we know that "greater is He that is in us than he that is in the world!"

I'm calling on every prayer warrior in our congregation and beyond:

- FAST AND PRAY for Earl's supernatural healing
- PRAY for Margaret's strength as she cares for him
- PRAY for protection from the enemy's attacks on this family
- PRAY for unity and reconciliation where there has been division

The prodigal son story doesn't end with the son staying in the far country. Let's pray for restoration and healing in every area of the Morrison family's life.

"He sent his word and healed them; he rescued them from the grave." - Psalm 107:20

Stand with us in faith!

#DeaconEarl   #HealingPrayers   #ProdigalSon #RestoreThisFamily

189 reactions 🙏 💜 👍 *92 comments 56 shares*

Dorothy Patterson (First Lady)

Posted 10 hours ago

My heart is so heavy tonight. I just got off the phone with Sister Margaret and Earl is really struggling.

Ladies, we need to rally around this precious family like never before. Margaret hasn't left the hospital in three days. She's exhausted and scared and trying to be strong for Earl.

Can we organize:

- Meals for when she gets home

- Hospital visits to keep her company
- Prayer coverage around the clock
- Practical help with bills and household needs

Also, I know there's been a lot of talk about the family situation that's been in the news. I'm not going to comment on that except to say this: Earl Morrison is a godly man who has served our church faithfully for 20 years. Right now, he needs our love and prayers, not our opinions about family matters.

Let's show what Christian love looks like in a crisis.

Praying for you, Margaret. You are not alone. 💕

#SisterMargaret #ChurchFamily #LoveInAction #PrayForEarl

98 reactions 🖤 🙏 😢 *67 comments 23 shares*

Millbrook Community Prayer Chain

Posted 12 hours ago

🔔 EMERGENCY PRAYER ALERT 🔔

Earl Morrison's condition has taken a serious turn. He's been moved to ICU and family has been called in.

WE NEED EVERY PRAYER WARRIOR AVAILABLE!

This is a CRITICAL moment. The battle is intense, but our God is MIGHTY TO SAVE!

Please drop everything and PRAY:

- For Earl's lungs to be healed and strengthened
- For his heart to be stable
- For miraculous turnaround in his condition
- For peace and strength for Margaret
- For divine intervention in this situation

Also praying that God would work in the hearts of

ALL family members during this difficult time. Sometimes crisis brings families together. Praying for reconciliation and healing in every area.

If you're reading this, please pray RIGHT NOW. Don't wait. Don't scroll past. PRAY!

Comment PRAYING so we know how many prayer warriors are standing with the Morrison family!

#CriticalPrayers #EarlMorrison #ICU #PrayRight Now #FamilyReconciliation

167 reactions 🙏 👍 💜 *203 comments 89 shares*

COMMENTS SECTION (Selected Comments):

Linda Johnson: Praying right now! Earl is such a good man. God please heal him! 🙏

Robert Davis: On my knees praying for Brother Earl. Also praying his son comes home where he belongs during this time.

Susan Miller: Just heard the news. Driving to the hospital now to sit with Margaret. She shouldn't be alone.

Michael Williams: Praying for healing and for family restoration. Crisis has a way of putting things in perspective.

Katherine Smith: Been praying all day. Also praying for that poor child who's been in the news. Families need to stick together, especially now.

Karen Anderson: Margaret Morrison is the strongest woman I know. Praying God gives her supernatural strength right now.

Beverly Adams: Why isn't his son here? I don't care what the issues are, you come home when your daddy is dying.

Jennifer Hebert: Maybe the son doesn't feel welcome. Sometimes families create their own divisions.

Praying for healing in all relationships.

Mark Stevens: Posted on our church page too. Getting prayer warriors from three counties involved!

Janet Thompson: Whatever has happened in that family, Earl Morrison needs prayers right now. That's what matters.

TRENDING TOPICS IN MILLBROOK: #PrayForEarl #MorrisonFamily #ICUPrayers #FamilyHealing #ComeHomeSon

---

LOCAL NEWS PICKUP:

- WHNT News 19: "Community Rallies Around Dying Deacon"

- The Huntsville Times: "Prayer Vigils Planned for Local Church Leader"

- AL.com: "Family Drama Overshadows Health Crisis in Small Town"

Document 53: Diary Entry

Written by Dale Morrison

Dated: February 11, 2020

Carmen called me this morning. She'd seen the Facebook posts about Dad being in ICU and thought I should know. I'd been staying off social media since the newspaper article came out - too many messages, too much attention, too overwhelming.

But when she read me Mama's post about Dad having trouble breathing, about him being so weak he can barely sit up, something inside me broke open.

He's dying. Really dying. And I'm 300 miles away, sitting in my tiny apartment, eating cereal for dinner, pretending I don't care.

But I do care. God help me, I still care.

I spent two hours pacing around my apartment, picking up my phone and putting it down again. I must have started to dial the hospital twenty times. What would I even say? "Hi, this is Dale Morrison. I know my father said he doesn't have a son, but could you tell me how he's doing?"

Would they even give me information? Would Mama want to hear from me? Would Dad get worse if he knew I called?

I finally called Janet from TransAtlanta. She came over with Chinese food and let me cry for an hour before I could even explain what was wrong.

"I want to go see him," I said through tears. "I want to hold my mama's hand and tell her she's not alone. I want to tell Dad I forgive him. I want to be there when..."

I couldn't finish the sentence.

"But?" Janet prompted gently.

"But what if he won't see me? What if I drive all that way and he turns me away from his deathbed? What if the last thing he says to me is that I'm not his child?"

Janet was quiet for a long time. "What if he doesn't say that? What if this is your chance to say goodbye?"

"What if it isn't?"

"Dale, you can't control how he responds. You can only control what you do. What does your heart tell you to do?"

My heart. My heart is a mess. It wants to run to that hospital and fight for my place in that room. It wants to demand that Dad see me, acknowledge me, love me before he dies. It wants to comfort Mama and be the child she needs right now.

But my heart also wants to protect me from more rejection. It remembers Dad's voice saying, "I don't have a son." It remembers years of disappointment, of hoping for love that never came. It's afraid of walking into that hospital room and having him use his last breath to reject me one more time.

I read the Facebook posts again. Bishop Patterson talking about the "prodigal son story" and praying for "family restoration." Part of me wanted to laugh. I'm not the prodigal son - I'm the child who was thrown out for being who I am. I'm the one who was told never to come back.

But another part of me wondered: what if he's changed? What if facing death has softened his heart? What if he wants to see me but is too proud to ask?

I called the hospital. My hands were shaking so badly

I could barely dial.

"I'm calling to check on Earl Morrison," I said to the nurse. "He's in ICU."

"Are you family?"

I paused. "I'm his... I'm Dale Morrison. His child."

"Oh honey, I'm so sorry. Your father is very sick. Are you coming to visit?"

She said it so naturally, like of course his child would be coming to visit. Like there was no question about whether I belonged there.

"I... I don't know. How is he?"

"He's stable for now, but it's been touch and go. Your mother's been here around the clock. I'm sure she'd love to see you."

Would she? Or would my showing up just add more stress to an already impossible situation?

After I hung up, I sat on my couch for another hour, staring at nothing. Finally, I called Mama's cell phone. It went straight to voicemail.

"Mama, it's... it's Dale. I heard about Dad being in the hospital. I'm... I'm praying for you both. I love you. Call me if you need anything. Or if... if you want me to come home."

I hung up and immediately regretted it. What if Dad hears the message? What if it makes him worse? What if Mama deletes it without listening?

But what if she needs to hear it?

Carmen texted me around 9 PM: "Any word from your mom?"

"No," I texted back. "I don't know what to do."

"You don't have to decide tonight. Sleep on it. Pray about it. The answer will come."

But I can't sleep. I keep thinking about Dad in that hospital bed, struggling to breathe. I keep thinking about Mama sitting in that uncomfortable chair, scared and alone. I keep thinking about all the things I never said, all the forgiveness I never offered, all the love I never got to give.

What if he dies and I never get to tell him I forgive him? What if he dies still believing I hate him? What if Mama spends the rest of her life thinking I didn't care enough to come home when it mattered?

But what if I go and he looks at me with those angry eyes one more time? What if he tells the nurses not to let me in? What if his last words to me are about what a disappointment I am?

I don't know which risk is worse - the risk of going and being rejected, or the risk of staying away and regretting it forever.

The girl in the mirror looks exhausted tonight. She's been crying for hours. Her eyes are red and swollen and she looks like the scared little kid she used to be, the one who just wanted her daddy to love her.

Maybe that's who I still am, underneath all the growth and healing and advocacy work. Maybe I'm still just a little girl who wants to go home to her parents, even if home was never safe.

Tomorrow I have to decide: do I get in my car and drive to Alabama, knowing I might be walking into more heartbreak? Or do I stay here in my new life, knowing I might be missing my last chance to say goodbye?

Either way, I'll have to live with the consequences for the rest of my life.

God, I wish Evelyn were here. She'd know what to do. She'd have the right words, the right piece of candy, the right way to help me see clearly.

All I can hear in my head is her voice: "You ain't God's mistake. You just ain't your daddy's idea of easy."

Maybe it's time to find out if that's still true, even when he's dying.

Maybe it's time to go home.

Or maybe it's time to finally let go.

I don't know yet.

But I have to decide soon.

Time is running out.

Document 54: Therapy Notes

Written by Constance Reynolds, LCSW

Dated: April 21, 2020

CONFIDENTIAL THERAPY SESSION NOTES

Client: Dale Morrison

DOB: November 3, 2001

Session Date: April 21, 2020

Session #: 7

Duration: 90 minutes (extended session at client request)

Therapist: Dr. Constance Reynolds, PhD, LCSW

PRESENTING CONCERN: Client called requesting emergency session due to family crisis. Father (Earl Morrison) is currently in ICU with terminal cancer. Client struggling with decision whether to return home to Alabama to see dying father who has previously rejected her identity and told her "never to come back."

CLIENT'S EMOTIONAL STATE: Client appeared visibly distressed upon arrival. Tearful, agitated, sleep deprived. Reports not eating well for past 48 hours. Experiencing conflicted emotions regarding father's condition and her potential response.

SESSION SUMMARY:

Presenting the Dilemma: Client began session by stating, "I don't know what to do, and I'm running out of time to decide." Explained that community is rallying around father with prayer requests, but she remains excluded from family narrative. Mother left voicemail message asking client to call but has not directly invited her home.

"Part of me wants to get in the car right now and drive to that hospital. Part of me thinks I'd be crazy to open myself up to more rejection when he's literally dying."

Exploring the "Want to Go" Side:

When asked what drives her desire to return, client identified several factors:

- Unfinished business with father ("I never got to tell him I forgive him")
- Concern for mother's wellbeing ("She's all alone and scared")
- Fear of lifelong regret ("What if I never get another chance?")
- Desire for closure ("I want him to know I don't hate him")
- Hope for deathbed reconciliation ("Maybe facing death changed his heart")

Client became tearful when discussing her continued love for father despite abuse: "I know it sounds crazy, but I still love him. Even after everything, he's still my dad."

Exploring the "Want to Stay" Side:

Client articulated equally compelling reasons for not returning:

- Self-preservation ("I can't handle being rejected again")
- Fear of making father's condition worse ("What if seeing me causes him more stress?")
- Concern about family dynamics ("What if I make it harder for my mom?")
- Protection of healing progress ("I've worked so hard to build self-worth")

- Past trauma triggers ("That hospital, that town - it all brings back the worst memories")

Processing Complex Grief: Client struggling with grieving someone who is still alive but emotionally unavailable. Discussed concept of "ambiguous loss" - mourning the father she never had while the actual father is dying.

"I'm not just losing him now. I lost him years ago when he decided he couldn't love who I really am. But somehow this feels different. More final."

Examining Fear of Rejection: Significant portion of session focused on client's fear that father will reject her even on his deathbed.

When asked what she would need to feel safe making the trip, client identified:

- Assurance that mother wants her there
- Plan for what to do if father refuses to see her
- Support system for emotional aftermath
- Clear boundaries about what she will/won't accept

Exploring Regret Scenarios:

Used decision-making exercise to explore potential regrets:

If you go and he rejects you: "I'd be hurt, but at least I'd know I tried. I'd know I offered forgiveness and love, even if he couldn't accept it."

If you stay and never see him again: "I'd always wonder. I'd wonder if he wanted to see me but was too proud to ask. I'd wonder if I could have given him peace."

Values Clarification:

Helped client identify core values driving this decision:

- Family loyalty vs. self-protection

- Forgiveness vs. boundaries
- Hope vs. realism
- Love vs. safety

Client noted: "I keep thinking about something Evelyn told me - that woman I met at the hospital. She said I wasn't unholy for being complicated. Maybe this situation is complicated too, and that's okay."

Discussing Mother's Needs: Client expressing significant concern for mother's emotional state. Recognizes mother as victim of father's controlling behavior. Wants to support mother but unsure if presence would help or hurt.

"My mom has never stood up to him. What if he makes her choose between seeing me and keeping peace with him?"

Religious/Spiritual Processing: Client referenced her faith journey and desire to respond as Christ would. Discussed concept of offering grace without expecting reciprocation.

"I've been learning that love doesn't always look like what we want it to. Maybe love in this situation means going, even if he can't love me back."

Safety Planning:

Due to client's emotional distress and big decision pending, created safety plan:

- Check-ins with TransAtlanta support system
- Plan for immediate departure if situation becomes abusive
- Lodging arrangements away from family home
- Return strategy if visit doesn't go well

Homework/Between Session Tasks:

1. Write letter to father (whether or not she delivers it)

2. Call mother directly to gauge receptiveness to visit

3. Create specific plan for trip logistics if she decides to go

4. Continue journaling about feelings and concerns

Clinical Impressions: Client demonstrating remarkable emotional maturity in processing complex family dynamics. Her ability to hold both love and boundaries simultaneously shows significant growth from early sessions. Decision ultimately represents healthy assertion of agency - either choice would be valid given her circumstances. Client's trauma history makes her hypervigilant about rejection, but she's also demonstrating increased capacity for risk-taking in service of important relationships. Her support system in Atlanta provides safety nets that didn't exist when she originally left home.

Treatment Plan: Continue processing family-of-origin issues. Support client's decision-making process without pushing toward specific outcome. Prepare for potential grief work regardless of which choice she makes. Schedule follow-up session within 48 hours to process decision and/or outcome.

Risk Assessment: Moderate emotional distress but good coping skills and strong support system. No immediate safety concerns. Client has realistic understanding of potential outcomes and good insight into her own needs and limitations.

Next Session: Scheduled for April 23, 2020 (48 hours) to process client's decision and provide support for chosen course of action.

Therapist Notes: This client continues to demonstrate remarkable resilience and wisdom. Her ability to consider multiple perspectives while maintaining self-compassion is impressive. Whatever she decides, she's approaching this decision from a place of strength rather than fear, which represents significant therapeutic progress. The complexity of loving someone who has hurt you while maintaining healthy boundaries is something many clients struggle with. Dale's processing of this dilemma could be instructive for future similar cases.

Dr. Constance Reynolds, PhD, LCSW Licensed Clinical Social Worker Specializing in LGBTQ+ Issues and Family Therapy
Date: April 21, 2020 **Time:** 11:30 PM

Document 55: Diary Entry

Written by Dale Morrison

Dated: April 23, 2020

I made my decision. I'm staying in Atlanta.

Tonight was the weekly TransAtlanta meeting, and I knew I had to tell everyone what I'd decided. I'd been carrying this weight for three days, and I needed my community to know where I'd landed.

Janet opened the meeting as usual, asking if anyone had urgent concerns to share. I raised my hand before I could lose my nerve.

"I need to tell you all something," I said, my voice shakier than I wanted it to be. "My father is dying in Alabama. He's in ICU and probably won't make it through the week. I've decided not to go see him."

The room got very quiet. I could feel everyone's eyes on me, but not in a judgmental way. More like they were holding space for whatever I needed to say.

"I know some of you might think I'm being selfish or cold. But I can't risk putting myself back in that environment. I can't risk having him reject me one more time while he's dying. I can't risk undoing all the healing I've done here with you all."

My voice broke a little on the last part, but I kept going.

"I've thought about it constantly. I've been to therapy. I've prayed about it. And I keep coming back to the same thing: I have to protect my peace. I have to protect the person I've worked so hard to become."

When I finished, the silence stretched for what felt

like forever. Then Carmen reached over and took my hand.

"Dale, that took incredible courage to share with us," she said. "Thank you for trusting us with this." That's when the responses started coming, and they were all over the place.

David, who'd been estranged from his family for two years, nodded emphatically. "I think you're making the right choice. Sometimes the healthiest thing you can do is not go back to the place that hurts you, even if it's family."

But Lisa had a different perspective. "I understand why you're scared, but I went home when my grandmother was dying, even though she'd disowned me. I'm glad I did. It gave me closure I didn't know I needed."

Marcus shared that he'd regretted not seeing his father before he died. "I was so angry at him for rejecting me that I stayed away. But now I wonder if I missed a chance for reconciliation."

On the other side, a new member named Alex said, "My father tried to have me committed when I came out. Going to his funeral was the worst mistake I ever made. His family blamed me for his heart attack. Sometimes staying away is self-preservation, not selfishness."

What amazed me wasn't that they had different opinions - it was that they all expressed them with love. Nobody told me I was wrong. Nobody made me feel guilty. They just shared their experiences and left space for mine to be different.

Janet, who's been facilitating these groups for years, finally spoke up. "Dale, there's no right or wrong answer here. There's only what's right for you, in your situation, with your history. What matters is that you're making this decision from a place of self-awareness, not from trauma or fear."

"But I am afraid," I admitted. "I'm afraid of regrets. I'm afraid of what people will think. I'm afraid that this makes me a bad daughter."

"Fear is information," said Carmen. "It tells us what we need to protect. You're not a bad daughter for protecting your mental health."

Then something happened that I'd never experienced before in my life. They went around the circle, each person saying something supportive about my decision, even the ones who might have chosen differently.

"I support you because you know yourself better than anyone else knows you."

"I support you because you've already survived so much, and you deserve peace."

"I support you because choosing your own well-being isn't selfish - it's necessary."

"I support you because you get to decide what love looks like in your life."

"I support you because you're not responsible for healing someone who spent your whole life hurting you."

By the time they'd all spoken, I was crying. Not sad tears, but overwhelmed tears. I'd never had people disagree with me and still support me. I'd never had a group of people honor my decision even when they might have made a different one.

"This is new for me," I said through my tears. "Having people support me even when they don't agree with me. In my family, love came with conditions. If you didn't do what they wanted, they withdrew their love."

"That's not love," Janet said gently. "That's control. Real love - healthy love - means supporting someone's right to make their own choices, even when those choices are hard to understand."

After the meeting, several people came up to me individually. Carmen gave me her phone number again and said to call her day or night if I needed to talk. David offered to drive me to Alabama if I changed my mind. Alex told me about a grief support group specifically for people dealing with estranged family members.

But it was what Janet said as I was leaving that hit me the most.

"Dale, you just experienced something that many people never get to experience. You shared a difficult, complicated decision with a group of people, and they supported your right to make that decision, even when they had different opinions. You got to disagree and still belong. That's what healthy community looks like."

She was right. I'd never experienced that before. In my family, disagreement meant rejection. In my church, questioning meant condemnation. But here, in this circle of folding chairs in a community center, I got to be imperfect and uncertain and still be loved.

I'm still sad about my father. I'm still scared about the regret I might feel. But I'm also proud of myself for making a decision based on what I need, not what others expect from me.

I'm staying in Atlanta. I'm choosing my peace over their expectations. I'm choosing my healing over their version of what a good daughter should do.

And for the first time in my life, I have a community

that supports me in that choice, even when it's complicated, even when it's hard to understand.

The girl in the mirror looks different tonight. She looks like someone who belongs somewhere. Someone who has people who love her even when she makes difficult choices. Someone who's finally learned the difference between conditional love and unconditional support.

She looks like someone who's home.

Tomorrow I'll call Dr. Reynolds and tell her about my decision. I'll probably cry some more. I'll probably second-guess myself a dozen times.

But I'll also remember sitting in that circle tonight, feeling held and supported and loved, exactly as I am.

That's worth staying for.

That's worth protecting.

That's home.

Document 56: Job Application

Written by Dale Morrison

Dated: April 28, 2020

ZENITH MARKETING SOLUTIONS EMPLOYMENT APPLICATION

Position Applied For: Administrative Assistant

Date: April 28, 2020

Referred by: Lisa Poltowski, Account Coordinator

PERSONAL INFORMATION

Name: Dale Morrison

Address: *234 Peachtree Street*, Apt 3B, Atlanta, GA 30309

Phone: (404) 555-0847 **Email:** dalemorrison2001@hotmail.com

Are you 18 years of age or older? Yes

Are you legally authorized to work in the U.S.? Yes

POSITION INFORMATION

How did you learn about this position? Employee referral - Lisa Poltowski

Desired salary: $30,000-$35,000 annually

Date available to start: Immediately

Are you available to work: Full-time ☑ Part-time ☐

EMPLOYMENT HISTORY

Previous Employer: Morrison's Family Construction **Position:** Stock Associate **Dates of Employment:** April 2018 - April 2019 **Supervisor:** Robert Morrison (Manager) **Phone:** (256) 555-0234

Reason for Leaving: Relocated to Atlanta **Duties:** Customer service, inventory management, cash handling, store maintenance

EDUCATION

School: Millbrook High School **Location:** Millbrook, AL **Graduation Date:** May 2019 **Degree/Diploma:** High School Diploma **GPA:** 3.4

SKILLS

- Proficient in Microsoft Office (Word, Excel, PowerPoint)
- 45 WPM typing speed
- Customer service experience
- Cash handling and POS systems
- Detail-oriented and organized
- Bilingual (English/Spanish - conversational)

REFERENCES

Janet Miller Director, TransAtlanta Support Services (404) 555-0912 *Professional reference - volunteer work*

Dr. Constance Reynolds Licensed Clinical Social Worker (404) 555-0745 *Personal reference*

INTERVIEW NOTES

Date: May 3, 2020

Interviewer: Patricia Nelson, HR Manager

Position: Administrative Assistant

Pre-Interview Notes: Candidate arrived 10 minutes early, professionally dressed, brought copies of resume and references. Lisa Poltowski provided positive internal recommendation, noting candidate's professionalism and strong work ethic.

INTERVIEW SUMMARY

Q: Tell me about yourself. A: "I recently moved to Atlanta from small-town Alabama to pursue better opportunities and build my career. I'm hardworking, detail-oriented, and excited about contributing to a company with strong values. I've been involved with community organizations here and am looking for a workplace where I can grow professionally while making a meaningful contribution."

Q: Why are you interested in working for Zenith Marketing? A: "Lisa Poltowski spoke highly of the company culture and the commitment to treating all employees with respect. I'm drawn to the collaborative environment and the opportunity to learn the marketing industry. I also appreciate that Zenith has clear nondiscrimination policies - that matters to me as someone who values inclusive workplaces."

Q: Your resume shows you worked at a family grocery store. How do those skills transfer to office work? A: "Customer service is universal - whether you're helping someone find the right product in a store or assisting a colleague with a project. I learned to multitask, handle pressure during busy periods, manage inventory systems, and communicate clearly with diverse customers. I also handled cash management and basic bookkeeping, which taught me attention to detail and accuracy."

Q: You mentioned valuing inclusive workplaces. Can you elaborate on what that means to you? A: "I believe everyone should be able to bring their authentic selves to work without fear of discrimination. I've experienced situations where people were judged based on assumptions rather than their qualifications and character. I'm looking for an environment where diversity is valued and where success is measured by performance and contribution, not by whether someone fits certain expectations."

Q: How do you handle stressful situations or conflicts? A: "I try to stay calm and focus on solutions rather than problems. In my previous job, we'd have rushes where multiple customers needed help simultaneously. I learned to prioritize, communicate clearly about wait times, and ask for help when needed. If there's a conflict, I believe in addressing it directly but respectfully."

Q: Where do you see yourself in five years? A: "I'd love to grow within the marketing field, possibly into project coordination or account management. I'm also interested in pursuing additional education - maybe business or communications courses. Long-term, I'd like to be in a position where I can mentor others and advocate for inclusive workplace practices."

Q: Do you have any questions for me? A: "What does success look like in this role? What opportunities are there for professional development? And can you tell me more about the company culture and how Zenith supports employee growth?"

POST-INTERVIEW EVALUATION:

Strengths:

- Professional presentation and communication skills
- Clear understanding of role requirements
- Genuine enthusiasm for inclusive workplace culture
- Good customer service background
- Mature approach to workplace challenges
- Strong references from professional contacts

Areas to explore:

- Limited office experience (but willing to learn)

- Recent move suggests some life transition (not necessarily negative)
- May need training on specific software/systems

Overall Impression: Candidate presents as mature, thoughtful, and professional. Strong customer service background translates well to administrative role. Clear values alignment with company culture, particularly around diversity and inclusion. References speak highly of character and work ethic. Would benefit from mentor during initial training period.

Recommendation: Hire, pending reference checks

REFERENCE CHECK NOTES

Janet Miller (TransAtlanta): "Dale is exceptional. She's professional, reliable, and has excellent interpersonal skills. She's been instrumental in our outreach efforts and demonstrates real leadership potential. Any employer would be lucky to have her."

Dr. Constance Reynolds: "I can speak to Dale's character and resilience. She's someone who approaches challenges with maturity and thoughtfulness. She's honest, hardworking, and committed to personal growth."

Document 57: Job Application Response
Written by Patricia Nelson
Dated: May 5, 2020

ZENITH MARKETING SOLUTIONS
Dale Morrison 234 Peachtree Street, Apt 3B
Atlanta, GA 30309

Dear Dale,

We are pleased to offer you the position of
Administrative Assistant with Zenith Marketing
Solutions. Your interview impressed our team, and we
believe you'll be an excellent addition to our company.

Position Details:

- Position: Administrative Assistant
- Start Date: Monday, May 11, 2020
- Salary: $45,000 annually
- Benefits: Health insurance
- Dental
- 401(k) with company match
- Annual 2 weeks PTO
- Paid sick leave
- Reporting to: Patricia Nelson, HR Manager

First Day Information: Please arrive at 9:00 AM on
your first day. We'll begin with orientation and introduce
you to your team. Lisa Poltowski has volunteered to be
your buddy during your first week to help you get settled.

We're excited to have you join our team and look forward to supporting your professional growth.

Sincerely,

Patricia Nelson, HR Manager

Zenith Marketing Solutions

Document 58: Diary Entry
Written by Dale Morrison
Dated: May 6, 2020

I got the job! I actually got the job!

When Patricia called this afternoon to offer me the position, I started crying right there on the phone. Happy tears, but I had to explain I wasn't upset - I was just overwhelmed with gratitude.

$45,000 a year. Benefits. Vacation time. A place where Lisa says people are judged by their work, not their personal lives. A place where I can be myself.

I keep thinking about that question Patricia asked about inclusive workplaces. Six months ago, I couldn't have imagined being in a job interview where I could talk about valuing diversity without fear. Where I could hint at my own experiences with discrimination and have it be seen as a strength, not a liability.

The girl in the mirror looks different tonight. She looks like someone with a future. Someone with a career. Someone who belongs in the professional world.

I start Monday. A new chapter begins.

Thank you, Lisa, for seeing something worth recommending. Thank you, Atlanta, for having companies that hire based on character instead of prejudice.

Thank you, God, for bringing me to exactly where I need to be.

Document 59: Text Message Conversation

Written by Bellsouth Mobile

Dated: May 6, 2020

TEXT MESSAGE CONVERSATION May 6, 2020

Lisa Poltowski (404) 555-0923
Dale Morrison (404) 555-0847

Lisa - 3:47 PM DALE!!! Patricia just told me!!! YOU GOT THE JOB!!! 🎉 🎉 🎉

Dale - 3:48 PM LISA I'M CRYING!! I can't believe it!! Thank you thank you THANK YOU!!

Lisa - 3:49 PM I am literally jumping up and down at my desk right now! My coworkers think I'm insane! 😄

Dale - 3:50 PM I called you as a reference and you got me HIRED! How did I get so lucky to have you as a friend??

Lisa - 3:52 PM Are you KIDDING me?? You got yourself hired! I just opened the door. You walked through it like the STAR you are! ⭐

Dale - 3:53 PM I'm shaking! $24,000! Benefits! A real job at a real company!

Lisa - 3:54 PM And we get to work together!!! This is going to be AMAZING! Patricia said I can be your buddy the first week!

Dale - 3:55 PM I don't know what I would do without you. Seriously. You've changed my life.

Lisa - 3:57 PM Stop making me cry at work!! 😭 You've changed MY life too! Watching you be so brave inspires me every day!

Dale - 3:58 PM We need to celebrate! Can I buy you dinner?? It's the least I can do!

Lisa - 3:59 PM YES! But I'M buying! This calls for somewhere fancy! You're getting your first REAL paycheck!

Dale - 4:01 PM Lisa no you've done too much already!

Lisa - 4:02 PM Nope! Final answer! We're celebrating my new coworker! 🍰 Cheesecake Factory at 7?

Dale - 4:03 PM OK but I'm getting dessert! 🍰

Lisa - 4:04 PM Deal! OMG I'm so excited I can barely focus on work! Patricia said you impressed everyone!

Dale - 4:06 PM I was so nervous! But everyone was so nice. Even when I talked about valuing inclusive workplaces...

Lisa - 4:07 PM See?? That's why Zenith is perfect for you! They WANT people who care about that stuff!

Dale - 4:09 PM I keep pinching myself. Six months ago, I was hiding in Alabama. Now I have a job, friends, a future!

Lisa - 4:11 PM And you DESERVE all of it! Every single bit! You worked for this!

Dale - 4:12 PM I'm going to make you proud. I promise.

Lisa - 4:13 PM Dale, I'm already proud. I was proud the day I met you. You're going to CRUSH this job!

Dale - 4:15 PM I have to call Janet and Carmen! They're going to freak out!

Lisa - 4:16 PM YES! Tell everyone! This is HUGE! Our whole TransAtlanta family is going to be so happy!

Dale - 4:18 PM I love that we have a family there. I love that you're part of it.

Lisa - 4:19 PM Found family is the BEST family! 💜 OK I really need to get back to work but I'm TOO EXCITED!

Dale - 4:21 PM Me too! I need to figure out what to wear on Monday! Professional clothes shopping this weekend?

Lisa - 4:22 PM ABSOLUTELY! I know all the best places! We're getting you the perfect first-day outfit!

Dale - 4:24 PM Lisa... thank you. For everything. For seeing something in me. For believing in me. For being my friend.

Lisa - 4:26 PM Stop it! You're going to make me ugly cry at my desk! 😭 😭 I love you, girl! You're going to change the world!

Dale - 4:27 PM I love you too! See you at 7! I'm going to be floating on air until then! ☁️

Lisa - 4:28 PM Me too! This is the BEST news ever! My friend is going to be my COWORKER! 🎉

Dale - 4:30 PM Your friend who's about to be the best administrative assistant Zenith has ever seen! 💪

Lisa - 4:31 PM THAT'S THE SPIRIT! See you tonight! Wear something celebratory! 🎉

Dale - 4:32 PM Already planning it! Thank you for making dreams come true! ✨

Lisa - 4:33 PM No - thank you for being brave enough to dream them! 💕

[Message delivery confirmations show all messages received]

[Call log shows Dale called Janet Miller at 4:35

PM - Duration: 12 minutes]

[Call log shows Dale called Carmen Rodriguez at 4:48 PM - Duration: 8 minutes]

[Call log shows Dale called Dr. Constance Reynolds at 5:02 PM - Duration: 6 minutes]

Document 60: Diary Entry

Written by Dale Morrison

Dated: June 2, 2020

Something happened at work today that I can't stop thinking about.

I've been at Zenith for exactly one week, and it's been incredible. Everyone has been so welcoming. Lisa introduced me to the whole team, Patricia has been checking in daily to make sure I'm settling in well, and I've actually been enjoying the work. Filing, scheduling meetings, managing databases - it all feels purposeful and professional in a way that stocking shelves never did.

But today, something shattered that perfect bubble.

I was in the break room around 2 PM, heating up my lunch in the microwave, when I heard voices from the table behind me. I wasn't trying to eavesdrop, but the conversation was loud enough that I couldn't help but overhear.

"I'm telling you, standards have really dropped around here," said a voice I recognized as Mark Stevens from accounting. He's one of the guys who barely acknowledged me when Lisa introduced us last week.

"What do you mean?" asked another voice - sounded like Brad from marketing.

"This whole 'inclusion amendment' thing they added to the employee handbook. Now they're hiring people just to check boxes instead of focusing on actual qualifications."

My blood ran cold. I knew they were talking about

me. I was probably the most recent hire, and I was the one Lisa had specifically mentioned benefited from the company's nondiscrimination policies.

"Like that new girl in admin?" Brad asked. "The one Lisa recommended?"

"Exactly. I mean, look at her. You can tell she's... different. Probably one of those diversity hires. I bet she doesn't even have the right experience."

Mark laughed. "Patricia's gone all liberal on us. Next thing you know, we'll be hiring based on whatever sob story people bring in instead of whether they can actually do the job."

"It's not fair to the rest of us who actually earned our positions," Brad added. "We worked hard to get here, and now they're just handing out jobs to make themselves look good."

I stood there frozen, my microwaved soup getting cold in my hands. Part of me wanted to turn around and confront them. Part of me wanted to run back to my desk and pretend I hadn't heard anything. But mostly, I felt sick.

Were they right? Had I only gotten the job because of the company's inclusion policies? Had Patricia hired me to fill some diversity quota rather than because I was qualified?

I slipped out of the break room without saying anything, my appetite completely gone. I spent the rest of the afternoon trying to focus on my work, but their words kept echoing in my head.

"You can tell she's different."

"Diversity hire."

"Doesn't have the right experience."

By 4 PM, I was spiraling. I kept second-guessing

every interaction I'd had since starting. When Patricia complimented my organizational skills, was she just being nice? When my supervisor said I was catching on quickly, was she surprised because she expected less from me?

But then I remembered something Dr. Reynolds had told me in therapy: "Other people's assumptions about you don't change your worth or your qualifications."

I looked at the work I'd completed in my first week. I'd reorganized the filing system, created a more efficient scheduling process, and caught several errors in the database that had been there for months. I'd done good work. Real work. Work that added value to the company.

I hadn't been hired because I was transgender. I'd been hired despite some people's prejudices about transgender people.

At 4:30, I decided. I walked to Patricia's office and knocked on her door.

"Dale! How are you settling in?" she asked, looking up from her computer with a smile.

"Actually, I need to talk to you about something that happened today," I said, sitting down across from her desk.

I told her everything. The conversation I'd overheard, the comments about inclusion policies, the implications about my qualifications. Patricia's expression grew more serious with each detail.

"I want you to know that I didn't just hear this and decide to tattle," I said. "I thought about it all afternoon. But I realized that if they're saying this about me, they're probably saying it about other people too. And if Zenith really values inclusion, then this kind of talk creates a hostile environment that undermines those values."

Patricia was quiet for a moment, then leaned forward. "Dale, first of all, thank you for bringing this to my attention. This is exactly the kind of thing I need to know about. Second, I want to be very clear about something: you were hired because you were the best candidate for the position. Period."

"But the inclusion policies—"

"The inclusion policies ensure that qualified candidates like you get fair consideration, not preferential treatment. Your interview was excellent, your references were outstanding, and your work this week has been exceptional. Mark Stevens, on the other hand, has been written up twice for unprofessional behavior."

She opened my personnel file and showed me my interview notes. "Look at what I wrote: 'Strong customer service background, excellent communication skills, genuine enthusiasm, mature approach to challenges.' None of that has anything to do with diversity hiring. That's about you being qualified."

I felt tears starting to form. "It's just... when you're different, you always wonder if people see your work or just your differences."

"I understand that concern," Patricia said gently. "But I need you to understand something: their prejudice is their problem, not yours. You earned this job. You're excelling at this job. Don't let their ignorance make you doubt yourself."

She paused, then continued. "I'm going to have conversations with both Mark and Brad tomorrow. This kind of talk is not acceptable at Zenith, and it won't be tolerated. We have these policies because we believe diversity makes us stronger, but more importantly, we have them because everyone deserves to work in an environment free from discrimination."

"What if they retaliate? What if they make things harder for me?"

"Then they'll be looking for new jobs. Dale, I want you to know that you have my full support. If anyone makes you feel unwelcome or questions your qualifications again, you come straight to me. This company is better because you're here."

As I walked back to my desk, I felt something I hadn't expected: pride. Not just in my work, but in my decision to speak up. Six months ago, I would have internalized those comments, let them eat away at my self-worth, maybe even quit to avoid further confrontation.

But I didn't do that. I stood up for myself. I stood up for other people who might face similar comments. I trusted that the company's values weren't just words on paper.

Lisa was waiting by my desk when I got back.

"Hey, you okay? You looked upset after lunch."

I told her what had happened, including my conversation with Patricia. Her face went through several expressions - anger, pride, determination.

"I'm so proud of you for reporting that," she said. "And I'm so sorry you had to hear it. But you know what? You just made this workplace better for everyone."

"How do you figure?"

"Because now Mark and Brad know that their behavior has consequences. Because Patricia knows these attitudes exist and can address them. Because the next person who gets hired won't have to wonder if people are questioning their qualifications behind their back."

She was right. By speaking up, I hadn't just protected myself - I'd helped protect the next person, and the person after that.

The girl in the mirror looks different tonight. She looks like someone who doesn't just survive workplace discrimination - she confronts it. Someone who knows her worth and won't let others diminish it. Someone who understands that belonging isn't just about being invited to the table, but about ensuring the table is welcoming for everyone.

Tomorrow, I'll go back to work with my head held high. I'll do my job well, as I have been. And if anyone has a problem with that, they can take it up with HR.

Because I belong here. I earned my place here. And I'm not going anywhere.

The girl in the mirror is finally learning to fight for herself.

It's about time.

Document 61: Mediation Notes

Written by Patricia Nelson

Dated: June 4, 2020

ZENITH MARKETING SOLUTIONS
HUMAN RESOURCES DEPARTMENT
CONFIDENTIAL MEDIATION SESSION
NOTES

Date: June 4, 2020 **Time:** 10:00 AM - 11:15 AM
Location: Conference Room B **HR Facilitator:** Patricia
Nelson, HR Manager **Participants:** Dale Morrison
(Complainant), Mark Stevens (Accounting), Brad
Johnson (Marketing) **Witness:** Michael Farmer, HR
Assistant (Note-taker)

SESSION PURPOSE: Mediation session to address
reported discriminatory comments made by Mark
Stevens and Brad Johnson regarding company inclusion
policies and Ms. Morrison's employment.

OPENING STATEMENT - PATRICIA Nelson:
"We're here today to address concerns that were brought
to my attention regarding comments made in the break
room on September 17th. Zenith Marketing Solutions is
committed to maintaining a respectful, inclusive
workplace for all employees. This session is an
opportunity for everyone to share their perspectives and
work toward a resolution that ensures our workplace
remains professional and welcoming."

INCIDENT REVIEW: Ms. Morrison reported
overhearing the following comments in the break room:

- References to "standards dropping" due to
inclusion policies

- Implications that she was a "diversity hire"

lacking qualifications

- Suggestions that inclusion policies prioritize "sob stories" over merit

- Comments about her being "different" and questions about her experience

STATEMENTS FROM INVOLVED PARTIES:

MARK STEVENS: "I want to start by saying I didn't mean anything personal against Dale. I was just expressing frustration about what I perceived as changes in hiring practices. I've been here for three years, and I've seen a lot of changes recently."

[Interrupted by Ms. Williams to clarify that personal intent doesn't negate professional impact]

"I understand that now. I guess I was concerned that... look, I worked really hard to get where I am, and sometimes it feels like newer policies might give advantages to certain groups."

[Asked to clarify what he meant by "certain groups"]

"Well, you know... people who might be hired to meet diversity requirements rather than purely on merit."

BRAD JOHNSON: "I feel like I got caught up in Mark's conversation. I don't really have strong feelings about this either way. I was mostly just agreeing with what Mark was saying without really thinking about it."

[Ms. Williams noted that passive participation in discriminatory conversations is still problematic]

"I understand that now. I should have either not participated or spoken up if I thought the conversation was inappropriate."

DALE MORRISON: "I want to be clear that I'm not trying to get anyone in trouble. But hearing those comments made me question whether I belong here, whether my work is valued, and whether other employees might face similar treatment. I reported this because I believe Zenith's values are more than just words in a handbook."

[Asked how the comments affected her work performance]

"It was hard to concentrate for the rest of that day. I found myself second-guessing every interaction, wondering if people were questioning my qualifications. It created anxiety about coming to work and participating in team activities."

COMPANY POLICY CLARIFICATION –

Patricia Nelson: "I want to clarify our hiring practices for everyone in this room. Our inclusion policies ensure that all qualified candidates receive fair consideration, regardless of their background. They do not lower standards or create quotas. Ms. Morrison was hired because she was the most qualified candidate for the position, as evidenced by her interview performance, references, and work quality during her first week."

DISCUSSION OF IMPACT:

Dale Morrison: "I've worked hard my entire life. I graduated high school, I have work experience, I interview well, and I do good work. To have that reduced to being a 'diversity hire' is insulting and hurtful. It also sends a message to other employees who might be different that they don't truly belong here."

Mark Stevens: "I honestly didn't think about it that way. I guess I made assumptions without knowing anything about your background or qualifications."

Brad Johnson: "I'm sorry, Dale. I can see how those comments would be hurtful and unprofessional."

RESOLUTION DISCUSSION:

Actions Required:

Mark Stevens:

- Formal written apology to Ms. Morrison
- Completion of diversity and inclusion training within 30 days
- Formal letter of reprimand placed in personnel file
- Agreement to refrain from similar comments or discussions
- Understanding that future incidents will result in progressive discipline up to and including termination

Brad Johnson:

- Verbal apology to Ms. Morrison (completed during session)
- Completion of diversity and inclusion training within 30 days
- Verbal counseling documented in personnel file
- Agreement to speak up if witnessing similar inappropriate comments in the future

Dale Morrison:

- Assured of company's full support for her continued employment
- Encouraged to report any future incidents immediately
- Offered additional resources if needed (EAP counseling, etc.)

COMPANY-WIDE ACTIONS:

- Review of break room policies and behavior expectations
- All-staff reminder about professional workplace conduct

- Enhanced new employee orientation regarding inclusion policies
- Consideration of additional diversity training for all staff

VERBAL APOLOGIES DURING SESSION:

Mark Stevens: "Dale, I owe you an apology. I made comments that were unprofessional and hurtful without knowing anything about you or your qualifications. I was wrong to question your hiring or make assumptions about your abilities. I'm sorry for creating an uncomfortable work environment for you."

Brad Johnson: "Dale, I'm sorry for participating in that conversation and for any hurt my comments caused. I should have been more thoughtful about the impact of my words."

Dale Morrison: "I appreciate both of your apologies. I hope we can move forward professionally and that this helps create a better workplace for everyone."

AGREEMENTS REACHED:

1. All parties agree to maintain professional conduct in all workplace interactions

2. Mark Stevens will provide written apology within 48 hours

3. Both Mark Stevens and Brad Johnson will complete required training

4. All parties agree to focus on collaborative, respectful working relationships going forward

5. Ms. Morrison agrees to continue bringing concerns to HR if needed

FOLLOW-UP ACTIONS:

- HR will monitor workplace dynamics for next 90 days

- Check-in meeting with Ms. Morrison scheduled for June 11, 2020
- Training completion deadline: June 30, 2020
- Review of this incident will be conducted at 6-month mark

SESSION CONCLUSION: All parties expressed understanding of expectations and commitment to professional conduct. Session concluded with reminder that Zenith Marketing Solutions values all employees and expects mutual respect in all interactions.

CONFIDENTIALITY REMINDER: All participants reminded that details of this mediation are confidential and should not be discussed with other employees.

POST-SESSION NOTES:

Ms. Morrison appeared satisfied with the resolution and expressed appreciation for the company's prompt response to her concerns.

Mr. Stevens seemed genuinely remorseful and indicated he had not considered the impact of his words on others.

Mr. Johnson appeared relieved to have the matter addressed and committed to being more mindful of his participation in workplace conversations.

HR Assessment: Situation appears resolved with appropriate corrective action taken. Will continue monitoring to ensure no retaliation occurs and that workplace environment remains positive for all employees.

DOCUMENTATION:

- Copy of notes filed in HR incident log
- Copies placed in personnel files of all parties

involved

- Training records to be updated upon completion
- Follow-up meeting scheduled in calendar system

Prepared by: Michael Farmer, HR Assistant **Reviewed by:** Patricia Nelson, HR Manager **Date:** June 4, 2020 **Time:** 2:30 PM

- **CONFIDENTIAL - HR USE ONLY -**

Document 62: Diary Entry

Written by Dale Morrison
Dated: May 12, 2021

It's been exactly one year since that awful day in the break room at Zenith, and I can hardly believe how much has changed.

I'm sitting in my new apartment - a real one-bedroom place in Virginia-Highland that I could afford after my promotion to Executive Assistant - writing this before my evening class. Yes, I'm in school now. Georgia State University, pursuing my bachelor's degree in social work with a focus on counseling. It's what I always dreamed of doing, and somehow, impossibly, I'm actually doing it.

Work has been incredible. After that mediation with Mark and Brad, something shifted at Zenith. Not just with them - though Mark actually became one of my strongest allies after completing his diversity training - but with the whole company culture. Patricia asked me to help develop their new employee orientation program, specifically the section on inclusion and workplace respect. My story, carefully anonymized, became part of their training materials.

Last month, I got promoted. More money, more responsibility, and Patricia told me it was because I'd shown "exceptional professionalism and leadership." When she said that, I thought about Dad, about all the times he told me I'd never amount to anything. Look at me now, Dad. I'm leading.

But the thing I'm most proud of is my work with TransAtlanta. Janet asked me to co-facilitate a support group for newly out transgender individuals, and it's become the most meaningful part of my week. Every Thursday evening, I sit in that same circle of folding chairs where I first felt seen and understood, and now I'm the one helping others feel that way.

Last week, a 16-year-old named Alex came to group for the first time. She was terrified, barely able to speak, and I saw myself two years ago in her eyes. She'd been kicked out by her family, was staying with a friend, and didn't know if she'd ever be able to live as herself.

I gave her the same thing Janet gave me: space to be heard, resources to stay safe, and hope that life could get better. By the end of the meeting, she was crying - not from pain, but from relief. "I thought I was the only one," she whispered.

"You're not alone," I told her, echoing Janet's words from that first night. "You never have to be alone again."

I've helped seventeen people navigate their coming out process this year. Seventeen. I keep a journal of their stories (with permission) because I want to remember each one. There's Marcus, who transitioned at his job and became a mentor for other trans employees. There's Sofia, who reconciled with her sister after I helped her write a letter explaining her identity. There's David, who started hormones and sent me a photo of his first real smile in years.

Each person I help feels like I'm healing a little more of my own story.

I'm also working with several local churches now, helping them understand how to be more affirming of LGBTQ+ members. It started when Pastor Wilson from the church Patricia attends asked me to speak to his congregation about my faith journey. I was terrified, but I talked about how being transgender deepened my relationship with God rather than separating me from it.

Afterward, three other pastors asked me to do workshops with their staff. One elderly woman came up to me after a presentation and said, "I have a granddaughter like you. I haven't spoken to her in two years because I didn't understand. But now I think I do. Will you help me write her a letter?"

We spent an hour crafting a message of love and acceptance. Two weeks later, she showed me a photo from her granddaughter's wedding - the first family event the granddaughter had attended in years.

That's when I knew I was exactly where God wanted me to be.

School is challenging but exciting. My professors don't know I'm transgender unless I choose to tell them, which is a strange kind of freedom. In my Human Development class, when we studied gender identity, I was able to speak from lived experience. My professor asked if I'd be willing to give a guest lecture next semester. Me, lecturing at a university. The girl who barely graduated from high school in small-town Alabama.

The hardest part of this year has been the continued silence from home. Mama never called me back after I left that voicemail about Dad being in the hospital the last time.

I have a family now - not the one I was born into, but the one I chose and the one that chose me back.

Speaking of family, Lisa got engaged last month! To a wonderful guy named James who treats her like a queen. She asked me to be in her wedding party, and when I cried and asked if she was sure, she said, "Dale, you're one of my best friends. Of course, I'm sure."

I'm going to be a bridesmaid. Me, in a bridesmaid dress, celebrating love with people who see me exactly as I am. If that's not a miracle, I don't know what it is.

The girl in the mirror looks so different than she did two years ago. She looks confident, purposeful, at peace. She looks like someone who belongs in the world, who has something valuable to offer, who deserves love and respect and happiness.

She looks like Dale - the real Dale, the one who was always there but was brave enough to come out and stay out.

Sometimes I think about that scared eighteen-year-old who got on a Greyhound bus with $3,200 and a heart full of terror and hope. I want to tell her: "It's going to be okay. More than okay. You're going to build a life more beautiful than you can imagine. You're going to help people. You're going to matter. You're going to be loved."

But maybe she already knew that. Maybe that's why she got on the bus.

Tomorrow, I start my second year of college. Tomorrow I'll go to work at a company where I'm valued and respected. Tomorrow evening, I'll sit in that circle of chairs and help someone else realize they're not alone.

Tomorrow I'll keep building the life I was always meant to live.

The girl in the mirror is finally home.

And she's just getting started.

Document 63: Call Log

Written by Bellsouth Mobile

Dated: May 24, 2021

BELLSOUTH WIRELESS DETAILED CALL LOG

Account Holder: Dale Morrison **Phone Number:** (404) 555-0847

Billing Period: April 25, 2021 **Statement Date:** May 24, 2021

OUTGOING CALLS TO (256) 555-0234 *[Margaret Morrison - Millbrook, AL]*

Date: May 25, 2021 Time: 2:47 PM **Duration:** 0:00:23 **Status:** No Answer/Voicemail **Notes:** Call went to voicemail after 4 rings

Date: May 25, 2021 Time: 7:15 PM **Duration:** 0:00:21 **Status:** No Answer/Voicemail **Notes:** Call went to voicemail after 4 rings

Date: May 26, 2021 Time: 11:30 AM **Duration:** 0:00:19 **Status:** No Answer/Voicemail **Notes:** Call went to voicemail after 3 rings

Date: May 26, 2021 Time: 6:45 PM **Duration:** 0:00:22 **Status:** No Answer/Voicemail **Notes:** Call went to voicemail after 4 rings

Date: May 26, 2021 Time: 12:15 PM **Duration:** 0:00:18 **Status:** No Answer/Voicemail **Notes:** Call went to voicemail after 3 rings

Date: May 26, 2021 Time: 8:30 PM **Duration:** 0:00:25 **Status:** No Answer/Voicemail **Notes:** Call went to voicemail after 5 rings

Date: May 27, 2021 Time: 10:15 AM **Duration:** 0:00:16 **Status:** No Answer/Voicemail **Notes:** Call went straight to voicemail

Date: May 27, 2021 Time: 4:20 PM **Duration:** 0:00:20 **Status:** No Answer/Voicemail **Notes:** Call went to voicemail after 4 rings

Date: May 27, 2021 Time: 9:45 PM **Duration:** 0:00:24 **Status:** No Answer/Voicemail **Notes:** Call went to voicemail after 5 rings

Date: May 28, 2021 Time: 1:30 PM **Duration:** 0:01:47 **Status:** Connected - Answered **Notes:** Call answered, conversation lasted 1 minute 47 seconds

Date: May 28, 2021 Time: 1:35 PM **Duration:** 0:00:15 **Status:** No Answer/Voicemail **Notes:** Call went straight to voicemail

Date: May 29, 2021 Time: 9:00 AM **Duration:** 0:00:17 **Status:** No Answer/Voicemail **Notes:** Call went straight to voicemail

Date: May 29, 2021 Time: 3:45 PM **Duration:** 0:00:19 **Status:** No Answer/Voicemail **Notes:** Call went to voicemail after 3 rings

Date: May 29, 2021 Time: 7:20 PM **Duration:** 0:00:21 **Status:** No Answer/Voicemail **Notes:** Call went to voicemail after 4 rings

Date: May 30, 2021 Time: 11:45 AM **Duration:** 0:00:16 **Status:** No Answer/Voicemail **Notes:** Call went straight to voicemail

Date May 30, 2021 Time: 5:30 PM **Duration:** 0:00:18 **Status:** No Answer/Voicemail **Notes:** Call went straight to voicemail

---

TOTAL CALLS TO (256) 555-0234: 15
TOTAL CALL TIME: 0:06:18
CALLS ANSWERED: 1
CALLS TO VOICEMAIL: 14

Document 64: Diary Entry

Written by Dale Morrison

Dated: May 30, 2021

I've been calling Mama every day this week. Fifteen calls. She answered once.

Friday afternoon, 1:30 PM. I almost dropped the phone when I heard her voice instead of the answering machine.

"Hello?" She sounded tired. Older.

"Mama? It's Dale."

Silence. Then: "I know."

"How are you? Are you okay? I've been worried about you. I heard Dad is in the hospital again."

"I'm... I'm managing."

"I know I should have called sooner. I just... I didn't know if you wanted to hear from me."

"Dale..." Her voice cracked. "I can't do this right now."

" I just want you to know I'm here. I'm in Atlanta, I'm doing well, and I love you."

"I have to go."

"Wait, Mama, please—"

The line went dead.

I called back immediately, but it went straight to voicemail. Every call since then has gone to voicemail. I think she's screening them now.

I know I should probably stop calling. Dr. Reynolds says I can't force someone to be ready for a relationship they're not prepared for. But she's my mama.

What if she needs me and is too proud to say so?

What if she's waiting for me to prove I won't give up on her the way everyone gave up on me?

Or what if I'm the painful reminder of everything that went wrong in that family, and my calls are making life harder?

I don't know. I just know I can't stop trying. Not yet.

Tomorrow I'll probably call again. And the day after that. Until she either tells me to stop or tells me she's ready to talk.

Because that's what love looks like sometimes. It looks like showing up even when the door doesn't open. It looks like leaving voicemails that may never be returned. It looks like hoping for connection even when you're met with silence.

The girl in the mirror looks sad tonight. But she also looks determined.

She's not giving up on her mother.

Even if her mother has given up on her.

Document 65: Facebook Post
Written by Multiple Individuals
Dated: May 30, 2021

FACEBOOK POSTS - EARL MORRISON'S PASSING

Margaret Morrison

Posted 6 hours ago

😢 💔 It is with a heavy heart that I announce the passing of my beloved husband, Earl Thomas Morrison. He went home to be with the Lord this morning July 26, 2021, at 6:47 AM, surrounded by peace.

The doctors said he had no more than 8 months when he was first diagnosed, but Earl lived for 1 year and 2 months. He was a fighter until the very end, never losing his faith or his determination to live life on his own terms.

Earl was a devoted husband of 32 years, a faithful deacon at Cedar Ridge Baptist Church, and a pillar of our community. He loved his family, his church, and his Lord with all his heart.

I know he is no longer in pain and is walking those golden streets with Jesus. God needed another angel, and He called Earl home.

Please keep me in your prayers during this difficult time.

"Precious in the sight of the Lord is the death of his faithful servants." - Psalm 116:15

#RIPEarlMorrison #GoneButNotForgotten #FaithfulServant

547 reactions 😢 ❤️ 🙏 234 comments 167 shares

Cedar Ridge Baptist Church

Posted 4 hours ago

🕊️ CELEBRATING A LIFE WELL LIVED 🕊️

It is with deep sorrow but also great hope that we announce the homegoing of our beloved Deacon Earl Morrison. Earl peacefully entered his eternal rest this morning after a courageous battle with cancer.

For over 20 years, Deacon Earl served our church family with dedication, wisdom, and unwavering faith. He was a true man of God who lived his convictions and inspired others through his example.

Even in his illness, Earl never stopped believing in God's goodness. He often said, "God's got a plan, and I trust Him completely." What a testimony of faith!

Earl exceeded every medical prediction through the power of prayer and his incredible will to live. The doctors said 14 months - God gave us over 2 years with this precious soul.

While we mourn his passing, we celebrate his victory! Earl is now in the presence of his Savior, healed and whole forever.

SERVICE INFORMATION:

VIEWING: 📍 Magnolia Funeral Home 📅 Friday, July 29, 2021 - 4:00-8:00 PM 📅 Saturday,

HOMEGOING SERVICE: 📍 Cedar Ridge Baptist Church 📅 Saturday, August 1, 2021 - 2:00 PM 👤 Officiated by Bishop William Patterson

BURIAL: 📍 Millbrook Memorial Gardens 📅 Immediately following service

In lieu of flowers, the family requests donations to the Cedar Ridge Baptist Church, a ministry Earl deeply supported.

"Well done, good and faithful servant." - Matthew 25:23

#DeaconEarl #HomegoingCelebration #WellDone

423 reactions 🙏 😢 🖤 *189 comments 234 shares*

Bishop William Patterson

Posted 3 hours ago

Saints, we have lost a giant of faith. Deacon Earl Morrison has gone home to glory.

I had the privilege of pastoring Earl for over 15 years, and I can say without hesitation that he was one of the most committed, faithful men I've ever known. His love for God, his family, and his church never wavered, even in his darkest hours.

When the doctors gave Earl 14 months to live, he looked them in the eye and said, "Doctors don't have the final say - God does." And God honored his faith by giving him over two years to continue his ministry and testimony.

Earl lived every day of those extra months with purpose and praise. He continued serving in whatever capacity he could, continued encouraging others, and continued proclaiming God's goodness.

What a way to finish the race! What a testimony of trust!

I will have the honor of officiating Earl's homegoing service on Saturday. It won't be a funeral - it will be a celebration of a life lived for Christ and a victory won through faith.

Earl Morrison fought the good fight, finished the race, and kept the faith. Now he wears the crown of righteousness.

See you on Saturday as we celebrate our brother's

graduation to glory!

"I have fought the good fight, I have finished the race, I have kept the faith." - 2 Timothy 4:7

#FoughtTheGoodFight   #EarlMorrison #VictoryInJesus

267 reactions 🙏 💜 👍 *98 comments 87 shares*

Magnolia Funeral Home *Posted 2 hours ago*

⚰️ FUNERAL ARRANGEMENTS ⚰️

EARL THOMAS MORRISON *October 12, 1962 – July 26, 2021*

The Morrison family and Magnolia Funeral Home announce the services for Mr. Earl Thomas Morrison, age 38, who passed away peacefully Thursday morning.

VISITATION: July 29, 2021 4:00 PM - 8:00 PM Magnolia Funeral Home 1247 Highway 14 West Millbrook, AL 36054

FUNERAL SERVICE: August 1, 2021 2:00 PM Cedar Ridge Baptist Church 567 Main Street Millbrook, AL 36054

INTERMENT: Millbrook Memorial Gardens Following funeral service

SURVIVING FAMILY: Loving wife of 32 years: Margaret (Maggie) Morrison Extended family and friends

Earl was a lifelong resident of Millbrook, faithful member and deacon of Cedar Ridge Baptist Church, and devoted employee of Morrison Manufacturing for 18 years. He will be remembered for his strong faith, his dedication to family and church, and his determination to live life on his own terms.

Memorial donations may be made to Cedar Ridge Baptist Church Building Fund.

#EarlMorrison #MillbrookMemorial #FuneralServices
156 reactions 😟 🙏 🤍 *67 comments 45 shares*

SELECTED COMMENTS:

Linda Johnson: Earl was such a good man. He helped us so much when Jim was out of work. Praying for Sister Margaret. 🙏

Robert Davis: Deacon Earl lived his faith every single day. What an example of trusting God through trials. He's healed now!

Susan Miller: 32 years of marriage - what a testimony of love and commitment. Praying for Margaret during this difficult time.

Michael Williams: Earl Morrison was a man's man and a God's man. He faced that cancer with more courage than anyone I've ever seen.

Katherine Smith: The way he exceeded every doctor's prediction shows that God still performs miracles. Earl's faith moved mountains.

Karen Anderson: I'll never forget Earl's testimony during his illness. He never complained, never lost hope. True faith in action.

Beverly Adams: Thinking of Margaret. Earl took such good care of her. She's going to need all of us now.

Mark Stevens: Earl gave me my first job at the plant. He was tough but fair. A real man of integrity.

Janet Thompson: That man lived every extra day God gave him with purpose. His legacy will live on through everyone he touched.

Dorothy Patterson: Earl Morrison was the definition of a faithful servant. Our church will never be the same without him.

TRENDING IN MILLBROOK:
#RIPEarlMorrison #DeaconEarl #FaithfulServant
#MillbrookStrong #HomegoingCelebration

FUNERAL HOME GUEST BOOK ONLINE:
247 signatures and memories posted

FLOWER ARRANGEMENTS ORDERED: *32
arrangements from various donors*

MEMORIAL DONATIONS: *$3,247 raised for
church building fund*

Document 66: Facebook Post

Written by Multiple Individuals

Dated: May 30, 2021

Dale Morrison

Posted 4 hours ago

I learned about my father's death through Facebook this morning.

Earl Thomas Morrison passed away yesterday at 6:47 AM. He was 39 years old, and he was my father, though none of the memorial posts mention that he had a child.

I've been sitting here for hours, staring at all the beautiful tributes to his faith, his dedication to family and church, his courageous battle with cancer. People are sharing memories of his kindness, his work ethic, his unwavering belief in God. And I'm grateful they're sharing these memories, because it helps me remember the man he could be at his best.

But I'm also heartbroken that I learned about his death the same way a stranger would - through social media posts from people who knew him. No phone call. No notification. Just the shock of scrolling through Facebook and seeing his photo with dates underneath.

I want to be angry. Part of me is angry. I'm his daughter, and I wasn't even mentioned in his obituary. I exist, but his story is being told as if I never did. Even in death, I've been erased from the family narrative.

But more than anger, I feel sadness. Sadness for the relationship we never had. Sadness for the father who couldn't see his daughter for who she really was. Sadness for the years of silence, the missed opportunities for reconciliation, the love that was there but could never find its way through the walls of fear and misunderstanding.

I also feel sad for him. Because in his final two years - the "bonus time" that everyone is celebrating - he chose to remain isolated from his own child. He had extra time that the doctors didn't predict, and he used none of it to build bridges or seek peace with his family. He died having never known the woman I became, never seen the life I built, never understood that I was exactly who God created me to be.

Here's what I wish he could have known:

I graduated from college last year with honors. I work for a company that values my contributions and respects my identity. I'm in graduate school studying to become a counselor so I can help other people navigate difficult family relationships and find their authentic selves.

I've helped dozens of people through my work with TransAtlanta. I've spoken at churches about faith and inclusion. I've been interviewed by newspapers and radio stations. I've made a difference in people's lives.

I have friends who love me unconditionally. I have a chosen family who sees me, celebrates me, and supports me through every challenge. I have a life filled with purpose, meaning, and joy.

I am a woman of faith. I believe in the same God my father served, and I believe that God loves me exactly as I am. I pray regularly, I read scripture, I try to live with love and compassion for others - including those who have hurt me.

I wish he could have seen all of this. I wish he could have known that his daughter turned out okay - more than okay. I wish he could have been proud of the person I became instead of mourning the person I never was.

But I also want to say this: I forgive him.

I forgive him for the rejection, for the silence, for the years of trying to change me instead of love me. I forgive him for the pain he caused and the relationship we never got to have. I forgive him because that's what Christians are called to do - to forgive as we have been forgiven.

This doesn't mean the hurt wasn't real or that the consequences of his choices don't matter. It means I'm choosing not to carry the weight of his rejection into my future. I'm choosing to remember that he was a human being who was afraid, who was limited by his understanding, who probably did the best he could with the tools he had.

I'm praying for his soul and for his peace. I'm praying for my mother, who is grieving alone and who has lost so much. I'm praying for healing for our family, even though it looks different than anyone expected.

To everyone who loved my father: thank you for seeing his good qualities and celebrating his life. Thank you for being there for him and for my mother during his illness. Thank you for the prayers and support you offered.

To anyone who is estranged from family: you are not alone in this complicated grief. It's possible to mourn someone who never fully accepted you, to love someone who couldn't love you back, to forgive someone who never apologized. Your feelings are valid, whatever they are.

And to my father, wherever you are now: I hope you finally understand that love doesn't have to look the way we expect it to. I hope you know that I never stopped being your child, even when you couldn't see me. I hope you're at peace.

Rest in peace, Dad. I love you, and I forgive you, and

I release you.

Your daughter, Dale Morrison

"Be kind to one another, tenderhearted, forgiving one another, as God in Christ forgave you." - Ephesians 4:32

#Grief #Forgiveness #FamilyIsComplicated #Faith #Love #RestInPeace #ChristianLove #Healing

1,247 reactions 💜 💀 🙏 💜 *347 comments 156 shares*

SELECTED COMMENTS:

Janet Miller (TransAtlanta): Dale, your grace and forgiveness in this moment is breathtaking. Your father's loss was not having the chance to know the incredible woman you became. Sending you love. 💜

Lisa Poltowski: I'm crying reading this. Your heart is so big, and your faith is so strong. He missed out on knowing an amazing daughter. We're here for you. 💕

Dr. Constance Reynolds: This is one of the most powerful examples of healing and forgiveness I've ever witnessed. You honor your faith and yourself with these words.

Carmen Rodriguez: Sister, you just taught me something about grace that I needed to learn. Thank you for sharing your heart so honestly. Love you. 🙏

Christina Rodriguez: I remember that scared kid who used to come into Walgreens. Look at the woman of faith you've become. Your father would have been proud if he could have seen past his fear.

Patricia Nelson: Dale, your professionalism and character at work reflect the same grace you're showing here. You're an inspiration to everyone who knows you.

Michael Farmer: Dale, your ability to respond to pain with love continues to amaze me. This post will help many people dealing with similar situations.

Alex Kim: You helped me through my own family estrangement. Now you're helping others through theirs. Your dad's legacy lives on in all the people you're helping heal.

Anonymous: I'm a parent who rejected my transgender child 5 years ago. Reading this makes me realize what I've lost and what I need to do to make it right. Thank you.

Rev. James Wilson: Dale, your faith testimony is more powerful than any sermon I've ever preached. This is what Christ's love looks like in action.

Margaret Morrison: I love you too.

[This comment has 456 likes and 234 replies]

Dorothy Patterson (First Lady) - *Posted 2 hours after original* Margaret Morrison, I saw your comment on this post. As Earl's Bishop's wife, I feel I must reach out to you privately. This is a difficult time and decisions about family relationships should not be made in grief. Please call me.

[45 likes, 89 replies]

Reply from Dale Morrison: Mrs. Patterson, with respect, my mother is free to make her own choices about her relationships. She's been making decisions about me for 20 years. I trust her judgment. *[234 likes]*

Reply from Linda Johnson: Dorothy, Margaret just lost her husband. Maybe let her grieve and love however she needs to. *[156 likes]*

Robert Davis - *Posted 2 hours after original* This is inappropriate. A man just died and his... this person... is making it all about themselves and their lifestyle choices. Earl Morrison was a good man who didn't deserve this kind of disrespect at his death.

[12 likes, 347 angry reactions, 123 replies]

Reply from Carmen Rodriguez: Robert, did you even read what she wrote? She honored her father and showed incredible grace. This is what forgiveness looks like. *[289 likes]*

Reply from Janet Thompson: A daughter grieving her father is not "inappropriate." The inappropriate thing is pretending she doesn't exist. *[178 likes]*

Reply from Dale Morrison: Mr. Davis, I'm sorry you feel that way. I was simply honoring my father and processing my grief. I meant no disrespect. *[567 likes]*

Beverly Adams - *Posted 3 hours after original* Margaret Morrison, I'm concerned about you. You're not thinking clearly in your grief. Earl would not want you to associate with this person who represents everything he stood against. Please talk to Bishop Patterson before you make any decisions you'll regret.

[8 likes, 234 angry reactions, 67 replies]

Reply from Katherine Smith: Beverly, that's Earl's child. Blood doesn't stop being blood because you don't understand someone's journey. *[145 likes]*

Reply from Margaret Morrison: Beverly, I buried my husband yesterday. I'm thinking more clearly than I have in years. This is my child, and I love her. *[1,203 likes, 234 heart reactions]*

Susan Miller - *Posted 3 hours after original* I have to say, I'm impressed by the grace and forgiveness shown in this post. Whether I understand this person's choices or not, this is what Christian love looks like. Earl raised her with strong values, and it shows.

[234 likes, 45 replies]

Reply from Michael Williams: You're right, Susan. The fruit of someone's character shows how they respond to pain. This shows good character. *[89 likes]*

Bishop William Patterson - *Posted 4 hours after original* This is a difficult time for our church family. While we mourn the loss of Deacon Earl, we must remember that grief affects everyone differently. However, I encourage all church members to seek Spiritual guidance before making life-changing decisions during this emotional time.

[67 likes, 234 comments]

Reply from Rev. James Wilson: Bishop Patterson, with respect, supporting one's child isn't a "life-changing decision" - it's what parents are called to do. This young woman has shown remarkable faith and grace. *[345 likes]*

Reply from Dale Morrison: Bishop Patterson, I appreciate your concern for your congregation. I'm not asking anyone to change their beliefs. I simply love my mother and forgive my father. *[234 likes]*

Karen Anderson - *Posted 4 hours after original* I knew Earl Morrison for 20 years. He was a good man, but he was also stubborn and proud. Maybe this is God's way of healing what Earl couldn't heal in life. Margaret, follow your heart.

[178 likes, 23 replies]

Mark Stevens - *Posted 5 hours after original* I don't pretend to understand everything about this situation, but I do understand forgiveness and grace. This post shows both. I'm sorry for your loss, Dale. Earl was a good man who made some hard choices.

[123 likes]

Reply from Dale Morrison: Thank you, Mark. That means a lot coming from you. *[67 likes]*

Christina Rodriguez - *Posted 5 hours after original* I've known Dale since she was a teenager. I watched her struggle with being rejected by the people who should have loved her most. What she's written here isn't just forgiveness - it's a miracle. Earl Morrison missed out on knowing an incredible daughter.

[456 likes, 34 replies]

Reply from Margaret Morrison: Thank you, Christina. You were always kind to her when others weren't. *[234 likes]*

MOST LIKED REPLY TO MARGARET MORRISON:

Dale Morrison: Mama, I love you so much. You're not alone. I'm here whenever you're ready. 🩶

[1,847 likes]

PRIVATE MESSAGES TO DALE *(Screenshots shared in diary entry)*

From: Margaret Morrison *Sent 6 hours after post* "Dale, can we talk? I have your number from your old voicemails. I'm ready now. I've been ready for a long time but didn't know how to start. Your post about your daddy helped me see that love doesn't have to look the way I always thought it did. Call me when you can. - Mama"

From: Janet Thompson *Sent 4 hours after post* "Honey, I knew your daddy since we were kids. He was scared of what he couldn't understand, but he would have been proud of the woman you became. Don't let the church busy bodies make you doubt that. - Mrs. Janet"

From: Katherine Smith *Sent 3 hours after post* "Dale, I helped deliver you when you were born. You were a beautiful baby then and you're a beautiful soul now. Your mama needs you, and you need her. Don't let anyone else tell you different."

Document 67: Diary Entry

Written by Dale Morrison
Dated: July 27, 2021

I can't believe what's happened in the last 24 hours. My post about Dad has been shared over 300 times. People from all over the country are commenting, sharing their own stories of family estrangement and reconciliation.

But the most important thing is Mama's comment. She called me her child. In public. On Facebook. Where everyone from Millbrook could see it.

Mrs. Patterson and Mrs. Adams are trying to convince her she's making a mistake, that grief is clouding her judgment. But some of the other church ladies are defending her - and me. Mrs. Thompson said I was raised with strong values, and it shows. Mrs. Anderson said maybe this is God's way of healing what Dad couldn't heal.

The private message from Mama made me cry for an hour. She's ready to talk. She's been ready but didn't know how to start. She said my post helped her see that love doesn't have to look the way she always thought it did.

I called her tonight. We talked for two hours. She cried. I cried. She told me she's been carrying guilt for three years about not protecting me from Dad's anger. She said she knew he was wrong but didn't know how to stand up to him.

"I was so scared of losing him that I lost you instead," she said. "That was the wrong choice."

She asked me to tell her about my life in Atlanta. About my job, my school, my friends, my advocacy work. She listened to all of it without interrupting, without judging. When I told her about helping other families reconcile, she said, "You're doing God's work, baby. I'm proud of you."

Proud of me. My mama said she's proud of me.

She wants to visit Atlanta. She wants to meet my friends, see where I live, and understand my life. She said she has a lot of learning to do, but she's ready to do it.

The church is divided about her supporting me. Bishop Patterson is trying to counsel her to "reconsider during this emotional time." But other people are saying that a mother's love for her child shouldn't need the Bishop's approval.

Mrs. Rodriguez sent me the sweetest message about how she's watched me grow up and how Dad missed out on knowing an incredible daughter. She said she's going to help Mama understand what it means to have a transgender child.

The girl in the mirror looks different tonight. She looks like someone whose family is finally healing. Someone whose mother chose love over fear, grace over judgment, relationship over reputation.

It took my father's death for my mother to find the courage to love me publicly. I wish it hadn't taken that long, but I'm grateful it happened at all.

Tomorrow I'm driving to Alabama to see Mama for the first time in over two years. We're going to visit Dad's grave together. We're going to start rebuilding what we never really had - a mother-daughter relationship based on truth and love.

The girl in the mirror is going home. Finally, really home.

Document 68: PTO Request
Written by Dale Morrison
Dated: July 27, 2021

ZENITH MARKETING SOLUTIONS
EMPLOYEE TIME OFF REQUEST

Employee Name: Dale Morrison **Department:** Administration

Employee ID: ZMS-2047 **Request Date:** July 27, 2021

Supervisor: Patricia Nelson, HR Manager

REQUEST DETAILS:

Type of Leave: Personal Time Off

Dates Requested: July 28 – August 4, 2021 (Monday through Friday) **Total Days:** 6 business days

Return Date: August 5, 2021

Reason for Request: Family emergency/bereavement. I need to travel to Alabama to spend time with my mother following my father's recent passing and to manage family matters that require my immediate attention.

Work Coverage Arrangements:

- Lisa Poltowski has agreed to manage urgent administrative tasks
- All scheduled meetings have been rescheduled or delegated
- Email autoreply will be set up directing urgent matters to Lisa
- All pending projects have been brought to completion or appropriate stopping points
- Client files have been organized and notes provided for continuity

Contact Information During Leave: Available by cell phone for emergencies: (404) 555-0847 Will check email once daily if urgent matters arise

Current Leave Balance:

- Personal Time Off: 8 days available
- Using 6 days, leaving 2 days remaining

Additional Notes: This trip involves reconciling with family after extended estrangement. The timing is critical as it follows my father's funeral and represents an important opportunity for family healing. I appreciate the company's understanding during this personal time.

EMPLOYEE SIGNATURE: *Dale Morrison*
DATE: July 27, 2023

SUPERVISOR APPROVAL SECTION:

Approved: ✓ Yes ☐ No

Supervisor Comments: Dale has been an exemplary employee and has handled a difficult family situation with remarkable professionalism. Her work is current, and she has made thorough arrangements for coverage. This time off is well-deserved and necessary for her personal well-being. I want to commend Dale for her maturity in handling both her professional responsibilities and personal challenges. She represents the best of Zenith's values in how she balances work and life priorities.

Take all the time you need, Dale. Family reconciliation is important work.

SUPERVISOR SIGNATURE: Patricia Nelson
DATE: July 27, 2021
TIME APPROVED: 11:30 AM

HR PROCESSING:

Payroll Notified: √ Yes **Leave Balance Updated:** √ Yes **Coverage Arrangements Confirmed:** √ Yes **Employee File Updated:** √ Yes

HR Notes: Employee has excellent attendance record and rarely uses personal time. Request approved without hesitation. Coverage arrangements are thorough and professional.

Processed by: Michael Farmer, HR Assistant **Date Processed:** July 27, 2021

Document 69: Email Correspondence

Written by Patricia Nelson and Dale Morrison
Dated: July 27, 2021

EMAIL CORRESPONDENCE:

FROM: Patricia Nelson pnelsoln@zenithmarketing.com

TO: Dale Morrison dmorrison@zenithmarketing.com

DATE: July 27, 2021, 11:45 AM

SUBJECT: Time Off Request Approved

Dale,

Your time off request has been approved immediately. I can't imagine how difficult this week has been for you, learning about your father's passing and then having this opportunity to reconnect with your mother.

Please don't worry about work at all. Lisa has everything under control, and we'll be fine. Focus on your family and on healing.

I saw your Facebook post yesterday, and I was moved by your grace and forgiveness. You continue to be an inspiration to all of us at Zenith. Your father would have been proud of the woman you've become, and I know your mother will be too.

Take care of yourself and give my regards to your mother. Safe travels.

Warmly, Patricia

FROM: Lisa Poltowski
lpoltowski@zenithmarketing.com
TO: Dale Morrison
dmorrison@zenithmarketing.com
DATE: July 27, 2021, 12:15 PM
SUBJECT: You've got this! 💪

Girl,

I'm so excited for you! I know this trip is going to be emotional, but I can't wait to hear how it goes with your mom. You've been praying for this opportunity for so long.

Don't you dare worry about work. I've got everything covered, and Patricia told everyone that you're managing a family situation, and we should support you 100%.

Pack something nice for meeting your mama - you want to look like the successful, amazing woman you are! But also pack tissues because you're probably going to cry happy tears.

I'm so proud of you for having the courage to go home and rebuild this relationship. Your mom is lucky to have a daughter like you.

Text me when you get there safely! Love you!

Lisa 💜

Document 70: Diary Entry

Written by Dale Morrison

Dated: July 27, 2021

Patricia approved my time off in less than an hour. She said I don't need to worry about work at all, that Lisa has everything covered, and that I should focus on family and healing.

She also said she saw my Facebook post and was moved by my grace and forgiveness. She said my father would have been proud of the woman I've become. Coming from Patricia, that means everything.

Lisa is so excited for me. She told me to pack something nice because I want to look like the successful woman I am when I meet Mama. She's right - I want Mama to see that I turned out okay, that I'm thriving, that she can be proud of me.

I can't believe I'm actually going home. Not just physically, but emotionally. After all these years of wondering if I'd ever have a relationship with my mother, it's finally happening.

The girl in the mirror looks nervous but hopeful. She's about to find out if home can be a place of love instead of rejection.

Tomorrow, I will drive to Alabama. Tomorrow, I will start building a real relationship with my mama.

Thank you, Zenith, for being the kind of workplace that supports the whole person, not just the employee. Thank you, Patricia, for understanding that sometimes work has to wait for life.

Thank you, God, for second chances.

Document 71: Diary Entry
Written by Dale Morrison
Dated: July 28, 2021

I'm writing this from my childhood bedroom in Millbrook, Alabama. I never thought I'd see this room again.

The drive from Atlanta took four hours, but it felt like traveling back in time. Every mile marker on I-20 brought back memories - good and painful ones mixed together like ingredients in a recipe I'd tried to forget.

When I pulled into the driveway at 1247 Maple Street, my hands were shaking so badly I could barely turn off the car. The house looked smaller than I remembered, and older. The paint was peeling on the front porch, and Dad's vegetable garden had gone wild with weeds.

But there was Mama, standing in the doorway, and when she saw me get out of the car, she started crying.

"Dale," she said, and the way she said my name - my real name - made my heart break and heal at the same time.

We stood there for a moment, just looking at each other. I was afraid to move, afraid she might change her mind, afraid this might all be a dream.

Then she opened her arms.

I ran to her like I was six years old again, and she held me so tight I could barely breathe. We both sobbed on that front porch where I used to sit and dream about escaping to somewhere I could be myself.

"My baby," she kept saying. "My baby girl. I'm so sorry. I'm so, so sorry."

"It's okay, Mama," I whispered. "I'm here now. We're here now."

The first few hours were awkward. We didn't know how to be together, how to fill twenty years of silence with conversation. She made sweet tea and cut pound cake, and we sat at the kitchen table where I used to do homework, both of us tiptoeing around the elephant in the room.

Finally, she looked at me and said, "Tell me about your life. Tell me everything. I want to know who my daughter really is."

So, I did. I told her about leaving on the Greyhound bus with $3,200 and a heart full of terror. I told her about TransAtlanta, about finding people who understood me. I told her about my job at Zenith, about school, and about my advocacy work.

I told her about the newspaper interview, about speaking at churches, about helping other families navigate what ours couldn't.

"You're famous," she said, half-laughing, half-crying. "My daughter is famous for helping people."

"Not famous, Mama. Just... useful. I think God gave me all that pain for a reason."

She nodded. "Your daddy always said God doesn't waste anything. Even hurt can become healing if you let it."

That's when I knew she was really listening, really trying to understand.

We talked until dinner time. She made fried chicken and mashed potatoes - my favorite meal from childhood - and we ate by candlelight because the dining room chandelier had burned out months ago and she hadn't bothered to fix it.

"I stopped caring about the house after your daddy got sick," she said. "Nothing seemed to matter much."

"It matters now," I said. "You matter. This place matters because it's where you are."

After dinner, she showed me Dad's room - they'd been sleeping separately for the last year because of his illness. His clothes were still in the closet, his Bible still on the nightstand.

"I haven't touched anything," she said. "I didn't know how to start."

"We don't have to start tonight," I said. "We have time."

That's when she asked the question I'd been dreading: "Do you want to see him? Your daddy? I mean... do you want to go to the cemetery?"

My throat closed up. "I don't know if I'm ready."

"We don't have to," she said quickly. "But... he's at peace now, Dale. Whatever anger he carried, whatever fear... it's gone. Maybe it's safe now to say goodbye."

So, this morning, we drove to Millbrook Memorial Gardens. Mama brought flowers - yellow roses, Dad's favorites. I brought something else: the piece of blue-wrapped candy Evelyn had given me at the hospital three years ago. I'd been saving it for a special occasion, and this felt like the right time.

His headstone was simple: "Earl Thomas Morrison. Beloved Husband and Servant of God." No mention of being a father, which stung a little but didn't surprise me.

I knelt down and placed the candy next to Mama's

flowers.

"What's that?" she asked.

I told her about Evelyn, about the woman who saw me in the hospital and called me "sugar" and gave me candy wrapped in blue paper. "She told me I wasn't unholy for being complicated. She helped me believe I could be transgender and still loved by God."

Mama started crying again. "I should have been the one to tell you that. I should have been your Evelyn."

"You're telling me now," I said. "That's what matters."

I talked to Dad's grave for a long time. I told him about my life, about the work I'm doing, about the people I'm helping. I told him I forgave him and that I hoped he understood now that love comes in all different shapes.

"I'm still your daughter," I said. "I was always your daughter. I hope you can see that now."

Mama took my hand. "He can see it," she said. "And if he can't, that's his loss, not yours."

We went to lunch at the diner downtown, and I saw several people I recognized from high school. A few stared, a few whispered, but Mrs. Johnson from the post office came over to our table.

"Dale Morrison," she said. "I saw your Facebook post about your daddy. That was the most beautiful thing I ever read. You're a credit to your raising."

Mama squeezed my hand under the table.

This afternoon, we went through some of Dad's things together. Mama let me keep his old Bible - the one he'd had since he was a teenager, full of underlined verses and margin notes. Some of the verses he'd marked were about love, about not judging others, about God's mercy being new every morning.

"He knew the right words," Mama said. "He just couldn't always live them."

"None of us can," I said. "That's why we need grace."

Tonight, we're going to look through photo albums. Mama wants to show me pictures from when I was little, and she wants to hear about my friends in Atlanta. She's particularly interested in Lisa, who she says sounds like "good people."

"I'd like to meet your friends," she said. "I'd like to see where you live, understand your world."

"You will," I said. "Whenever you're ready."

As I'm writing this, Mama is in the kitchen making hot chocolate the way she used to when I was small - with extra marshmallows and a dash of vanilla. In a few minutes, we're going to sit on the couch and look at baby pictures and fill twenty years of silence with stories and laughter and probably more tears.

But good tears this time. Healing tears.

The girl in the mirror looks different tonight. She looks like someone who's finally come home - not to this house, necessarily, but to this relationship. She looks like a daughter who's been welcomed back, a prodigal who's been embraced instead of being judged.

She looks like someone whose family is finally whole again, even though it's smaller than it used to be.

Tomorrow we're going to visit Dad's grave again, and then we're going to start planning Mama's trip to Atlanta. She wants to see my apartment, meet my friends, maybe even come to a TransAtlanta meeting.

"I have a lot to learn," she said. "But I want to learn. I want to understand your world so I can be a good mother to the daughter I have, not the child I thought I wanted."

That might be the most beautiful thing anyone has ever said to me.

The girl in the mirror is finally home.

And home, it turns out, was always supposed to be about love.

We just had to find our way back to it.

Document 72: Diary Entry

Written by Dale Morrison

Dated: July 29, 2021

I wasn't going to go to the viewing. Mama and I would visit Dad's grave later and have our private goodbye. That was the plan. But this morning at breakfast, Mama looked at me across the table and said, "Dale, do you want to go see your daddy one more time? At the funeral home?"

"Mama, I don't think that's a good idea. You saw the Facebook comments. Half the church thinks I shouldn't even exist, let alone show up at Dad's viewing."

"Well, the other half thinks you should," she said firmly. "And more importantly, I think you should. You're his daughter. You have every right to be there."

I thought about it all morning. Part of me wanted to stay hidden, to avoid the stares and whispers and judgments. But another part of me - the part that's learned to stand up for herself - knew Mama was right.

So, at 3:30 PM, I put on my best black dress - the one I'd bought for job interviews - and drove with Mama to Magnolia Funeral Home.

I should have been prepared for the reactions, but somehow, I wasn't.

The moment we walked in, conversations stopped. People turned to stare. I heard whispers that weren't quite whispers:

"Is that really..." "I can't believe she had the nerve..." "In a dress, no less..." "Poor Margaret..."

Mama took my arm and held it tight. "Hold your head up," she whispered. "You belong here."

We walked to the front of the room where Dad's casket was. He looked peaceful, younger somehow than he had in the last few years. I touched his hand and whispered, "I love you, Daddy. I forgive you. I hope you're at peace now."

When we turned to find seats, I could feel every eye in the room on us. Some people looked curious, some looked sympathetic, but many looked disgusted or angry.

Mrs. Henderson, who'd been Dad's supervisor at the plant, deliberately turned her back when we walked past. Mr. Davis, who I remember from church, shook his head and muttered something under his breath.

But it was Mrs. Caldwell, one of the church deacons' wives, who said the thing that cut the deepest.

As we walked past her row, she looked me up and down with obvious disdain and said, just loud enough for everyone around to hear: "God don't like ugly."

The words hit me like a physical blow. I stopped walking, my face burning with shame and hurt. For a moment, I was that scared teenager again, being told by adults that God disapproved of me.

But before I could respond, Mama stepped forward.

"You know what, Delores?" Mama said, her voice carrying across the suddenly silent room. "He ain't too fond of cute either. And honey, the way you just spoke to my daughter wasn't cute at all."

The room went dead quiet. Mrs. Caldwell's mouth dropped open.

"This is my child," Mama continued, loud enough for everyone to hear. "My daughter. She came here to pay her respects to her father, same as all of you.

- 274 -

If you have a problem with that, you can take it up with me."

I'd never seen my mother stand up to anyone like that. Not to Dad, not to the church ladies, not to anyone. But there she was, defending me in front of the entire community.

A few people started murmuring, but Mrs. Johnson from the post office started clapping. Then Mrs. Rodriguez joined in. Then a few others.

"That's right, Margaret," Mrs. Johnson said. "Family is family."

Mama led me to the front row, where the family was supposed to sit. There was a moment of hesitation - would people accept me there? Did I really belong in the front row?

Mama didn't hesitate. She moved her purse and Dad's brother's jacket to make room for me right next to her.

"Sit down, baby," she said. "This is where you belong."

So, I sat in the front row at my father's viewing, next to my mother, who had just publicly claimed me as her daughter in front of everyone who'd ever questioned my existence.

Bishop Patterson stood up to give the eulogy. I braced myself, wondering if he'd make some comment about family or about God's plan that would be a veiled reference to me.

But he didn't. He talked about Dad's work ethic, his love for the church, his dedication to his family. When he said "family," he looked right at Mama and me.

"Earl Morrison was a man who loved deeply, even when that love was complicated," Bishop Patterson said. "He was human, which means he made mistakes. But he was also faithful, and he is now at peace with his Creator, who sees and understands all things."

It wasn't an apology exactly, but it felt like an acknowledgment. An acknowledgment that Dad was complicated, that families are complicated, that love doesn't always look the way we expect it to.

After the service, people started filing past the casket to pay their final respects. Some stopped to speak to Mama and me.

Mrs. Rodriguez hugged me and said, "Your daddy would be proud of the woman you've become." Mrs. Thompson squeezed my hand and said, "Welcome home, honey."

But others walked past without acknowledging me at all. Mrs. Caldwell left without speaking to anyone in our row.

The biggest surprise came from Mark Stevens, Dad's coworker from the plant. He stopped in front of me and said, "Dale, I want you to know that your father talked about you."

My heart stopped. "He did?"

"Near the end, when he was really sick. He said he had regrets. He said there were things he wished he'd done differently. He never said exactly what, but... I think he missed you. I think he was sorry."

I started crying then. Not because I believed Dad had completely changed his mind about me, but because maybe, in his last days, he'd felt some small measure of regret about how things had ended between us.

"Thank you for telling me that," I whispered.

After everyone left, Mama and I sat alone with Dad for a few more minutes.

"I'm proud of you," she said. "For coming tonight. For holding your head up. For being gracious even when people weren't gracious to you."

"I'm proud of you too, Mama. For standing up for me. For making room for me. For claiming me as your daughter in front of everyone."

She took my hand. "You are my daughter. You've always been my daughter. I'm sorry it took me so long to say it out loud."

We drove home in comfortable silence, both of us exhausted but somehow lighter. When we got to the house, Mama made us hot chocolate, and we sat on the porch even though it was cold.

"Do you think Dad really had regrets?" I asked.

"I think your daddy was a complicated man who loved in complicated ways," she said. "Maybe he couldn't say he was sorry while he was alive, but maybe that's what Mark was trying to tell you. Maybe Dad found his peace before he died."

"You're not unholy for being complicated." Evelyn's words are still coming back to me.

I hope that's true. I hope in his final days, Dad found some way to make peace with having a daughter he couldn't understand but couldn't stop loving.

The girl in the mirror looks different tonight. She looks like someone who survived a trial by fire and came out stronger. Someone who faced a hostile crowd and held her ground. Someone whose mother stood up for her when it mattered most.

She looks like someone who belongs in the front row of her own family's story.

Tomorrow is the funeral service at the church. I'm nervous about going back to Cedar Ridge Baptist

Church, to the place where I was hurt so badly. But Mama will be with me, and I've learned that having one person who truly sees you and loves you is worth more than having a crowd that tolerates you.

The girl in the mirror is ready for whatever comes next.

She's not hiding anymore.

She's not apologizing for existing anymore.

She's just living as herself, with dignity and grace, exactly as God made her.

And that, it turns out, is enough.

Document 73: Obituary

Written by Magnolia Funeral Home and First Lady Dorothy Patterson

Celebrating the life of
Deacon EARL THOMAS MORRISON

Sunrise: April 5, 1962 - *Sunset:* July 26, 2021

Sunday, August 1, 2021

Cedar Ridge Baptist Church

892 Old Montgomery Road

Millbrook, AL 36054

Bishop William 'Willie' Patterson, Eulogist,

Gracious host, and presiding

Obituary

Earl Thomas Morrison, 60, of Millbrook, passed away at his home on July 26, 2021.

Earl was born in Millbrook to the late Thomas and Ruby Morrison. He was a lifelong member of Cedar Ridge Baptist Church, where he served as a deacon for over twenty years. Earl was known for his strong faith, his dedication to traditional family values, and his unwavering commitment to Biblical principles.

For thirty-five years, Earl worked at Morrison Construction, the family business founded by his father. He was respected by his colleagues for his work ethic and diligence. Earl believed in the value of hard work and passed this belief on to all who knew him.

Earl was a devoted husband to his wife of thirty-two years, Margaret (Maggie) Morrison. He was a loving father who worked tirelessly to provide for his family and guide them in the ways of the Lord. Earl enjoyed hunting, fishing, and spending time outdoors. He was an avid supporter of the local high school football team and rarely missed a game.

Earl is survived by his beloved wife, Margaret Morrison, his sister, Linda Morrison-Hughes (Robert) of Birmingham, numerous cousins, nieces, and nephews, and his church family at Cedar Ridge Baptist Church.

Earl was preceded in death by his parents and his brother, David Morrison.

Funeral services will be held at 11:00 AM on

Sunday, August 1, 2021, at Cedar Ridge Baptist Church, with Rev. William Patterson officiating. Burial will follow at Millbrook Memorial Gardens.

In lieu of flowers, the family requests donations be made to the Cedar Ridge Baptist Church Building Fund or the Millbrook High School Football Booster Club.

"Well done, good and faithful servant."
- Matthew 25:23

God's Garden

God looked around his Garden and found an empty place.
He then looked down upon his earth and saw your loving face.
He put his arms around you and lifted you to rest.
His Garden must be beautiful; he always takes the best.

He knew that you were suffering, he knew you were in pain.
And knew that you would never get well on earth again.
He saw your path was difficult, he closed your tired eyes,
He whispered to you "Peace be Thine" and gave you wings to fly.

When we saw you sleeping so calm and free of pain,
We would not wish you back to earth to suffer once again.
You've left us precious memories, your love will be our guide,
You live on through your children, you're always by our side.

It broke our hearts to lose you, but you did not go alone.
For part of us went with you on the day God called you home.

Author Unknown

- 282 -

Order of Service

Processional
Selection...Cedar Ridge Baptist Church Praise Team
Prayer of Comfort...…First Lady Dorothy Patterson
Special Prayer Song…………. Sister Kira Plummer
Scripture Reading
Old Testament…………. Sister Kariny Humphries
New Testament……….......Sister Shandell Wyche
Selection………………. Sister Carolyn Northcutt
Open Remarks……….………. Family and Friends
Selection………...……...Sister Quanteria Wiseman
Words of Comfort……..... Bishop William Patterson
Acknowledgements………Magnolia Funeral Home
Removal of Flowers
Final Glance
Recessional

Active Pallbearers
Family and Friends

Flower Attendants
Family and Friends

Acknowledgements

Our hearts have been made to rejoice

during the passing of our loved one by

the many acts of kindness extended to our family.

Your prayers and all expressions of love and
sympathy are greatly appreciated.

May God's blessings of peace and love cover each
of you.

- The Family

Final Rites Entrusted To:

Magnolia Funeral Home name

1247 Heritage Boulevard, Millbrook, AL 36054
phone number (334) 555-0892

Fax (334) 555-0893

"Honoring Life, Celebrating Legacy"

Our Family Serving Yours Since 1943

Document 74: Diary Entry
Written by Dale Morrison
Dated: August 4, 2021

I'm writing this from a rest stop somewhere between my two homes. I've been in Alabama for eight days, and it feels like I've lived a whole other lifetime.

This morning, Mama and I had breakfast one more time at the little kitchen table where I used to do homework. She made pancakes and bacon, and we talked about everything and nothing, both of us trying to avoid the fact that I was leaving in a few hours.

"I don't want you to go," she said finally, her voice small.

"I don't want to go either," I said. "But I have to get back to work, back to school. My life is in Atlanta now."

"I know. I'm proud of the life you've built. I just... I wish I could have been part of building it with you."

"You're part of it now, Mama. That's what matters."

We spent the morning looking through more photo albums. She showed me pictures of me as a baby, as a toddler, as a young child before everything got complicated. In every photo, I was smiling, and she was smiling at me.

"You were such a happy baby," she said. "Always laughing, always curious about everything."

"I was happy then," I said. "I felt loved."

"You were loved. You are loved. I'm sorry I let

you forget that for so long."

Around noon, we had to talk about the elephant in the room - the obituary. I'd seen it in the Millbrook Gazette, and my name wasn't mentioned anywhere. It listed Dad's survivors as "his beloved wife Margaret" and "extended family and friends." No mention of a daughter. No mention of me at all.

"Dale, I need to tell you something," Mama said, her face getting red. "I saw the obituary too, and I was shocked. I never told them to leave you out."

"I figured as much," I said. "It's okay, Mama."

"No, it's not okay. I called the funeral home to ask what happened. Mr. Williams said that Dorothy Patterson - Bishop Patterson's wife - had come by and asked them to remove 'the child's information' from the obituary. She said it would be 'less painful for the family' if they kept it simple."

I felt that familiar stab of hurt, but it was duller now. Less sharp. "She made that decision for us?"

"She did. And I told Mr. Williams that it was not our decision to make, and that Dorothy Patterson had no right to speak for our family. I'm so sorry, baby. I should have been more involved in the arrangements. I should have made sure you were included."

"Mama, don't worry about it. Some folks don't change. Mrs. Patterson has been trying to erase me from this family for years. At least now we know where we stand."

But I was thinking about more than just the obituary. I was thinking about the whole week - the viewing, the funeral service, the way people looked at me.

- 286 -

"You know what was interesting?" I said. "When I walked up to Dad's casket to say my final goodbye, I looked at Bishop Patterson. I expected to see that familiar look - the one that said he wanted to cast demons out of me. But he didn't look like that. He looked... uncomfortable. Maybe even a little ashamed."

"Really?"

"Yeah. Like maybe he knew what they did to me was wrong, but he's in too deep to admit it now. Like maybe he's been carrying his own regrets about that night."

I paused, remembering the way he'd avoided eye contact, the way he'd shifted uncomfortably when I knelt by the casket.

"I'm going to need more time to process what happened to me in that church," I said. "To really address it, to really heal from it. But seeing him look away instead of looking through me... that felt like progress."

"And what about the other people? The ones who were unkind?"

I laughed, remembering. "Well, people still tried to look down their noses at me. The difference was that this time it was harder because I was in heels."

Mama burst out laughing. "Dale Morrison, you are something else."

"I'm serious! Mrs. Caldwell is only about five-foot-two, and I was wearing three-inch heels. She had to crane her neck up to give me a disapproving look. Kind of took the power out of it."

We laughed until we cried, and then we just cried.

"I'm going to miss you so much," she said.

"I'm going to miss you too. But Mama, this isn't goodbye. This is hello. This is the beginning of us having a real relationship."

"Promise me you'll call. Every week."

"I promise. And you promise me you'll come to visit Atlanta. I want to show you my apartment, introduce you to my friends, and take you to my favorite restaurants."

"I promise. Though I might need you to help me understand some things. I still have a lot to learn about... about all of this."

"We have time to learn together. That's what families do - they learn together."

When it was time to leave, we both started crying again. She walked me to my car and hugged me so tightly I thought she might never let go.

"I love you, Dale Morrison," she said. "I love the woman you've become, and I'm sorry I missed so much of you becoming her."

"I love you too, Mama. Thank you for fighting for me. Thank you for making room for me in the front row. Thank you for being my mother."

"I've always been your mother. I just forgot how to show it for a while."

I drove away watching her in my rearview mirror, standing in the driveway waving, getting smaller and smaller until I turned the corner.

But the amazing thing is, I don't feel like I'm losing her again. I feel like I'm finally taking her with me. For the first time in my life, I'm leaving Alabama with my mother's love instead of her rejection.

The drive back to Atlanta was completely different from the drive there. I wasn't nervous or scared. I was excited to get home to my life, but also excited to include Mama in that life.

I called Lisa from the road to tell her about everything that happened. She cried when I told her about Mama defending me at the viewing.

"Dale, your mom sounds amazing. I can't wait to meet her."

"You will. She's coming to visit next month."

"Really? Oh my God, I need to plan a dinner party! I need to make sure she knows how much we all love you!"

That's my Lisa. Always thinking about how to make people feel welcomed and loved.

I also called Janet from TransAtlanta. She wants me to share my story at the next support group meeting - not the painful parts, but the healing parts. The reconciliation parts.

"Dale, you've just proved that families can change, that love can overcome fear, that it's never too late to build bridges. That's a message our community needs to hear."

She's right. For so long, my story was about rejection and survival. Now it's about reconciliation and healing. Both parts are important, but the healing part might help other people hope for their own healing.

The girl in the mirror looks different tonight. She looks like someone who went home and came back with more than she left with. She went home with questions and came back with answers. She went home with wounds and came back with healing.

She looks like someone who finally has a mother who sees her, loves her, and fights for her.

She looks like someone who's finally, truly, completely

home - both in Atlanta and in her family.

Tomorrow, I go back to work, back to school, back to my advocacy work. But I go back carrying my mother's love with me, carrying the knowledge that I'm not alone in this world, carrying the hope that other families can find their way back to each other too.

The girl in the mirror is finally whole.

And she's just getting started living as her whole self.

The best is yet to come.

Document 75: Diary Entry

Written by Dale Morrison

Dated: August 12, 2021

Tonight was one of the most meaningful TransAtlanta meetings I've ever been part of. Janet asked me to share about my trip to Alabama, specifically the reconciliation aspects, and I think it ended up being exactly what several people in the group needed to hear.

The meeting started as usual with introductions and check-ins. We had three new members tonight - a 19-year-old trans woman named Maya who'd been kicked out by her parents six months ago, a 24-year-old trans man named Jordan who hadn't spoken to his family in three years, and a 45-year-old woman named Patricia who was two years into her transition but still completely estranged from her adult children.

All three of them looked so defeated when they talked about their families. That familiar pain in their eyes - the pain of being rejected by the people who were supposed to love you most.

"I keep thinking they'll come around," Maya said during check-in. "But it's been six months, and they won't even take my calls."

"My sister sent me a Christmas card last year addressed to my old name," Jordan said. "Like I don't exist anymore."

"My daughter told me I was dead to her," Patricia said, her voice barely above a whisper. "She said I chose my 'lifestyle' over my family. But I didn't choose this. I just chose to stop dying inside."

I could see Janet looking at me, and I knew she was

thinking the same thing I was: they needed to hear that reconciliation was possible, even when it seemed hopeless.

"Dale," Janet said, "would you be willing to share about your recent experience with your mother?"

I took a deep breath. "I'd be honored."

I told them about the three years of silence after I left Alabama. About calling my mother dozens of times and getting voicemail. About learning of my father's death through Facebook. About the decision to stay in Atlanta instead of going to the hospital when he was dying.

"For three years, I believed my family was lost to me forever," I said. "I grieved the relationship with my mother like she was dead, because in my life, she might as well have been."

I saw Maya nodding. Jordan was leaning forward, listening intently.

Then I told them about my Facebook post after Dad died, about my mother's comment, about the phone call that changed everything.

"The thing is, I had to be willing to risk more rejection," I said. "When I called her back, she could have hung up on me. When I decided to go to Alabama, she could have changed her mind. Every step of the way, I had to choose hope over self-protection."

"But what if she had rejected you again?" Patricia asked. "How do you survive that?"

"The same way I survived the first rejection," I said. "With the support of chosen family. With therapy. With the knowledge that other people's inability to love me doesn't change my worth."

I told them about the viewing, about Mrs. Caldwell's

cruel comment, about my mother standing up for me in front of the entire community.

"My mother found her voice," I said. "But she couldn't find it until my father died. Sometimes the person who's preventing reconciliation isn't the person you're trying to reconcile with - it's someone else entirely."

Carmen, who's been in the group for years, spoke up. "That's so true. My father wanted to accept me, but my stepmother wouldn't let him. It took her getting sick and realizing life was short for her to stop interfering."

"So how do you know when to keep trying and when to let go?" Maya asked.

That was the hardest question, and I thought about it for a long time before answering.

"I think you keep trying as long as you can without destroying yourself," I said. "For me, I had to build a strong enough foundation in Atlanta - good friends, therapy, work I loved - before I could risk reaching out again. I had to know I'd be okay if they rejected me."

"But also," added David, who's been estranged from his family for four years, "you have to be willing to accept that some people can't or won't change. Dale's story is beautiful, but not every story ends with reconciliation. And that's okay too."

I nodded. "David's absolutely right. I got lucky. My mother was ready to change, and my father's death gave her permission to do it. But even if she hadn't been ready, I would still be okay. I have a family here, with all of you. I've learned that love doesn't have to come from the people who share your DNA."

Jordan raised his hand. "But how do you deal with grief? Even when you have chosen family, you still mourn the family you lost."

"You let yourself grieve," I said. "You don't rush it, you don't apologize for it, you don't let anyone tell you to 'get over it.' Losing family - even when they're still alive - is a real loss. It deserves to be mourned."

Lisa, who's been coming to meetings occasionally since her engagement, spoke up. "I've watched Dale go through this whole journey, and what I've learned is that she never stopped loving her family, even when they couldn't love her back. That's what made reconciliation possible when the opportunity came."

"But loving them doesn't mean accepting abuse," I clarified. "I forgave my father, but I also protected myself from him. Love and boundaries can coexist."

We talked for another hour about the practical aspects of reconciliation - how to reach out safely, how to set boundaries, how to manage expectations, how to deal with partial acceptance versus full acceptance.

Maya asked, "What if they want to reconcile but they won't use your chosen name or pronouns?"

"That's where boundaries come in," I said. "You get to decide what you can and can't live with. For me, being called by my name was non-negotiable. I'd rather have no relationship than a relationship built on denying who I am."

"My mother still slips up sometimes," said Carmen. "But she catches herself and apologizes. There's a difference between someone who's trying and someone who's refusing."

Patricia, the woman whose daughter had cut her

off, was quiet for most of the discussion. Finally, she spoke up.

"I keep thinking I should write her a letter," she said. "But I'm afraid she'll just throw it away."

"She might," I said gently. "But she might not. And even if she throws it away, you'll know you tried. Sometimes that's all we can do - love people from a distance and hope they'll be ready someday."

"What would you put in the letter?" Janet asked.

Patricia thought for a moment. "That I love her. I'm sorry she's in pain. That I'm not going anywhere, and when she's ready to talk, I'll be here."

"That sounds perfect," I said. "That's exactly what my mother needed to hear from me - that I wasn't going anywhere, that I was still her child, that love was still available if she wanted it."

As the meeting was winding down, Maya came up to me.

"Thank you for sharing your story," she said. "I'm not ready to reach out to my parents yet but knowing that reconciliation is possible... it gives me hope."

"Take your time," I said. "Build your foundation first. Make sure you're strong enough to handle whatever response you get. And remember - you're not trying to win them back. You're offering them the opportunity to know the real you. If they can't take that opportunity, that's their loss."

Jordan also approached me as people were leaving. "I think I'm going to call my sister," he said. "Not my parents, but my sister. She was always the more open-minded one."

"Start where you can," I said. "Sometimes one person in the family becomes the bridge to the others."

As I was packing up to leave, Janet pulled me aside.

"Dale, that was beautiful," she said. "You gave people hope without giving them false expectations. That's a hard balance to strike."

"I just told the truth," I said. "The truth is that reconciliation is possible, but it's not guaranteed. The truth is that family love can overcome fear, but it takes courage from everyone involved."

Driving home tonight, I thought about how different my story could have been. If my mother hadn't been ready to change, if my father's death hadn't created an opening for healing, if I hadn't built a strong enough support system to risk reaching out - any of those factors could have led to a different ending.

But I also thought about the people in group tonight who are still hoping, still grieving, still trying to figure out how to love family members who can't love them back. Their stories aren't finished yet. Maya might get a call from her parents next Christmas. Jordan's sister might surprise him. Patricia's daughter might read that letter and realize she misses her parents.

Or none of those things might happen. And that would be okay too, because they all have chosen family who sees them and loves them exactly as they are.

The girl in the mirror looks thoughtful tonight. She looks like someone who's learned that sharing your healing can help others believe in their own potential for healing. She looks like someone who's found her purpose in turning pain into hope.

She looks like someone who's finally understood that the best thing you can do with a happy ending is share it with people who are still writing their stories.

Tomorrow I'll probably get calls or emails from people in group, wanting to talk more about reconciliation or boundaries or hope. And I'll be here for them; the same way Janet and Carmen and Lisa were here for me when I needed to believe that love was possible.

The girl in the mirror is home. And now she's helping other people find their way home too.

That's what family does - chosen family, blood family, or both.

We help each other come home.

ATLANTA JOURNAL-CONSTITUTION FOLLOW-UP INTERVIEW TRANSCRIPT

Date: May 15, 2022 **Reporter:** Michael Farmer, Staff Writer **Subject:** Dale Morrison - Follow-up on Family Reconciliation **Location:** Java Jive Coffee Shop, Virginia-Highland

---

Farmer: Dale, thank you for agreeing to this follow-up interview. When we spoke over a year ago, you were estranged from your family. A lot has changed since then.

Morrison: It has. My father passed away in July, and my mother and I have reconciled. It's been a journey of healing that I never expected to take.

Farmer: You've been speaking at conferences about something you call "complicated grief." Can you explain what that means?

Morrison: Complicated grief is what happens when you lose someone who never fully saw or accepted you. When my father died, I had to grieve not just his death, but also the relationship we never had. I had to mourn the father who couldn't see his daughter, while also honoring the man who gave me life.

Farmer: That must be incredibly difficult psychologically.

Morrison: It is. You're grieving someone who caused you pain, which brings guilt. You're mourning missed opportunities for reconciliation. You're processing love and hurt simultaneously. It's not the straightforward grief people expect.

Farmer: How do you begin to process that kind of loss?

Morrison: First, you have to give yourself permission to grieve however you need to. Some days I missed my father terribly. Other days I was angry at him. Some days I felt relief that the conflict was over. All of those feelings were valid.

Farmer: You've said that your father "couldn't see" you. Do you think he was just stubborn, or was there something deeper going on?

Morrison: I think my father was afraid. He had a very specific idea of what family should look like, what children should be like. When I didn't fit that mold, he didn't know how to handle it. Fear made him rigid when he could have chosen love.

Farmer: But surely at some point, intelligent people have to take responsibility for their prejudices. I mean, your parents had eighteen years to figure out that they were damaging their child.

[Long pause]

Morrison: Michael, I need to correct something there. My parents aren't unintelligent or uncaring people. They're human beings who were limited by their understanding and their fear. A wise woman once told me that some folks aren't unholy for being complicated - they're just complicated.

Farmer: I apologize. I didn't mean to—

Morrison: No, it's okay. But this is important. When we demonize people who've hurt us, we lose the opportunity to understand what went wrong and how to heal it. My father wasn't evil. He was scared and stubborn and raised in a way that didn't give him tools to love someone like me. That doesn't excuse the harm, but it helps explain it.

Farmer: That's a remarkably gracious perspective. How did you arrive at that understanding?

Morrison: Through a lot of therapy, a lot of prayer, and some very wise people who taught me that holding onto bitterness only hurts me. The same woman who told me about not being unholy for being complicated also said that sugar works better than vinegar when you're trying to heal something sweet.

Farmer: "Sugar works better than vinegar." I like that. Tell me about your mother's transformation. What changed for her?

Morrison: My father's death gave her permission to make choices she couldn't make while he was alive. But also, seeing my response to his death - the grace I tried to show even in my pain - helped her see that I was still the child she'd raised to have good values. I hadn't become someone different. I'd just become myself.

Farmer: What was it like going back to Alabama for the funeral?

Morrison: Terrifying and healing at the same time. Some people in the community were hostile. Others were surprisingly supportive. But the most important thing was my mother standing up for me publicly. She made it clear that I was her daughter and I belonged there.

Farmer: How has your relationship with your mother evolved since then?

Morrison: We talk every week now. She's planning to visit Atlanta next month. We're building a relationship we never had - a mother-daughter relationship based on honesty and acceptance. She's learning about my world, and I'm learning to trust her love again.

Farmer: What advice would you give to other people dealing with complicated grief?

Morrison: Don't rush it. Don't let anyone tell you how to feel or how long to feel it. Find people who understand that grief isn't always straightforward. And remember that you can love someone and be hurt by them at the same time. Both things can be true.

Farmer: You're also speaking to families who are struggling to accept LGBTQ+ children. What do you tell them?

Morrison: I tell them that love doesn't require understanding. You don't have to understand your child's journey to love them through it. I also tell them that they have a choice: they can spend energy trying to change their child, or they can spend energy building a relationship with the child they actually have.

Farmer: And if they're coming from a religious background that sees being transgender as sinful?

Morrison: I tell them that God is bigger than their theology. I tell them that the same God who created diversity in nature created diversity in humanity. And I tell them that their child's relationship with God is between their child and God - not between their child and them.

Farmer: You've become quite an advocate. Was that always your plan?

Morrison: Not at all. I just wanted to survive, to build a life where I could be myself. But I learned that my pain had purpose when I could use it to help other people heal. Every family I help reconcile, every young person I help find hope - that gives meaning to everything I went through.

Farmer: What's next for you?

Morrison: I'm finishing my social work degree. I want to specialize in family therapy, particularly working with families who are navigating gender identity issues. I also want to continue training religious leaders who want to be more affirming.

Farmer: Any final thoughts for our readers?

Morrison: Just this: families are complicated, love is complicated, and people are complicated. But that doesn't make any of us unholy. Sometimes the most sacred thing you can do is love someone exactly as they are, even when you don't understand them. And sometimes the most courageous thing you can do is keep your heart open to love, even when it's broken.

[Post-Interview Notes]

Farmer: Dale, I want to apologize again for my comment about your parents. You handled that with such grace.

Morrison: Thank you for being open to correction. That's how we all learn and grow.

Farmer: This woman you keep quoting - about being complicated not being unholy, and sugar working better than vinegar - she sounds like she had a profound impact on you.

Morrison: Evelyn. Her name was Evelyn. I only met her once, but she saw me when I couldn't see myself. Sometimes God sends angels in the most unexpected packages.

Farmer: Well, it sounds like you've become someone's angel too.

Morrison: I hope so. We all need someone to remind us that we're not unholy for being complicated. We're just humans, trying to figure out how to love well.

[Reporter's Reflection Notes] Subject continues to demonstrate remarkable emotional maturity and wisdom. Her ability to find grace in difficult circumstances and to extend compassion even to those who have hurt her is noteworthy. Story angle: How personal healing can become a platform for helping others heal. This follow-up piece will focus on the journey from victim to advocate, and the power of choosing understanding over bitterness.

Planned publication: Sunday, May 22, 2022 - Front page, Living section **Title consideration:** "From Rejection to Reconciliation: A Daughter's Journey Home"

Document 77: Atlanta Journal Article

Written by Michael Farmer

Dated: May 22, 2022

THE ATLANTA JOURNAL-CONSTITUTION SUNDAY, May 22, 2022 - LIVING SECTION

From Rejection to Reconciliation: A Daughter's Journey Home

Local advocate, Dale Morrison, speaks about 'complicated grief' and the healing power of grace

By Michael Farmer, Staff Write

ATLANTA - In a quiet coffee shop in Virginia-Highland, Dale Morrison sits across from me with the same thoughtful presence she had when we first met 16 months ago. But something fundamental has changed. The young woman who once spoke about survival now speaks about healing. The advocate who once focused on finding acceptance now helps others extend it.

Morrison, 20, has become a prominent voice in discussions about family reconciliation, faith, and what she calls "complicated grief" - the unique pain of losing someone who never fully saw or accepted you.

"When my father died, I had to grieve not just his death, but also the relationship we never had," Morrison explains. "I had to mourn the father who couldn't see his daughter, while also honoring the man who gave me life."

Since our last interview, Morrison's life has been transformed by tragedy and grace in equal measures. Her father, Earl Morrison, died of cancer on July 26, 2021, leading to an unexpected reconciliation with her mother, Margaret, after three years of estrangement.

"My father's death gave my mother permission to make choices she couldn't make while he was alive," Morrison says. "But also, seeing my response to his death - the grace I tried to show even in my pain - helped her see that I was still the child she'd raised to have good values."

Morrison's journey from rejection to reconciliation began with a Facebook post about her father's death that went viral, garnering over 1,000 reactions and comments from across the country. The post, which demonstrated remarkable forgiveness toward a father who had rejected her transgender identity, caught the attention of families nationwide.

"I got messages from kids who said they weren't suicidal anymore because they read my story," Morrison says, her voice catching slightly. "Parents reached out asking how to rebuild relationships with estranged children. That's when I realized my pain had purpose."

The term "complicated grief" has become central to Morrison's advocacy work. She explains it as the psychological challenge of mourning someone who caused significant pain while they were alive.

"You're grieving someone who hurt you, which brings guilt. You're mourning missed opportunities for reconciliation. You're processing love and hurt simultaneously," she says. "It's not the straightforward grief people expect."

Morrison's approach to healing emphasizes grace over bitterness, understanding over condemnation. When asked about her father's rejection, she offers a perspective that seems wise beyond her years.

"My father wasn't evil. He was scared and stubborn and raised in a way that didn't give him tools to love someone like me. That doesn't excuse harm, but it helps explain it."

This philosophy comes from what Morrison calls her "foundational teaching" - wisdom shared by an elderly woman named Evelyn who befriended her during a difficult period. "She told me that some folks aren't unholy for being complicated - they're just complicated. And that sugar works better than vinegar when you're trying to heal something sweet."

Morrison's reconciliation with her mother has become a beacon of hope for other families navigating similar challenges. Margaret Morrison now calls her daughter weekly and is planning her first visit to Atlanta next month.

"We're building the relationship we never had - a mother-daughter relationship based on honesty and acceptance," Morrison says. "She's learning about my world, and I'm learning to trust her love again."

The impact of Morrison's story extends far beyond her personal life. She now speaks at conferences about complicated grief and family reconciliation, trains religious leaders on LGBTQ+ inclusion, and counsels families through TransAtlanta, a local support organization.

Dr. Constance Reynolds, a therapist who has worked with Morrison, calls her approach "revolutionary in its simplicity."

"Dale has learned to hold space for the full complexity of human relationships," Reynolds explains. "She can love someone who hurt her, forgive someone who never apologized, and find grace for people who couldn't extend grace to her. That's not just psychological healing - that's spiritual maturity."

Morrison's advice to families struggling with LGBTQ+ acceptance is both practical and profound: "Love doesn't require understanding. You don't have to understand your child's journey to love them through it. You have a choice: spend energy trying to change your child or spend energy building a relationship with the child you actually have."

For those dealing with their own complicated grief, Morrison offers this guidance: "Don't rush it. Don't let anyone tell you how to feel or how long to feel it. Find people who understand that grief isn't always straightforward. And remember that you can love someone and be hurt by them at the same time."

Morrison is currently finishing her social work degree at Georgia State University, specializing in family therapy. Her goal is to work professionally with families navigating gender identity issues while continuing her advocacy work.

"Every family I help reconcile, every young person I help find hope - that gives meaning to everything I went through," she says.

As our conversation concludes, Morrison reflects on the unexpected direction her life has taken. "I just wanted to survive, to build a life where I could be myself. But I learned that my pain had purpose when I could use it to help other people heal."

Her final words echo the wisdom that has guided her journey: "Families are complicated, love is complicated, and people are complicated. But that doesn't make any of us unholy. Sometimes the most sacred thing you can do is love someone exactly as they are, even when you don't understand them."

In a world that often demands choosing sides, Dale

Morrison offers a different path - one of grace, understanding, and the radical belief that love can overcome fear, even when it takes time to find its way home.

Morrison will be speaking at the Southern Conference on Family Healing on March 15-16 at the Georgia World Congress Center. For more information about TransAtlanta support services, visit www.transatlanta.org.

Document 78: Impact Metrics

Written by Michael Farmer

Dated: June 5, 2022

IMPACT METRICS - TWO WEEKS AFTER PUBLICATION:

Media Coverage:

- Reprinted in 23 newspapers across the Southeast
- Featured on Good Morning America
- Interviewed by NPR's "Fresh Air"
- Discussed on The Oprah Winfrey Show (taped segment)
- Featured in Christianity Today magazine

Community Response:

- 2,000+ letters to the editor (75% positive)
- Article shared 25,000+ times on social media
- TransAtlanta website crashed from traffic increase
- 15 new support groups started nationwide using Dale's materials

Speaking Engagements:

- 12 conference invitations
- 8 university speaking requests
- 6 religious organizations requesting training
- 4 book publishers expressing interest

Document 79: Impact Metrics

Written by Michael Farmer

Dated: June 5, 2022

LETTERS TO THE EDITOR - PUBLISHED May 25 10, 2022

"A Mother's Perspective" *Your article about Dale Morrison moved me to tears. I am a mother who rejected my transgender son five years ago. Reading about Dale's grace toward her father and her mother's courage to change has inspired me to reach out to my child. Some wounds can be healed if we're brave enough to try. - Anonymous, Savannah*

"Complicated Grace" *As a pastor, I was challenged by Dale's approach to forgiveness and understanding. She's taught me that love doesn't require theological agreement - it requires courage. I'm changing how I counsel families in crisis. - Rev. Michael Johnson, First Methodist, Columbus*

"Hope for Healing" *I lost my daughter to suicide three years ago because I couldn't accept her transgender identity. Reading Dale's story makes me wish I had been as brave as her mother. Please, parents - don't wait until it's too late. Love your children while you can. - Sarah K., Birmingham*

"Professional Insight" *As a family therapist, I see Dale Morrison's approach as groundbreaking. Her concept of "complicated grief" gives language to an experience many clients struggle with. This article should be* *required reading for mental health professionals. - Dr. Angela Jackson, LCSW*

NATIONAL MEDIA RESPONSES:

Good Morning America - June 5, 2022 *Diane Sawyer:* "Dale Morrison's story challenges us to think differently about forgiveness, family, and faith. Her message that 'families are complicated but not unholy' is resonating with viewers across America..."

NPR Fresh Air - June 8, 2022 *Terry Gross:* "What strikes me about Dale Morrison is her refusal to demonize people who have hurt her. In our polarized culture, her approach to healing offers a different model for handling conflict..."

Christianity Today - June 2022 Issue *"Morrison represents a new voice in conversations about faith and sexuality - one that emphasizes grace over judgment, relationship over theology. Her influence is growing among progressive evangelical leaders..."*

ACADEMIC INTEREST:

Emory University Theology Department

- Invited Dale to guest lecture on "Theology of Complicated Relationships"
- Three doctoral students requesting interviews for dissertations
- Proposal for case study on reconciliation methodology

Georgia State University Social Work Program

- Dale's approach incorporated into family therapy curriculum
- Research study proposed on "complicated grief" in LGBTQ+ families
- Field placement opportunities created at TransAtlanta

Document 80: Diary Entry

Written by Dale Morrison

Dated: June 15, 2022

I can't believe the response to Michael's article. My phone hasn't stopped ringing. TransAtlanta's voicemail is full every day with people wanting to share their stories or ask for help.

The most amazing part is the letters from parents. So many people say they're going to reach out to estranged children, that they're going to choose love over fear. If my story helps even one family heal, everything I went through was worth it.

But there was one letter that broke my heart. A mother in Birmingham who lost her transgender daughter to suicide three years ago. She wrote, "I wish I had been as brave as your mother." I've been crying about that letter for days.

I'm realizing that my story isn't just about me anymore. It's about every family that's struggling, every parent who's afraid, every kid who thinks they'll never be loved for who they are.

Evelyn was right - we're not unholy for being complicated. We're just humans, trying to figure out how to love well. And sometimes, if we're very lucky, we get the chance to show other people that love is always possible, even when it seems impossible.

The girl in the mirror looks different now. She looks like someone whose pain became purpose, whose story became hope for others.

She looks like someone who finally understands what it means to turn wounds into wisdom.

She looks like someone who's ready for whatever comes next.

Document 81: Diary Entry
Written by Dale Morrison
Dated: June 22, 2022

Mama is coming to Atlanta tomorrow, and I'm more nervous than I've been about anything in years.

She's been planning this trip for two months, ever since we talked about it during my visit home. We've been making our weekly phone calls, and she's been asking questions about my life here - about my friends, my apartment, my work, my advocacy work. But talking about it and seeing it are two very different things.

I spent all day today cleaning my apartment until it sparkled. Lisa came over to help me rearrange furniture and make sure everything looked perfect.

"Dale, relax," she said, watching me fold the same dish towel for the third time. "Your mom is going to love seeing your life here. She's going to be so proud of what you've built."

"But what if she's overwhelmed? What if meeting everyone from TransAtlanta is too much? What if she sees my life and realizes she doesn't really understand it?"

Lisa stopped me and took my hands. "Your mom chose to come here. She chose to learn about your world. Give her credit for that courage."

The plan for the weekend is ambitious, maybe too ambitious. Tomorrow evening I'm picking her up from the airport, and we're having a quiet dinner at my apartment. Saturday, I'm taking her to brunch with Lisa and a few coworkers from Zenith. Saturday afternoon, we're going to the TransAtlanta community center so she can see my advocacy work.

Saturday evening, Janet is hosting a small dinner party with some of the support group members. Sunday morning, we're going to Rev. Wilson's church - the one where I've been speaking about faith and inclusion. Sunday afternoon, she flies home.

It's a lot. Maybe too much. But Mama said she wanted to see everything, to understand my whole life. "I missed three years of watching you grow up," she said during our last phone call. "I want to catch up as much as I can in one weekend."

I keep thinking about how different this is from my childhood, when bringing friends home was always complicated. Dad would interrogate them, make them uncomfortable, judge whether they were "good influences." Mama apologized for his behavior later, but she never stood up to him in the moment.

Now she's coming to my home, to meet my chosen family, to see the life I built without them. And instead of judging, she's asking to understand.

The girl in the mirror looks anxious tonight, but also excited. She looks like someone who's about to introduce the most important people in her life to each other. She looks like someone whose two worlds are finally going to meet.

Tomorrow, I find out if love really can bridge any gap.

Document 82: Diary Entry
Written by Dale Morrison
Dated: June 23, 2022

Mama is here, asleep in my bedroom while I write this from the couch. The day was everything I hoped it would be and nothing like I expected.

Her flight was delayed by two hours, so I spent most of the afternoon pacing around the airport, checking my phone, reorganizing my purse, and generally driving myself crazy with nerves.

When she finally walked out of the gate, I barely recognized her. She'd gotten her hair cut and styled, and she was wearing a new outfit - nice jeans and a sweater I'd never seen before. She looked younger, more confident, more like the woman I remembered from before Dad got sick.

"Dale!" she called out, and I ran to her like I was six years old again.

"Mama, you look beautiful," I said, hugging her tight.

"I wanted to look nice for your city," she said, laughing. "I went shopping in Montgomery before I came. Figured I should dress the part."

On the drive to my apartment, she peppered me with questions about everything we passed.

"Is that where you work? Is that the school you go to? Oh, my goodness, look at all these people!" She was like a tourist, but also like a mother trying to picture her daughter's daily life.

When we got to my building, she got quiet as we climbed the stairs to the third floor.

"This is it," I said, unlocking the door. "This is

home."

She walked into my little one-bedroom apartment and just stood there, taking it all in. My books on the shelves, my TransAtlanta certificates on the wall, photos of me with Lisa and Carmen and Janet, my college diploma, the interview clippings Patricia had framed for me.

"Oh, Dale," she whispered. "Look what you built."

She spent twenty minutes looking at every photo, asking about every person. When she got to the picture of me speaking at the podium at a conference, she started crying.

"I'm so proud of you," she said. "I'm so proud of the woman you became, and I'm so sorry I wasn't here to watch it happen."

"You're here now," I said. "That's what matters."

We had dinner at my little kitchen table - takeout from my favorite Thai restaurant because I was too nervous to cook. Mama had never had Thai food before, but she tried everything and declared the pad Thai "surprisingly delicious."

"Tell me about your friends," she said. "I want to know about everyone I'm going to meet tomorrow."

So, I told her about Lisa, about how she recommended me for the job at Zenith and has been like a sister to me. About Janet, who runs TransAtlanta and was the first person to make me feel like I belonged somewhere. About Carmen, who's been transitioning for five years and shows me what's possible. About Dr. Reynolds, who's helped me heal from so much trauma.

"They sound like wonderful people," Mama said. "They sound like family."

"They are family," I said. "Chosen family."

She was quiet for a moment. "I'm glad you had family when I couldn't be family to you."

After dinner, we sat on my couch, and she asked me to see more photos. I showed her pictures from TransAtlanta meetings, from my speaking engagements, from graduation, from work events. In every photo, I was smiling.

"You look happy," she said. "Really, truly happy."

"I am happy," I said. "It took a while to get here, but I am."

"I can see that. And I can see why you fought so hard to get here."

As she was getting ready for bed, she looked around my apartment one more time.

"This feels like you," she said. "Everything here feels like the Dale I remember from when you were little but grown up. Does that make sense?"

It made perfect sense. This apartment, this life, this community - it's who I was always meant to be, if I'd been allowed to grow up as myself.

The girl in the mirror looks peaceful tonight. Day one went better than I dared to hope. Mama isn't overwhelmed or judgmental or uncomfortable. She's curious and proud and present.

Tomorrow, we meet my chosen family. Tomorrow, she sees me in my element, advocating and helping and being myself fully.

I think she's going to love them. More importantly, I think they're going to love her.

Document 83: Diary Entry

Written by Dale Morrison

Dated: June 24, 2022

Today was perfect. Actually perfect.

We started with brunch at Murphy's in Virginia-Highland. I was so nervous about Mama meeting Lisa that I could barely eat my eggs benedict. But within five minutes, they were talking like old friends.

"Mrs. Morrison," Lisa said, "I have to tell you, Dale is one of the most remarkable people I've ever met. When she started at our company, she just lit up every room she walked into."

"She's always been special," Mama said. "I just forgot how to see it for a while."

Lisa told Mama about the workplace incident with Mark and Brad, about how I handled it with such professionalism and grace. Patricia from HR, who joined us halfway through brunch, told Mama about my promotion and how I'd helped develop their new employee training program.

"Your daughter is going to be running companies someday," Patricia said. "She has this gift for bringing people together and helping them understand each other."

I watched Mama's face light up with pride. This was her daughter they were talking about - successful, respected, making a difference in the world.

After brunch, we went to the TransAtlanta community center. I was worried this might be too much for Mama - seeing the support group space, meeting transgender people at different stages of their journeys. But she surprised me.

Janet gave us a tour of the facility, explaining the different programs we offer. When we got to the meeting room where I facilitate my support group, Mama asked if she could sit in one of the chairs.

"This is where my daughter helps people," she said to Janet. "This is where she turns her pain into purpose."

Janet's eyes filled with tears. "Your daughter is one of our most gifted facilitators. She has this ability to hold space for people's grief and hope at the same time."

We met Carmen, who was there preparing materials for the next day's meeting. I was nervous about this introduction - Carmen is further along in her transition than I am, more obviously feminine, and I wasn't sure how Mama would react.

But Carmen was her usual warm, funny self, and within minutes she and Mama were laughing about something. When we were getting ready to leave, Carmen pulled me aside.

"Dale, your mom is wonderful. She asked me about my family, about my transition, about what it was like when I first came to group. And she listened - really listened. You can tell where you get your heart from."

The dinner party at Janet's house was the real test. Janet had invited six people from the support group - Carmen, David, Lisa (who's become an honorary member), Alex (who's been coming for eight months now), Maya (the teenager who came to group right after I shared my reconciliation story), and Jordan (the trans man who decided to call his sister).

I was terrified that Mama would be overwhelmed meeting so many transgender people at once, that she'd say something unintentionally hurtful, that she'd feel out of place.

Instead, she was perfect.

She asked thoughtful questions. She listened to people's stories without judgment. She thanked Maya for being brave enough to live authentically so young. She told David about a cousin of hers who'd always been "different" and how she wished she'd understood more about it at the time.

But the moment that made me cry was when Jordan started talking about calling his sister after hearing my story about reconciliation.

"It worked," he told Mama. "I called her, and she cried, and she said she'd been wanting to reach out but didn't know how. We're rebuilding our relationship because of what your daughter shared with us."

Mama reached across the table and took Jordan's hand. "I'm so glad," she said. "Every family deserves to heal when they can."

After dinner, Janet pulled me into the kitchen while Mama was looking at photo albums with the others.

"Dale, your mother is remarkable," she said. "Do you see how naturally she connects with people? Do you see how she's not trying to fix anyone or change anyone? She's just loving them."

"She's learning," I said.

"No, honey. She's not learning how to love. She already knows how to love. She's just learning how to love without fear."

The drive home was quiet. Mama seemed to be processing everything she'd seen and heard.

"Those are good people," she finally said. "Really good people."

"They are. They saved my life, Mama. When I had no family, they became my family."

"I'm grateful to them," she said. "I'm grateful they took care of my daughter when I couldn't."

Now she's asleep in my bed, and I'm on my couch, writing about the most wonderful day I've had in years. Tomorrow, we will go to church together - something I never thought would happen.

Tomorrow, she flies home, but she's not leaving the same person who came.

The girl in the mirror looks radiant tonight. She looks like someone whose worlds have collided beautifully, whose family - blood and chosen - has come together in love.

She looks like someone who's finally, completely, whole.

Tomorrow is the last day of Mama's visit, but it's not an ending. It's the beginning.

A beginning of a mother and daughter who finally see each other clearly, love each other fully, and belong to each other completely.

The girl in the mirror is home. All the way home.

Document 84: Diary Entry

Written by Dale Morrison
Dated: June 28, 2022

Something happened today that I'll never forget. Mama got to see me do what I was born to do, and I got to see her understand - really understand - who her daughter has become.

We were getting ready to leave Janet's house after the dinner party when my phone rang. I almost didn't answer it because I didn't want to be rude, but I recognized the number - it was Alex, the teenager who'd been coming to TransAtlanta meetings for about eight months.

"I'm sorry," I said to everyone. "This is one of the kids from group. I should take this."

I stepped into Janet's hallway, and Mama followed me, looking concerned.

"Dale?" Alex's voice was shaky, scared. "I'm sorry to call so late, but I didn't know who else to call."

"It's okay, Alex. What's happening?"

"My foster mom found out. About me being trans. Someone from school called her and told her they saw me at the support group meeting last week."

My heart sank. Alex had been placed in a conservative Christian foster home six months ago after aging out of the system. The family seemed nice enough, but Alex had been careful not to tell them about being transgender.

"What did she say?" I asked.

"She said I have to choose. I can either 'get right with God' and stop this 'transgender nonsense,'

- 325 -

or I have to find somewhere else to live. She gave me until tomorrow morning to decide."

I could hear Alex crying on the other end of the phone. Mama was watching my face, and I could see her piecing together what was happening.

"Alex, listen to me," I said, switching into my counselor voice. "You're going to be okay. We're going to figure this out. Are you safe tonight?"

"Yeah, she said I can stay tonight. But Dale, I don't have anywhere to go. I don't have any money. I don't know what to do."

I looked at Mama, who nodded toward Janet's living room. She understood that this was important.

"Alex, I want you to take some deep breaths with me, okay? In for four counts, hold for four, out for four. Can you do that?"

We breathed together over the phone while I thought quickly about resources.

"Now, I want you to remember what we've talked about in group. What do we know about your identity?"

"That... that it's not wrong," Alex said, voice still shaky but a little steadier.

"That's right. You are exactly who God made you to be. One person's inability to understand that doesn't change your truth. What else?"

"That I'm not alone."

"That's right. You have a whole community of people who love and support you. Janet, Carmen, me - we're all here for you. You're not facing this alone."

I spent the next twenty minutes talking Alex through the immediate crisis. I gave them Janet's emergency number and the number for a transgender-friendly housing program. I promised to call first thing in the morning to help coordinate temporary housing and longer-term support.

"Alex, I want you to remember something," I said as we were finishing the call. "You've survived everything that's brought you to this point. You're stronger than you know, braver than you feel, and more loved than you realize. This is scary, but you're going to get through it."

"Thank you, Dale. I don't know what I would do without you."

"You'll never have to find out. Get some sleep, and I'll call you first thing in the morning."

When I hung up, Mama was standing in the hallway, tears streaming down her face.

"What?" I asked, suddenly worried. "Are you okay?"

"Dale Elizabeth Morrison," she said, her voice thick with emotion. "Do you have any idea what I just witnessed?"

I was confused. "Mama, I'm sorry about the interruption. That was Alex, one of the teenagers in our support group. They're in crisis and—"

"Baby, stop." She took my hands. "I just watched my daughter save someone's life."

"I didn't save anyone's life. I just—"

"Yes, you did." She was crying harder now. "I watched you take a scared, desperate child who was about to lose their housing for being who they are, and I watched you help them breathe. I watched you remind them of their worth. I watched you give them hope when they had none."

She paused, wiping her eyes with her sleeve.

"I watched you be exactly who God called you to be."

That's when I started crying too.

"Dale, I need you to understand something," Mama continued. "I just heard you do what I should have done for you when you were Alex's age. I heard you tell a frightened child that they were exactly who God made them to be, that they weren't alone, that they were stronger than they knew."

She was right. Twenty minutes earlier, I'd given Alex everything I'd needed to hear when I was eighteen and terrified and sleeping on a bus to Atlanta.

"You turned your pain into purpose," she whispered. "You took everything that hurt you and used it to heal someone else. That's not just counseling, baby. That's ministry."

We stood in Janet's hallway, both of us crying, while the dinner party continued in the living room.

"I'm so proud of you," Mama said. "And I'm so sorry that you had to learn how to do that because no one did it for you."

"Mama—"

"No, let me say this. I failed you when you needed me most. But watching you just now, seeing how you show up for other people's children the way I should have shown up for you... I see that God didn't waste your pain. He used it to make you into someone who could save other people from drowning."

We rejoined the dinner party, but the mood had shifted. Janet had quietly explained to everyone what had happened, and they were all in crisis response mode, making calls and coordinating resources for Alex.

"This is what we do," Carmen explained to Mama. "This is what family does. When one of us is in crisis, all of us respond."

Mama watched as our chosen family mobilized to help a kid in need. She saw Janet make calls to emergency housing resources. She saw David offer to drive across town to pick up Alex if needed. She saw Maya, who's only seventeen herself, text other transgender teenagers to let them know about the emergency hotline.

"This is your ministry," Mama said to me as we were getting ready to leave. "This community, this work, this calling - this is your ministry."

She was right. I'd been thinking of my advocacy work as helping people, as giving back, as using my experiences to make a difference. But watching it through Mama's eyes, I realized it was more than that.

It was ministry. It was showing up for God's children who'd been told they weren't worthy of love. It offered grace to people who'd been given judgment. It was creating family for people whose families had abandoned them.

In the car on the way home, Mama was quiet for a long time.

"I need to tell you something," she finally said. "When your daddy was sick, toward the end, he asked me about you."

My breath caught. "He did?"

"He asked if I thought you were happy. If I thought you were safe. If I thought you'd found people who cared about you." She paused. "I told him I didn't know because I hadn't been brave enough to find out."

"Mama..."

"But now I know. You're not just happy and safe and loved. You're exactly who you were meant to be. And I think... I think your daddy would be proud of that, if he could see it."

When we got home, I called Janet to check on Alex. They'd found temporary housing for the next few days and were working on longer-term placement with a trans-friendly family.

"Dale," Janet said, "I want you to know that your mother spent the rest of the evening asking questions about how she could help support our work. She asked about volunteering, about donating, about what parents need to know to support their transgender children."

"Really?"

"She said watching you help Alex tonight showed her what she wanted to do with her second chance at being your mother. She wants to help other parents learn to love their children the way she's learning to love you."

The girl in the mirror looks different tonight. She looks like someone whose mother finally sees her calling, her gifts, her purpose. She looks like someone whose pain has been transformed into ministry, whose wounds have become wisdom.

She looks like someone whose mother is proud - not just of who she's become, but of how she's used her becoming to help others.

Tomorrow, we go to church together, and then Mama flies home. But she's not leaving the same person who came. She's leaving as someone who's seen her daughter's ministry firsthand.

She's leaving as someone who finally understands

that God didn't make a mistake when He made me.

She's leaving as someone who wants to help other parents see their children the way she's finally learned to see hers.

The girl in the mirror is beloved. Seen. Understood. Called. Supported.

The girl in the mirror is home.

Document 85: Diary Entry

Written by Dale Morrison

Dated: July 31, 2022

Today I took my mother to church for the first time in four years. The last time we were in a sanctuary together, I was being held down by deacons who thought they could pray the transgender out of me. Today, I walked into Riverside Community Church with my head held high, my mother's arm linked through mine.

I was nervous about this part of the weekend more than anything else. Church has been such a source of trauma for me, and even though I've been speaking at Riverside for six months now, bringing Mama felt different. More vulnerable. More loaded with history.

But Mama had specifically asked to go to church with me during her visit.

"I want to see where you worship," she said during one of our phone calls. "I want to understand how you've rebuilt your relationship with God after everything that happened."

Rev. Wilson had been excited when I told him Mama was coming.

"I'd love to meet the woman who raised such a remarkable daughter," he'd said. "And I think she'd love to see how her daughter is helping our congregation grow in love and understanding."

We got to Riverside at 9:45 AM for the 10 AM service. It's a beautiful church - contemporary but warm, with big windows that let in natural light and an altar that feels welcoming rather than intimidating. Nothing like the dark, imposing sanctuary of Cedar Ridge Baptist Church.

"This feels different," Mama said as we walked in. "Lighter somehow."

"Wait until you meet the people," I said.

And that's when it started. People I'd gotten to know over the past six months began greeting us, and I watched Mama's face change as she realized how welcome I was here.

"Dale!" called out Mrs. Patterson (no relation to Bishop Patterson from Millbrook, thankfully). "So good to see you! And you must be Dale's mother. We've heard so much about you."

"This is Margaret Morrison," I said, my voice filled with pride. "Mama, this is Mrs. Patterson. She coordinates the church's social justice ministry."

"Mrs. Morrison, your daughter has been such a blessing to our congregation," Mrs. Patterson said, taking Mama's hands. "Her talks about faith and inclusion have opened so many hearts, including mine."

Dr. Rodriguez, who chairs the theology committee, came over next.

"Dale, I was hoping you'd be here today. And Mrs. Morrison, what a pleasure to meet you. Your daughter has helped us understand that God's love is even bigger than we thought it was."

I watched Mama's eyes fill with tears as person after person told her how much my presence meant to them, how my story had changed their understanding, how my advocacy work was helping the church become more loving and inclusive.

"I never knew," she whispered to me as we found seats. "I never knew you were making such a difference."

The service began with contemporary worship music - guitars and drums, nothing like the traditional hymns I'd grown up with. But there was something familiar about it too. The joy, the reverence, the sense of community.

"This is how I always imagined church should feel," Mama said during the opening prayer. "Like everyone belongs here."

Rev. Wilson's sermon was about the woman at the well - the Samaritan woman who was shunned by her community but welcomed by Jesus. He talked about how Jesus crossed social boundaries to show love, how he didn't let other people's prejudices determine his compassion.

"Sometimes," Rev. Wilson said, looking directly at me and Mama, "God sends us people who challenge our assumptions about who is worthy of love. These people are gifts, even when they make us uncomfortable. They expand our understanding of God's grace."

I felt Mama squeeze my hand.

During the pastoral prayer, Rev. Wilson said something that made me cry: "We thank you, God, for sending us prophets and teachers in unexpected packages. Help us to recognize your love in all its forms and help us to love as widely and deeply as you love us."

After the service, Rev. Wilson made a point of coming over to us.

"Mrs. Morrison," he said, "thank you for sharing your daughter with us. She's taught us so much about what it means to love unconditionally."

"She's taught me that too," Mama said. "I'm still learning, but she's a patient teacher."

"The best teachers usually are," Rev. Wilson replied.

As we were leaving, Mama was quiet, processing everything she'd experienced.

"Dale," she said as we got in the car, "I need to apologize to you."

"For what?"

"For letting you think that God didn't love you. For letting you think that faith and your identity couldn't coexist." She was crying now. "I just spent an hour in a church where people love you exactly as you are."

"Mama—"

"No, let me finish. I let your father's fear and the church's ignorance convince me that God was disappointed in you. But God isn't disappointed in you, Dale. God is proud of you. And so am I."

We sat in the church parking lot, both of us crying.

"I want to do better," she said. "I want to learn more about inclusion, about how to support transgender people, about how to help other parents see their children the way I'm learning to see you."

"Mrs. Patterson mentioned that they have a group for parents of LGBTQ+ kids," I said. "Maybe you could connect with them, learn from other parents who've been on this journey."

"I'd like that," she said. "I'd like to help other parents find their way to love instead of fear."

Now Mama is packing for her flight home, and I'm sitting here thinking about everything that's happened this weekend. She came to Atlanta as a mother trying to understand her daughter. She's leaving as a woman who's seen God's love in action, who's witnessed ministry firsthand, who's ready to help other families find their way to acceptance.

The girl in the mirror looks different tonight. She looks like someone who's been blessed by her mother's presence, affirmed by her mother's love, and challenged by her mother's faith in her potential.

She looks like someone who might be called to something even bigger than she thought.

She looks like someone whose mother finally sees her exactly as God sees her - beloved, called, and worthy of celebration.

Tomorrow Mama flies home, but she's not leaving me. She's taking me with her in her heart, and I'm carrying her love with me as I step into whatever God has planned next.

The girl in the mirror is beloved. She's called. She's supported by both her chosen family and her birth family.

And she's ready to say yes to whatever God asks of her next.

Even if it's bigger and scarier and more wonderful than anything she's ever imagined.

The girl in the mirror is home. All the way home.

And now she's ready to help other people find their way home too.

Document 86: Airline Ticket
Written by Delta Airlines
Dated: August 1, 2022

DELTA AIR LINES ELECTRONIC BOARDING PASS

PASSENGER: MORRISON/MARGARET M (MRS) **FROM:** Atlanta, GA (ATL) - Hartsfield-Jackson **TO:** Montgomery, AL (MGM) - Regional Airport

FLIGHT: DL 1247

DATE: Monday, August 1, 2022

DEPARTURE: 3:45 PM (Gate A12)

ARRIVAL: 4:32 PM (Local Time)

SEAT: 14A (Window)

CONFIRMATION: R7KM9P

BOARDING GROUP: 2

BOARDING TIME: 3:15 PM

IMPORTANT REMINDERS:

- Arrive at gate 30 minutes before departure
- Valid ID required for boarding
- Carry-on restrictions apply

DALE'S HANDWRITTEN NOTE ON BOARDING PASS:

Thank you for the most beautiful weekend of my life. Thank you for seeing my world, loving my friends, and celebrating my calling. Thank you for being proud of who I've become.

I love you more than words can say.

Safe flight home. Call me when you land.
Your daughter, Dale 🤍

Document 87: Letter to Dale; Written on the plane

Written by Margaret Morrison

Dated: August 1, 2022 at 30,000 ft

Dale,

I'm flying home from the most eye-opening weekend of my life. Three days ago, I thought I was going to visit my daughter in Atlanta. Instead, I discovered that my daughter is exactly who God called her to be, and I've been blessed to witness her ministry firsthand.

I watched Dale save a teenager's life with a phone call. I watched her facilitate healing in a room full of people who society has rejected. I watched her be celebrated in a church for her gifts, her wisdom, her calling.

I met her chosen family - people who love her unconditionally, who've supported her through everything I failed to support her through. They welcomed me not because I deserved it, but because I'm Dale's mother. They showed me grace I don't deserve.

Earl, if you could see her now. If you could see what she built, who she's become, how many people she's helped··· I think even you would be proud.

I'm going home with work to do. I want to help other parents learn what I've learned. I want to keep other families from losing what we almost lost forever.

My daughter might be called to ministry. Real, official ministry. And I want to support her however I can.

The plane is landing soon. Dale made me promise to call as soon as I get home. For the first time in four years, I'm excited to tell my child about my day, to share my thoughts, to be her mother in all the ways I should have been all along.

God is good. Second chances are real. Love really can overcome fear.

And my daughter – my beautiful, gifted, called daughter – is going to change the world. I just know it.

Love,

Mom

Document 88: Email Correspondence

Written by Sarah James and Dale Morrison

Dated: October 15, 2022

TEXT MESSAGES – August 1, 2022

Margaret - 5:15 PM Landed safely. Thank you for the most wonderful weekend. I love you so much.

Dale - 5:16 PM I love you too Mama! So glad you came. Already missing you!

Margaret - 5:18 PM I keep thinking about what Rev Wilson said about seminary. Have you thought about it more?

Dale - 5:20 PM I have actually. It feels scary but right. Like maybe this is what I've been moving toward all along.

Margaret - 5:22 PM Then I think you should pray about it. And know that whatever you decide, I support you 100%.

Dale - 5:24 PM Thank you Mama. For everything. For this weekend, for loving my friends, for seeing my calling.

Margaret - 5:26 PM Thank you for showing me how to love without fear. You're an amazing daughter and an even better teacher. 🩶

Dale - 5:28 PM Talk tomorrow? Same time as always?

Margaret - 5:29 PM Wouldn't miss it. Sweet dreams baby girl. I'm so proud of you.

Dale - 5:30 PM Sweet dreams Mama. I love you. 🩶

Document 89: Email Correspondence

Written by Sarah James and Dale Morrison
Dated: October 15, 2022

EMAIL CORRESPONDENCE

FROM: Sarah.James@harpercollins.com
TO: dalemorrison2001@hotmail.com
DATE: October 15, 2022, 9:47 AM
SUBJECT: Book Proposal - HarperCollins Interest

Dear Ms. Morrison,

I hope this email finds you well. My name is Sarah James, and I'm a Senior Editor at HarperCollins Publishers. I've been following your advocacy work with great interest, particularly after reading your interviews in the Atlanta Journal-Constitution and seeing your recent appearance on The Oprah Winfrey Show.

Your story of family reconciliation and faith-based healing has resonated with readers across the country, and we believe it could reach an even wider audience in book form. We would like to discuss the possibility of you writing a memoir for HarperCollins.

Based on our preliminary discussions, we're envisioning a book that tells your complete story - from your childhood in Alabama through your transition, family estrangement, advocacy work, and eventual reconciliation with your mother. We're particularly interested in your unique perspective on faith and LGBTQ+ identity, as well as your insights on "complicated grief" and family healing.

We believe this book could serve as both inspiration and practical guidance for families navigating similar challenges. The market for authentic, hopeful memoirs in this space is significant and growing.

If you're interested in exploring this opportunity, I'd love to schedule a phone call to discuss our vision for the project and answer any questions you might have. We're prepared to move quickly on this if there's mutual interest.

I can be reached at (212) 555-0134 or at this email address. I look forward to hearing from you soon.

Best regards,

Sarah James Senior Editor,

Inspirational Memoirs HarperCollins Publishers

10 East 53rd Street

New York, NY 10022

Document 90: Diary Entry

Written by Dale Morrison
Dated: October 16, 2022

I can't believe I'm going to be a published author. Dale Morrison, the girl who barely graduated high school, is going to have a book in bookstores across America.

Sarah James seems wonderful - very respectful, very understanding of what this story means to the transgender community. She emphasized that they want the real story, not a sanitized version.

"People need to see the messy parts," she said. "That's what makes healing believable."

The advance is life-changing money. I could quit my job at Zenith and write full-time. I could go to seminary without worrying about debt. I could help TransAtlanta expand their programs.

But more than the money, this is a chance to reach families I could never reach through speaking engagements. Parents who would never come to a conference might pick up a book from a bookstore. Kids who feel hopeless might find it in a library.

I'm terrified of writing 90,000 words about my life. What if I run out of things to say? What if my story isn't interesting enough for a whole book? What if I can't write well enough?

But I keep thinking about that woman in Dallas whose daughter died. Maybe if this book had existed two years ago, her daughter would still be alive. Maybe some parents will read it and choose love over fear. Maybe some kids will read it and choose hope over despair.

That's worth being scared for.
That's worth everything.
The girl in the mirror looks like an author tonight.
She's still getting used to it.

Document 91: Book Deal Letter

Written by Sarah James
Dated: October 20, 2022

FORMAL CONTRACT LETTER
HARPERCOLLINS PUBLISHERS
10 East 53rd Street
New York, NY 10022

Ms. Dale Morrison
234 Peachtree Street, Apt 3B
Atlanta, GA 30309

Dear Ms. Morrison,

Following our productive phone conversation on June October 18, 2022, I'm pleased to present you with our formal offer for your memoir project, tentatively titled "A Woman Named Dales: In the Shadows pf Grace."

CONTRACT TERMS:

Book Details:

- Length: 80,000-100,000 words
- Delivery Date: October 2024
- Publication Date: June 2025
- Format: Hardcover, paperback, and digital editions

Financial Terms:

- Advance: $225,000 (paid in three installments)
  - $75,000 upon signing
  - $75,000 upon delivery of final manuscript

- $75,000 upon publication

- Royalties: 10% of net receipts for hardcover, 7.5% for paperback
- Digital rights: 25% of net receipts

Marketing Support:
- National book tour (15-20 cities)
- National media campaign
- Social media promotion
- Potential tie-ins with your existing speaking engagements

Editorial Support:
- Dedicated editor (Sarah James)
- Cover design and marketing materials
- Research assistance if needed

Rights:
- Publisher retains hardcover, paperback, and digital rights
- Author retains film/TV rights
- International rights to be negotiated separately
- Audio book rights included

Additional Considerations:
- Author maintains the right to review and approve all marketing materials
- Publisher agrees to sensitivity review by LGBTQ+ advocacy organizations
- Percentage of proceeds may be donated to TransAtlanta (author's choice)

Timeline:
- Contract execution: By October 31, 2022
- First draft completion: August 30, 2023

- Final manuscript delivery: October 31, 2024
- Publication: June 2025

Ms. Morrison, we believe your story has the potential to change lives and heal families across America. Your unique voice - combining personal narrative with practical wisdom - is exactly what readers are seeking at this moment.

We're committed to supporting you throughout this process and ensuring that your message reaches the widest possible audience. Our marketing team is already excited about the possibilities for promoting this book through faith-based and LGBTQ+ communities, as well as mainstream media.

Please review the attached contract carefully. We've also included a detailed outline template to help you structure your narrative, though you should feel free to organize the material in whatever way feels most authentic to your experience.

If you have any questions or concerns, please don't hesitate to contact me directly at (212) 555-0134. We're hoping to have this contract finalized by the end of the month so we can begin the exciting work of bringing your story to the world.

Thank you for considering HarperCollins as your publishing partner. We believe this book will have a significant impact on countless readers who need to hear your message of hope and healing.

Looking forward to collaborating with you,
Sarah James, Senior Editor,
Inspirational Memoirs
HarperCollins Publishers
Enclosures:

- Full contract
- Sample marketing timeline
- Author guidelines and expectations

Document 92: Diary Entry

Written by Dale Morrison
Dated: October 20, 2022

I got offered a book deal today. A real book deal, with a real publisher, with real money attached to it.

The editor from HarperCollins called this morning while I was at work. She'd read both of my newspaper interviews and seen the transcript from my Oprah appearance last month. She wants me to write a memoir about my journey - from rejection to reconciliation, from survival to advocacy.

"We think your story could help thousands of families," she said. "Maybe hundreds of thousands."

The advance they're offering is more money than I make in two years at Zenith. Enough to quit my job and write full-time. Enough to go to seminary without worrying about student loans. Enough to help TransAtlanta expand their programs.

I should be thrilled. Six months ago, I was just Dale Morrison, administrative assistant and part-time advocate. Now I'm getting calls from publishers, speaking at conferences across the country, consulting with organizations about inclusion policies. My calendar is booked through October with speaking engagements.

But sitting here tonight, I feel... overwhelmed. And a little lost.

This morning I was Dale, the girl who helps run support groups and works a steady job. Tonight, I'm Dale Morrison, potential author, national spokesperson, "transgender advocate and reconciliation expert" as the booking agents call me.

I don't know how to be that person.

Success started slowly. After the second newspaper interview, I got invited to speak at three conferences. Then five. Then ten. The speaking fees started small but have grown to the point where I make more from one weekend conference than I used to make in a month.

Companies are hiring me to train their HR departments. Churches are paying me to help them become more inclusive. Universities want me to lecture about faith and identity. I've been on six radio shows, three TV programs, and that segment on Oprah that aired to 20 million people.

Everyone wants the Dale Morrison story. Everyone wants to know how I turned rejection into reconciliation, how I maintained my faith, how my family healed. They want a hopeful ending, inspiration, the proof that love can overcome fear.

And I want to give it to them. I really do. But I'm starting to feel like I'm becoming a symbol instead of a person.

Last week at a conference in Dallas, a woman came up to me after my talk and said, "You're so lucky your story has a happy ending. My transgender daughter killed herself two years ago. I wish she could have been strong like you."

I didn't know what to say. How do you tell someone that you're not stronger than their daughter, just luckier? How do you explain that the only difference between me and her child might have been timing, or geography, or one person showing up at the right moment?

I've been having a hard time at the TransAtlanta meetings lately. Not because the people there aren't supportive - they're thrilled about my success. But I feel like I can't be vulnerable anymore. I can't share my struggles or fears because people look at me like I should have figured it out.

"Dale's the success story," I heard Maya say to a new member last week. "If you want to see what's possible, look at Dale."

But I don't feel like a success story. I feel like a scared 21-year-old who's been asked to represent an entire community, who's supposed to have answers for situations she's never faced, who's expected to be perpetually grateful and endlessly inspiring.

Lisa noticed I've been different. We had lunch yesterday, and she asked me point-blank: "Are you okay? You seem exhausted."

"I am exhausted," I admitted. "I love the work, I love helping people, but I feel like I'm losing myself in it. Everyone wants Dale Morrison the advocate. I don't know how to just be Dale anymore."

"You know what I think?" Lisa said. "I think you need to turn down some speaking engagements. I think you need to remember that you can't save everyone, and you don't have to try."

She's right, but it's hard. Every time I get a call from a desperate parent or a suicidal teenager, every time someone tells me my story gives them hope, I feel obligated to say yes. How do you turn down the opportunity to save someone's life?

But I'm burning out. I haven't written in my diary consistently in two months because I'm always traveling or preparing talks or responding to emails from people who need help. I missed my weekly call with Mama twice last month because of conference schedules. I haven't been to my own therapy appointments in three weeks.

The money is nice - I'll admit that. For the first time in my life, I'm not worried about rent or groceries. I can afford nice clothes for speaking engagements, I can take Mama out to dinner when she visits, I can donate to TransAtlanta and other organizations.

But I'm also starting to understand something I never expected: success can be as isolating as failure, just in different ways.

When I was broken and unknown, I felt like no one saw me. Now that I'm successful and recognized, I feel like everyone sees me, but no one knows me. They see Dale Morrison as the advocate, the inspiration, the symbol of hope. They don't see Dale as the person who still gets scared, who still struggles, who still needs support sometimes.

Patricia at work has been incredibly understanding. She's given me flexible time off for speaking engagements and told me my job will be there when I figure out what I want to do. But I can see the writing on the wall - I can't keep doing both. I'm going to have to choose between the security of a steady job and the uncertainty of full-time advocacy.

The book deal feels like a sign. Maybe this is what I'm supposed to do. Maybe God is opening this door so I can help more people, reach more families, create more healing.

But I'm scared of losing the parts of my life that keep me grounded. I'm scared of becoming so focused on helping everyone else that I forget to take care of myself. I'm scared of becoming famous for my trauma instead of being known for my humanity.

Dr. Reynolds, when I finally made it to a therapy

appointment last week, said something that stuck with me: "Dale, you've spent so much energy learning to be seen that you might have forgotten how to be still."

She's right. I've gone from invisible to highly visible almost overnight, and I don't know how to find the balance.

Carmen called me tonight after I told her about the book offer.

"Dale, this is incredible! You could help so many people with a book."

"I know," I said. "But I'm scared I'm going to lose myself in all of this."

"What do you mean?"

"I mean everyone wants me to be the success story, the inspiration, the proof that everything works out. But what if I have bad days? What if my relationship with my mom isn't perfect? What if I make mistakes? What if I'm just human?"

Carmen was quiet for a long time. "Dale, maybe that's exactly what people need to see. Maybe they need to know that success doesn't mean perfection, that healing doesn't mean never struggling again."

Maybe she's right. Maybe the book could be honest about the messy parts, the ongoing challenges, the reality that healing is a process, not a destination.

The girl in the mirror looks tired tonight. She looks like someone who's been given more than she asked for and doesn't quite know what to do with it. She looks successful and overwhelmed, grateful and scared, hopeful and exhausted all at the same time.

She looks like someone who needs to make some decisions about what kind of life she wants to build with this unexpected platform she's been given.

Tomorrow, I need to call the editor back about the book deal. I need to decide whether I'm ready to quit my job and become a full-time author and speaker. I need to figure out how to stay grounded while reaching for opportunities I never imagined.

But tonight, I'm just going to be Dale. Not Dale Morrison the advocate or the inspiration or the symbol. Just Dale, sitting in her apartment, writing in her diary, trying to figure out how to manage success with the same grace she learned to handle rejection.

The girl in the mirror is blessed. She knows that. She's grateful for every opportunity, every platform, every chance to help people heal.

She just needs to remember that she's still a person worthy of love and care, even when she's not inspiring anyone, even when she's not changing the world.

She needs to remember that being human isn't a failure. It's the whole point.

The girl in the mirror is learning how to be successful without losing herself.

It's harder than she thought it would be.

But she's going to figure it out.

She always does.

Document 93: Diary Entry

Written by Dale Morrison

Dated: October 22, 2022

I signed the book contract today. My hands were shaking as I wrote my name on each page, but I did it.

"A Woman Named Dale: In the Shadows of Grace" will be published by HarperCollins in spring/summer 2025. 24 months to write the book that tells my story - the whole story, not just the inspiring parts.

The decision took me a week of soul-searching, phone calls, and sleepless nights. But I finally realized something: I've been given this platform for a reason, and it would be selfish to turn away from it just because it feels overwhelming.

The phone calls helped me see clearly.

Mama cried when I called her about the offer.

"Dale, honey, this means your story is going to help so many families. Families like ours, who lost their way but found their way back. You have to do this."

Dr. Reynolds was more cautious. "This is wonderful, Dale, but I want you to think about what it means to put your entire life story in print. Your trauma, your healing, your family's mistakes - it will all be public forever. Are you ready for that level of exposure?"

That gave me pause. Am I ready for strangers to read about the worst night of my life at Cedar Ridge Baptist Church? About Dad's rejection? About sleeping on a bus with $3,200 and a heart full of terror? About those first desperate weeks in Atlanta?

But then I called Janet, and she said something that changed my perspective: "Dale, you've been telling pieces of your story to help people heal for months now. This just means you can help more people at once. And maybe, just maybe, some kid who's about to give up will find your book in a library and realize they're not alone."

That's when I knew I had to say yes.

Lisa was practical, as always. "Get a lawyer to look at the contract," she said. "And Dale? Don't quit your job until you've actually written the book. Writing is hard work, and you need security while you figure out if you can do this."

She's right. Patricia at Zenith has agreed to let me work part-time while I write. Twenty-five hours a week instead of forty, which gives me time to write but keeps me grounded in normal life.

Carmen had the best reaction. "Girl, you're going to be on bookshelves! In Barnes & Noble! I'm going to buy ten copies just to see your name in print."

But it was Sarah's vision for the book that really convinced me. When we talked on the phone yesterday, she said, "Dale, we don't want a sanitized inspiration story. We want the real story - the pain, the struggle, the setbacks, the ongoing work of healing. People need to see that reconciliation isn't a fairy tale ending. It's daily choice to keep loving even when it's hard."

That's exactly what I want to write. Not "Dale Morrison's Amazing Success Story" but "Dale Morrison's Complicated Human Story." The story of a girl who got lucky in some ways and unlucky in others, who made mistakes and learned from them, who found healing not because she was special but because she refused to give up on love.

I want to write about Evelyn, the woman who gave me candy wrapped in blue paper and told me I wasn't unholy for being complicated. I want to write about the night at Cedar Ridge Baptist Church when they tried to pray the transgender out of me. I want to write about sleeping in the bus station on my first night in Atlanta. I want to write about finding TransAtlanta, about meeting Lisa, about learning to see myself through loving eyes.

I want to write about Dad's funeral, about being erased from his obituary, about Mama's courage to defend me in front of the whole community. I want to write about our reconciliation - not as a perfect happy ending, but as the beginning of learning to love each other honestly.

Most of all, I want to write about complicated grace. The grace that lets you forgive someone who never apologized. The grace that lets you love someone who couldn't love you back. The grace that lets you keep hoping for healing even when healing seems impossible.

The advance is $225,000. More money than I've ever seen in my life. The first check, $75,000, will be deposited when they receive my signed contract.

I want to give $5,000 to TransAtlanta. They saved my life, and now I can help them save other lives. Janet almost cried when I told her.

"Dale, that's incredibly generous, but you don't have to—"

"Yes, I do," I said. "You gave me a family when I didn't have one. You gave me hope when I had none.

You gave me the skills to help other people heal. This money came from telling my story, and my story doesn't exist without TransAtlanta."

The writing process terrifies me. Eighty thousand words about my life? I've never written anything longer than a five-page college paper. But Sarah says they'll provide support - an editor to help structure the narrative, research assistance if I need it, professional guidance through the whole process.

"Most first-time authors feel overwhelmed," she said. "But you've been telling your story for months. You know what resonates with people. Trust yourself."

The deadline is October 2024. 24 months to excavate my entire life, to make sense of pain and healing, to find the words that might help other families find their way back to each other.

Eighteen months to write the book I wish had existed when I was eighteen and terrified and alone.

The girl in the mirror looks different tonight. She looks like someone who's about to undertake the biggest challenge of her life. She looks scared and excited and determined all at once.

She looks like an author.

Tomorrow, I will start writing. Tomorrow, I begin the work of turning my life into something that might save someone else's life.

The girl in the mirror is ready.

She's been getting ready for this her whole life, even though she didn't know it.

Time to find out what grace looks like on the page.

Time to find out if complicated stories can become

healing stories when they're told with love.
The girl in the mirror believes they can.
She's about to prove it.

Document 94: Phone Call Transcript

Written by Bellsouth Mobile
Dated: October 23, 2022

PHONE CALL TRANSCRIPT Dale Morrison & Margaret Morrison October 23, 2022 - 7:30 PM

Dale: Mama? Are you sitting down?

Margaret: Well, I am now. What's wrong? You sound funny.

Dale: Nothing's wrong. Something's... something's really good actually. I got a call today from a publisher. From HarperCollins.

Margaret: HarperCollins? The book people?

Dale: Yes, the book people. Mama, they want to publish my story. They want me to write a book about everything - about leaving Alabama, about transitioning, about our reconciliation. Everything.

[Long pause]

Margaret: Dale Elizabeth Morrison.

Dale: Yes ma'am?

Margaret: Are you telling me that my daughter is going to be a published author?

Dale: If I say yes to their offer, then... yes. Yes, I am.

Dale: Mama? Are you okay? Why are you crying?

Margaret: I'm more than okay, baby. I'm so proud I can't even find the words. A book! A real book with your name on it!

Dale: It's scary, Mama. They want me to tell the whole story. The good parts and the hard parts. The parts about Dad, about the church, about... everything.

Margaret: Good. People need to hear the whole story. People need to understand what happens when families let fear win, and what happens when they choose to love instead.

Dale: But Mama, that means writing about Dad's rejection, about the night at church, about us not talking for three years. Are you okay with the whole world knowing about our mistakes?

Margaret: Honey, if our mistakes can help other families not make the same ones, then yes. Absolutely yes. Your daddy's gone, and he can't be hurt by what's written about him. But there are fathers living out there who might read your book and realize they still have time to love their children.

Dale: I didn't expect you to be so supportive.

Margaret: Dale, three months ago I watched you help a

suicidal teenager find hope with a phone call. I've seen what happens when you tell your story. If a book means you can help more people like that, then I think it's exactly what God wants you to do.

Dale: The money is... it's a lot of money, Mama.

Margaret: How much?

Dale: Seventy-five thousand dollars.

[Long pause]

Margaret: Sweet Jesus.

Dale: I know, right? I could quit my job and write full-time. I could go to seminary. I could buy a house.

Margaret: You could do all of that. But Dale, let me tell you something - don't you go spending that money before you've earned it. Writing a book is hard work. You make sure you can actually do it before you go make big life changes.

Dale: Yes ma'am. Lisa said the same thing.

Margaret: Lisa's got good sense. So, what's the book going to be called?

Dale: "Complicated Grace: A Daughter's Journey from Rejection to Reconciliation."

Margaret: That's perfect. That's exactly what we've been living - complicated grace.

Dale: Mama, I need to ask you something. The book is going to include our story - our reconciliation, your visit to Atlanta, how we rebuilt our relationship. Are you comfortable with that being public?

Margaret: Dale, our story is a miracle. If it can help other mothers find their way back to their children, then I want the whole world to know about it.

Dale: Even the parts where you made mistakes?

Margaret: Especially those parts. Honey, I'm not ashamed of making mistakes. I'm ashamed of how long it took me to fix them. If some other mother reads about my failures and decides to do better, then my failures served a purpose.

Dale: You know people in Millbrook are going to read this book, right? People from Cedar Ridge Baptist Church, people who knew Dad.

Margaret: Let them read it. Let them see what their judgment cost our family and let them see what grace gave us back. Maybe some of them will learn something.

Dale: What if Bishop Patterson gets upset about how I write about the church?

Margaret: [firmly] Bishop Patterson had his chance to

show Christian love to a child in crisis, and he failed. If he doesn't like how that looks in print, maybe he should have acted differently.

Dale: Mama, you sound so... strong. So sure.

Margaret: I am sure. I'm sure that God gave you this gift for a reason. I'm sure that your story needs to be told. And I'm sure that I'm proud to be your mother, whether you write a book or not.

Dale: I love you so much.

Margaret: I love you too, baby. Now, when do you have to give them an answer?

Dale: They want to know by the end of next week.

Margaret: And what's your heart telling you?

Dale: [long pause] My heart is telling me that scared eighteen-year-old girl who got on a bus with three thousand dollars, and a prayer needs someone to write her story. She needs someone to tell the world that she mattered, that her pain had purpose, that her healing was possible.

Margaret: Then you write that story, Dale. You write it for her, and for every other scared kid who needs to know they're not alone.

Dale: What if I can't do it? What if I'm not good enough to write a whole book?

Margaret: Dale Elizabeth, you've been telling stories your whole life. You told me the story of who you really were when you were just a child. You told your chosen family the story of where you came from. You told me the story of forgiveness when your daddy died. You know how to tell stories that heal people.

Dale: How did I get so lucky to have you as my mother?

Margaret: We both got lucky, baby. We got lucky that love was stronger than fear, that grace was bigger than our mistakes, that it's never too late to come home to each other.

Dale: That's going to be in the book, you know. That conversation.

Margaret: Good. Let people know that miracles still happen. Let them know that families can heal. Let them know that sometimes the best thing you can do with your pain is turn it into someone else's hope.

Dale: I think I'm going to say yes.

Margaret: I think you should. I think this is what you've been moving toward your whole life.

Dale: Will you help me? When I'm writing about our story, will you tell me if I get it right?

Margaret: Of course I will. We'll write it together - the story of how a mother and daughter found their way back to each other.

Dale: Mama?

Margaret: Yes, baby?

Dale: Thank you for becoming the mother I needed you to be.

Margaret: Thank you for waiting for me to figure out how to love you right.

Dale: I'll always wait for you, Mama. That's what daughters do.

Margaret: And I'll always fight for you now. That's what mothers do.

Dale: I love you.

Margaret: I love you too, my sweet girl. My daughter, the author.

Dale: [laughing] I like the sound of that.

Margaret: So, do I. So, do I.

Document 95: Diary Entry

Written by Bellsouth Mobile

Dated: November 10, 2022

I'm sitting here staring at a check for $75,000 made out to Dale Elizabeth Morrison, and I can't stop crying.

It came in the mail today with a letter from Mama. When I saw the envelope from Morrison Construction Company, I thought it was probably some paperwork Dad had left behind that needed my signature. I almost didn't open it right away.

I should have known better. Mama doesn't do anything halfway.

The letter was written in her careful handwriting:

My dearest Dale,

I've been thinking about your book and your ministry work, and I realize you need more than just my emotional support. You need financial freedom to pursue what God is calling you to do.

Morrison Construction Company has been in our family for five generations. Your great-great-grandfather started it in 1897, and every Morrison man since then has worked to build its reputation. We've always been known for quality work, fair dealing, and honest business practices.

After your father died, everyone expected me to hand the company over to his brother Joe or maybe sell it to the employees. But the truth is, it belongs to you. You're the next generation. You're a Morrison.

I know you don't want to run a construction company, and honestly, I don't want to run it either. So, I sold it to the employees - they know the business, they care about the reputation, and they'll treat our customers right.

The enclosed check is your inheritance, baby. It's five generations of Morrison hard work, converted into freedom for you to do the work you were born to do.

Don't you dare feel guilty about this. Don't you dare think you don't deserve it. You are building something more important than houses and office buildings. You are building hope. You are building healing. You are building bridges between families and between people and God.

Use this money to write your book without worry. Use it to go to seminary if that's what God calls you to do. Use it to help TransAtlanta serve more people. Use it to buy yourself a house where you can host gatherings and create community.

Or use it to sit still for a while and figure out what comes next. You've been through more in 20 years than most people go through in a lifetime. You've earned the right to breathe.

I love you, and I'm proud of you, and I believe in what you're building.

Your mother, Margaret Morrison

PS - The employees wanted me to tell you that they're proud to carry on the Morrison *name. They know about your work, and they think you're a credit to the family.*

I called her immediately, of course. I was sobbing so hard I could barely speak.

"Mama, I can't accept this. This is your security, your future—"

"Dale Elizabeth Morrison, don't you dare tell me what I can and can't do with my own money," she interrupted. "That company was built on the backs of Morrison men for five generations. Well, you're a Morrison, and you're building something that matters more than anything we've ever built."

"But Mama, the family legacy—"

"Baby, you ARE the family legacy now. You're taking the Morrison name places it's never been. You're making it mean something it never meant before."

She paused, and I could hear her getting emotional.

"Your great-great-grandfather built houses so families would have shelter. Your great-grandfather built churches so communities would have places to worship. Your grandfather built schools so children would have places to learn. Your father built hospitals and office buildings so people could work and heal."

"And you," she continued, her voice getting stronger, "you're building hope. You're building acceptance. You're building love where there used to be fear. That's not less than what they did, Dale. That's more."

I didn't know what to say. I've never had this kind of money. I've never had the kind of freedom that comes with not having to worry about rent or groceries or whether I can afford to take unpaid time off to write.

"What am I supposed to do with all this?" I asked.

"Whatever God tells you to do with it," she said simply. "But Dale, let me tell you what I hope you'll do first."

"What's that?"

"I hope you'll quit worrying about money and focus on your calling. I hope you'll write the most beautiful, honest book you can write. I hope you'll help more families find their way back to each other. And I hope you'll remember that you're not just Dale Morrison anymore - you're Dale Morrison, representative of five generations of people who believed in building things that last."

After we hung up, I sat in my apartment for two hours just looking at the check. A quarter of a million dollars. More money than I ever imagined having.

But more than the money, it's what the money represents. It's Mama's complete belief in me and my work. It's her recognition that what I'm doing matters. It's her investment in my future and in the people I'm trying to help.

I called Lisa, because I had to tell someone.

"Dale, oh my God! Your mom sold the family business for you?"

"She said I'm building something more important than construction."

"She's right. Dale, do you realize what this means? You can write your book without any financial pressure. You can take time to really think about seminary. You can help TransAtlanta in ways you never could before."

She's right. I've been so focused on the overwhelming nature of the gift that I haven't thought about the opportunities it creates.

I could give TransAtlanta enough money to expand their programming significantly. I could create a scholarship fund for transgender young people who want to go to college. I could buy a house with space for support group meetings and community gatherings.

Or I could just breathe for a while. For the first time in my adult life, I could make decisions based on calling rather than survival.

I called Janet next.

"Dale, this is incredible. Your mother just gave you the freedom to become who you're truly meant to be."

"I don't even know what that looks like yet."

"That's okay. You have time to figure it out now. You have the luxury of discernment."

Tonight, I'm going to call Dr. Reynolds to talk about how to handle this kind of sudden wealth responsibly. I want to make sure I'm making decisions from a healthy place, not from overwhelm or guilt.

But right now, I'm just sitting here, grateful. Grateful for a mother who sees my calling so clearly that she'd sell a five-generation family business to support it. I am grateful for the freedom to write my book without worrying about paying rent. Grateful for the opportunity to help TransAtlanta serve more people.

Grateful for the Morrison name and what it's always meant - building things that last.

The girl in the mirror looks different tonight. She looks like someone who's been trusted with something precious. She looks like someone whose family believes in her completely.

She looks like someone who's been given the freedom to become exactly who God created her to be.

Tomorrow I'm going to start making a plan. A plan for the book, for my education, for my ministry, for my future. A plan that honors both where I came from and where I'm going.

But tonight, I'm just going to sit here and feel loved. Loved by a mother who sold everything to invest in her daughter's dreams. Loved by a family legacy that's been transformed into something new and beautiful.

The girl in the mirror is wealthy now. Not just in money, but in love, in support, in possibility.

She's ready to build something that will last for generations.

She's ready to make the Morrison name mean something even more beautiful than it ever meant before.

The girl in the mirror is free.

And freedom, it turns out, feels like the most precious gift of all.

Document 96: Letter to Janet and the TransAtlanta Family

Written by Dale Morrison

Dated: December 20, 2022

Dear Janet and the TransAtlanta Family,

I need to update you on something I promised a few months ago. When I got my book advance, I told Janet I wanted to donate $5,000 to TransAtlanta to help expand our programming.

I'm writing to apologize because I can no longer make that donation.

I can't donate $5,000 because I want to donate $15,000 instead.

My mother recently sold our family's construction company and gave me the proceeds. She said I'm building something more important than buildings - I'm building hope. She's right, and TransAtlanta is where I learned how to build hope from the ground up.

This organization saved my life. You gave me family when I didn't have one. You taught me that my pain could have purpose. You showed me how to turn survival into service.

The enclosed check represents five generations of Morrison family work, now transformed into support for the work we do together. Use it to expand the youth program, to hire more staff, to reach more families, to save more lives.

Use it to build hope.

With all my love and gratitude,
Dale Morrison

PS - Janet, you once told me that we're not just surviving anymore - we're thriving. This donation is proof that you were right.

Document 97: Real Estate Contract
Written by Jadyn Jones
Dated: December 30, 2022

PURCHASE AND SALE AGREEMENT
Georgia Association of Realtors®

PROPERTY: 1847 Briarcliff Road NE, Atlanta, GA 30306

BUYER: Dale Elizabeth Morrison

SELLER: Robert and Susan Chen

PURCHASE PRICE: $385,000.00

DOWN PAYMENT: $50,000.00

CLOSING DATE: December 30, 2022

PROPERTY FEATURES:

- 3 bedrooms, 2.5 bathrooms
- 2,100 square feet
- Large living room with fireplace
- Guest suite with private entrance
- Home office with built-in bookcases
- Screened back porch
- Quiet neighborhood, walking distance to Virginia-Highland

FINANCING: 30-year conventional mortgage, $385,000 loan amount

LENDER: SunTrust Bank at 6.25% interest

CONTINGENCIES SATISFIED:

Home inspection completed December 15, 2022

Financing approved December 1, 2022

Appraisal: $427,000 (December 15, 2022)

SIGNATURE (buyer): *Dale Morrison*
Date: 12/30/2022

SIGNATURE (relator): *Jacob Hayes*
Date: 12/30/2022

Document 98: Diary Entry

Written by Dale Morrison
Dated: December 30, 2022

Finally - a real home! Room for Mama when she visits, office space for writing, and a guest room where she can have her morning coffee and watch the birds.

The Morrison family is putting down roots in Atlanta.

Closing in two weeks. I can't believe I'm going to be a homeowner at 20 years old.

This house feels like the beginning of something beautiful.

Document 99: Foreword of New Book

Written by Dale Morrison

Dated: May 9, 2025

PUBLISHED BOOK
A WOMAN NAMED DALE
In the Shadows of Grace

By Dale Morrison

FOREWORD

Some people are born loud. I was born written.

From the time I could hold a pencil, I was writing myself into existence. First in crayons on construction paper, then in ballpoint pens in school notebooks, finally in careful cursive in journals I hid under my mattress. I wrote because I had to. I wrote because the girl living inside my body had things to say that my voice couldn't yet speak.

I wrote myself through childhood in small-town Alabama, where being different was dangerous and being different in the way I was different was unthinkable. I wrote myself through adolescence, when my body betrayed my spirit and my family couldn't understand why their son was disappearing before their eyes. I wrote myself through the night they tried to pray the girl out of me, through the morning I packed everything I owned in a duffel bag, through the afternoon I bought a one-way ticket to anywhere that wasn't there.

I wrote myself onto a Greyhound bus with $3,200 and a heart full of terror and hope. I wrote myself into Atlanta, into a tiny apartment, into a job that paid just enough to keep me alive while I figured out how to live.

I wrote myself into friendship, into family, into love. I wrote myself through transition - not just the physical one, but the spiritual one, the emotional one, the long journey from survival to joy.

I wrote myself through three years of silence from the family that raised me, through the kind of grief that has no name because the person you're mourning is still alive. I wrote myself through forgiveness - the kind that has to be chosen over and over again, the kind that doesn't wait for apologies, the kind that loves people exactly as they are even when they can't love you back.

I wrote myself back into my mother's heart and she wrote herself back to mine. Together, we wrote a new story about what family means, about what love looks like when it chooses courage over fear.

But mostly, I wrote myself home. Home to my body, home to my spirit, home to my calling, home to the truth that was always there waiting for me to be brave enough to live it.

This book is the story of a girl who wrote herself into existence and discovered that she had been real all along. It's the story of rejection and reconciliation, of broken places that heal stronger, of grace that shows up in the most unexpected packages. It's the story of what happens when you refuse to let other people's fear determine your future.

It's the story of a woman named Dale, and how she learned that being born different isn't a mistake - it's a calling.

Some people are born loud, demanding attention, taking up space, making noise until the world has no choice but to notice them.

I was born written, quiet but persistent, putting words on paper until those words became life, until that life became a story, until that story became a bridge for other people trying to find their way home.

This is that bridge.

Welcome to my story. Welcome to your story. Welcome home.

Dale Morrison

Atlanta, GA
May 9, 2025

ACKNOWLEDGEMENTS

This book would not exist without the generosity, wisdom, and courage of many people who helped bring Dale's story to life.

To my sensitivity readers, who shared their lived experiences with grace and honesty—thank you for trusting me with your stories and for guiding me toward authenticity. Your voices made this book better, truer, and more worthy of the community it hopes to serve.

To the online LGBTQ+ archives and organizations—this work stands on the foundation you built with your courage.

To my writing community, who listened to endless readings of diary entries and TikTok posts, who helped me understand the difference between documents and scenes, and who never once suggested I write something easier—your faith in this story sustained me through every revision.

To the librarians and archivists throughout my life who showed me how documents tell the deepest truths, and to the families who have walked similar journeys and shared their wisdom along the way.

To my students, who teach me daily about resilience, authenticity, and the power of finding your voice on the page.

To my children, who gave me space to disappear into Dale's world for months at a time, who brought me snacks during long writing sessions, fed the dog when I forgot, and who never stopped believing their mom was writing something important. You are my greatest teachers and my biggest cheerleaders.

And to my best friend, my husband, who was willing to stand still at random moments while I shared my fears with writing this story. He took over dinner duties when I was deep in documents, and never once questioned why I needed to tell this story. Thank you for being my first reader, my constant support, and my home. This book is better because you believed in it from the very first page.

What if there was a woman named Dale?

Finally, to every family still writing their way back to each other—may you find the grace to see past fear to love. Know God's love always wins in the end.

AUTHOR'S NOTE

This book began with a simple question: What there was a woman named Dale?

As a high school English teacher, I spend my days helping students find their voices on the page. I've learned that sometimes the most honest writing happens when we think no one is reading—in journals, in letters never sent, in the margins of our lives (or our textbooks). These private documents often contain more truth than any polished essay.

Dale Morrison's story emerged from my desire to explore how families break and heal, how faith and love can coexist with deep pain, and how some people write themselves into existence one document at a time. While Dale is fictional, her journey reflects the experiences of countless LGBTQ+ individuals and their families navigating rejection, reconciliation, and the complicated grace that makes healing possible.

The epistolary format—telling a story entirely through documents—felt essential to Dale's narrative. Her diary entries, letters, social media posts, and official records create an intimate archive of a life lived courageously. I wanted readers to feel like they were discovering real papers, real evidence of a real person's journey from survival to purpose.

This story required extensive research and the generous guidance of sensitivity readers from the LGBTQ+ community. Their insights helped ensure that Dale's experience, while fictional, honors the truth of what many transgender individuals and their families have endured. Any remaining shortcomings are mine alone.

To readers who see themselves in Dale's story: you are not alone. To parents struggling to love beyond their fear: grace is possible. To families still writing their way back to each other: love recognizes love, eventually.

Stories have the power to change hearts, bridge divides, and remind us of our shared humanity. If Dale's journey helps even one family find their way back to love, then every document in this collection will have served its purpose.

Some people are born loud. Some are born written. All deserve to be read with love.

Kae R. Nelson

Las Vegas, Nevada 2025

READING GROUP GUIDE

DISCUSSION QUESTIONS

1. Format and Storytelling

How does the epistolary format—telling the story entirely through documents—affect your reading experience? What do you learn from Dale's private writings that you might not have discovered through traditional narrative?

2. Family Dynamics

Examine the relationship between Dale and her parents throughout the story. How do Earl and Margaret each handle Dale's identity differently? What moments show the complexity of their love and rejection?

3. Faith and Identity

How does the novel portray the intersection of faith and LGBTQ+ identity? Discuss the role of Cedar Ridge Baptist Church versus other faith communities Dale encounters. Can faith and acceptance coexist?

4. The Power of Words

Dale's viral Facebook post about "complicated grief" becomes a turning point. Why do you think this post resonated so widely? How does writing serve as both survival tool and healing mechanism throughout the story?

5. Chosen vs. Blood Family

Compare Dale's relationship with her biological family to her chosen family in Atlanta. What does the novel suggest about different types of family bonds? How do both play essential roles in Dale's journey?

6. Mother-Daughter Reconciliation

Trace Margaret's evolution from rejection to acceptance. What specific moments or documents show her changing perspective? Do you find her transformation believable? Why or why not?

7. The Complexity of Forgiveness

Dale writes, "My father died today. I loved him. He couldn't love me back. I forgive him anyway." Discuss the concept of "complicated grief." How can love and hurt coexist? Is forgiveness always possible or necessary?

8. Southern Culture and Setting

How does the Alabama setting influence the story? Discuss the role of place in shaping family expectations, community responses, and Dale's need to leave and eventually return.

9. Documents as Truth

The narrator states that "documents tell the truest stories because they capture us as we really were, not as we wish we had been." Do you agree? How do Dale's private writings reveal different aspects of her personality and growth?

10. Hope and Healing

Despite dealing with heavy themes like rejection, abuse, and grief, the novel ultimately celebrates healing and hope. How does the author balance darkness with light? What gives this story its hopeful ending?

THEMES FOR FURTHER EXPLORATION

• The power of authentic self-expression

• Religious trauma and spiritual healing

• The evolution of family acceptance

• Written communication as emotional connection

• Southern LGBTQ+ experiences

• Chosen family and community support

• Complicated grief and forgiveness

• The courage required for living authentically

WRITING AND REFLECTION ACTIVITIES

• **Write your own "document"**— a diary entry, letter, or social media post—about a pivotal moment in your life or family history.

• **Research LGBTQ+ history in your own community.** What resources exist for families navigating acceptance?

• **Discuss:** If you could write a letter to any character in the book, who would it be and what would you say?

ABOUT THE AUTHOR

Kae R. Nelson is a storyteller who traded the humid summers of the South for the desert heat of Las Vegas, where she now lives with her family, one loyal dog, and a garden that refuses to cooperate. Armed with an MFA in Creative Writing and Literary Arts from the University of Alaska Anchorage, her collegiate work has graced the pages of *Understory*, the university's annual anthology of achievement, and the *Alaska Women Speak Journal*, where she explored the complexities of southern womanhood and her rebellion against its traditional expectations. By day, Kae shapes young minds as a high school English Literature Arts teacher, and by night (and weekends, and summer breaks), she crafts the kind of stories that make readers forget they have anywhere else to be. *A Woman Named Dale* marks her debut as a novelist, introducing readers to a voice that's both authentically southern and refreshingly unconventional. When she's not grading papers or wrestling with plot points, you might find Kae in her small Las Vegas backyard, optimistically tending to plants that seem determined to test her patience.

www.ingramcontent.com/pod-product-compliance
Lightning Source LLC
Chambersburg PA
CBHW070903260626
47162CB00007B/2548